End of the Wild

Shipwrecked in the Pacific Northwest

Jason Taylor

Lone Tree Press
First Edition

Cover by Cakamura DSGN Studio

To order additional copies, please send an email to endofthewild@gmail.com

to my family
without whom this story could never have happened

PART 1: THE SHIPWRECKED

CHAPTER 1

"Oh shit, oh shit, oh shit!"

Ian leapt from his bunk, Amy's panicked shouts echoing in his ears, but it was already too late. With a massive shudder, barnacle-covered rocks punched through the wooden hull and a torrent of cold water poured into the boat.

The impact threw him to the floor, hands and knees wet, the smell of brine in his nose. He pulled himself to his feet, fighting for balance, and flung himself up the companionway stairs into the cockpit. Amy stood in shock, eyes wild, face drained of all color, one earbud dangling, bassline thumping from the music she'd been listening to.

"Oh shit Ian, what just happened? I think I'm..." and then she collapsed, her eyes glazing over and rolling back into her head as her body crumpled to the cockpit floor.

Stunned, barely able to stay on his feet himself, Ian stared wide-eyed at Amy's prone form. The boat was in violent motion, the lurching of a mortally wounded animal. The air around them was filled with the sound of raging wind and crashing waves, accompanied by groans and sharp cracks, as his boat, his only real love in this world, tore itself apart.

Feeling the boat heave under him again, he braced himself, feet wide, one hand on the binnacle, struggling to gain control of his thoughts. First, situational awareness. Second, understand threats to the boat and crew. Third, take action.

There was still daylight, skies leaden, wind twenty knots or more judging by the size of the swells and the wind-driven spray. Sails were up, the wind driving them hard onto the rocks. No way to get them down, not now. Instruments? All dead. Could he use the engine to pull them off the rocks? Did he even want to? Back in the water the boat might quickly sink, no telling how large the hole was. He glanced down below, water was already up to the seat bottoms in the salon. Not good. Not good at all.

He could feel the panic rising, a paralyzing helplessness that could kill them both. He clenched his jaw against it. Tried to breathe through it. The boat was shifting, pummeled by the churning waves that were driving them further onto the rocks, the wind unrelenting, the angle quickly becoming perilous, the ocean far too close on the starboard side. Panic rising again, he moved himself carefully to the high side of the boat, further from the water.

Suddenly it clicked into place. His panic dropped out of him, right out the bottom of his stomach, through his feet, and it was gone. He saw it clearly now. His boat was dead. Well and truly dead. Water was coming in over the side now, and down below he could see it was as high as the galley sink. The boat's movements were sluggish; she was in her final death throes, it wouldn't be much longer.

He grabbed Amy, pulling her over the high side, down the slippery hull and into the rocks. Water thrashed around them, freezing cold, taking his breath, no way to breathe, not now, keep moving. Falling, he scrabbled forward with one arm, crablike, pulling Amy behind him, feeling the barnacles tearing into his hands and knees. He was battered forward until he collapsed just beyond the tide line, just past the reach of the ocean, a tiny figure lost among the huge driftwood trees that lay upon the beach like the thigh bones of a giant, thrown there by something even larger and even less concerned with a puny human life.

When he came to again, he was aware that he was shivering. His limbs were numb and stiff, his hands felt like clubs, and they looked like raw meat. Amy. Where was Amy?

He sat up suddenly, too fast for his sluggish blood, and had to cradle his head in his hands for three long beats while his vision cleared and the ringing in his ears faded. Amy was a dark heap of sand-covered, sodden clothing to his left. In front of him the ocean beat on the rocks, sending up plumes of spray. Timeless. No sign of a mast. No sign of his boat. She was completely gone.

Behind him was forest – dark roots reaching out from the verge and plunging deep into the sand to hold fast against the perpetual wind and spray. He was sitting on a beach, white with crushed shells. A midden. Evidence of an ancient First Nations village site, the detritus of centuries of the living who had long ago faded into oblivion.

He crawled over to Amy and touched her arm. "Amy, wake up."

She looked at him with blank eyes and he could feel the panic churning inside him again. There was nothing in those eyes. It wasn't Amy looking back at him, it was a raw senselessness, her face slack. He clamped down, pushing the panic back as he felt the edges of his vision start to shrink, his chest pulling at him. Pulling at him to run, to yell, to do something. He shook her hard, yelled, "Amy!" She blinked once, slowly. A few more fast blinks and she was back, falling into him, hugging him hard, shuddering, and making incoherent noises that might have been words.

"Amy, we've got to figure out what to do next." He could see her pull herself together. She was strong, he knew that, had seen it before. She'd been scared on this trip, had bitten off more than she could chew, but she'd stuck with it, hadn't complained, and had learned quickly. She bore up when it was cold, did what was needed when the weather turned and the wind and waves rose up. He had been exhausted today, and he'd started to trust her. That's why he'd agreed to get some sleep while she took a turn at the helm and kept the boat sailing north, putting miles under the keel.

Ian shook these thoughts from his head. It was time to focus on what they needed to do to survive. He took quick stock. They had the clothes on their backs. No radio. No ditch bag. No food or knife or matches. They both had shoes, thank the gods for that. His habit of sleeping off-watch fully dressed had helped him there. They were alive, battered, cut, and freezing, but alive. That was enough for now.

The beach they were on was a crescent roughly one hundred feet from point to point, hemmed in on both sides by walls of blocky, black rocks that reached out and descended into the ocean. He closed his eyes and visualized the last view of the GPS chart before going to sleep.

"Amy, how long was I sleeping before we hit?"

"Only a couple of minutes. Ian, I swear to God, I don't know what happened. The fog came in so quickly and there was something out there... Something that reached out to me... I don't know how to explain it."

"Something out there? What are you talking about?"

Amy's eyes lost focus, as she turned inward, trying to remember, trying to put it into words. "I don't know. I just... it was like I was somewhere else. I thought I was in a forest. Oh my God, I sank your boat. Ian, I'm so sorry."

"You fainted after we ran aground. You're still disoriented. Let's focus on what we need to do to get out of this mess, ok?"

Amy compressed her lips and nodded.

They had been a few miles south of Hurst Island when he'd given Amy the helm, so that must be where they were now – south shore of Hurst Island. The bad news was that it was a Provincial Park, preserved as wilderness. The good news was that there was supposed to be a lodge on the north side of the island, maybe six miles away. He tried to remember what he'd read. He knew it was only open during the summer and it was well into the Fall now, but maybe there would be a caretaker around who could help them.

They made their way to the top of the rocks on the eastern point. Twenty feet up, they had a better view over the beach with a panoramic view of the ocean to the south. Queen Charlotte Strait reached off to the horizon, a clear line of fading light. To the east were the snow-capped mountains of the mainland. To the west, the heavy forests of Vancouver Island – wild and inhospitable and as good as unreachable without a boat – the water cold enough to kill even if the seas were calm. The channel looked especially deadly at the moment, heaped into vicious, steep-sided waves, the tops blown off in whorls of spray by wind opposing a strong tide.

Six miles to the lodge. Just six miles. They could do that in a few hours, right? Ian turned from the ocean and looked into the dense forest lining the beach, considering what they should do. As he scanned the treeline he saw something moving in the trees. Right at the edge of the beach, just past the bushes, there was definitely something. He squinted his eyes and focused on it. Could there be someone else on the island?

"Hello? Hello! Anyone there?" He walked a few steps to get a closer look and the figure melted into the gloom of the trees, becoming indistinct in the waning light. He felt the hair rising on his arms as goosebumps erupted. He shook it off, feeling the fear subside as he rationalized what he'd seen. There was no one else around. The wind and the shadows were playing tricks on him.

To the east the sky was fading to a deep purple, to the west it was streaked with a riot of color. The light was fading fast and the air cut hard into their wet clothes. Six miles in this terrain? That could take a full day. They needed to find a place to shelter for the night.

CHAPTER 2

"Do you think another boat will find us?" Amy had pulled herself together but she was shivering, leaning in, using him as a windbreak.

"I hate to say it, but no, I don't think so. There are not many boats out this time of year and they'd have to come in close to see us. Not much chance of that."

She turned away from the ocean and looked into the forest, "What are we going to do? How are we going to get home?"

"The island isn't that big, only a few miles wide, and maybe six miles long. We can walk to the lodge on the other side and get help there, but we won't make it tonight. There's no point trying to make it in the dark, we'd risk getting lost or hurt."

"Ok. I'm freezing, let's see if we can find some shelter."

There was a cliff behind them, inaccessible, so she hopped down the rocks and back onto the beach. Ian noticed that her clothes were starting to dry, salt stains showing bone white on her back and legs as she pushed past the thicket of leaves and branches hard up against the rock wall. He hopped down to follow her, careful on the slippery rocks, wincing painfully when he had to use his hands to stabilize himself. He stood briefly on the beach, looking at the spot where Amy had disappeared into the forest.

"Ian, come on!" He could hear her but couldn't see anything clearly in the penetrating gloom past the trees. There wasn't a single break in the vegetation along the entire length of the beach. Up against the rocks, where she had gone through, was the weakest point, so he followed her in.

Past the first line of trees and bushes, the forest opened

up to widely-spaced trees of massive size. Dried leaves, rotting sticks, and ancient nurse logs, the bones of a primeval forest, littered the forest floor. He could hear wind blowing through the tops of the trees, but he could no longer feel it.

The rock wall from the beach continued to his right, small trees and other vegetation growing sideways out of it, larger trees on top. To his left was a swampy depression filled with huge ferns and the gigantic hairy leaves of skunk cabbage. The ground he was on was solid, earthy, and dry. Looking back through the gloom he could make out the white of the beach, nearly glowing, the ocean heaving beyond. He realized that if there were someone on the beach now, he would be able to see them perfectly but they'd have no idea he was watching from within the dark forest.

"Ian! Are you coming? I found something."

She was looking at him and he could just barely see her face as a lighter colored shape floating in the dark. The light was falling fast as he hurried over to find her standing at the base of a huge red cedar tree, the top shattered off thirty feet up, a hole in the trunk leading into an empty space inside. She was brushing away spider webs and a crust of dirt and loose bark around the edges of the hole, working her way inside. With one more glance back, he followed her in.

The hollowed-out space was about five feet across, slightly damp, fragrant, and tapered to a close with almost enough room to stand up in, if you didn't mind getting chunks of decomposing cedar in your hair. He could see Amy sitting, curled up against the far wall, so he sat down next to her, snuggled in, and tried to get comfortable. He could feel the warmth from her body relaxing him, their body heat making the space noticeably warmer, their shivering starting to fade.

"Ian, I think we should stay here for the night. It feels safe. We can start walking in the morning."

***

She was a keeper, as his Mom would have said. Not his type, but when she'd walked up the dock in Victoria he hadn't been able to look away. She was swaying her hips a little and when she saw he was looking, she had given him a big, winning smile, teeth perfectly even and little crinkles in the corners of her eyes showing that she smiled often and with genuine feeling. Must be an American, nobody else in the world has teeth like that. Like expensive dental work was a God-given right that every gangly twelve-year-old was entitled to without question.

"Hey, are you Ian?"

"Yeah, that's right. And you are?"

"Amy," she held out her hand to shake. Her eyes were a deep green contrasting strikingly against red hair, pulled efficiently out of the way in a ponytail. She was standing there, arm straight, hand out, confidently holding his gaze, waiting. He reached out his hand and grabbed hers. It was smooth, cool to the touch, delicate, with a firmer grip than he'd expected. Her smile got bigger and that's when he noticed the gold flecks deep in her irises, reflecting the sun behind him.

After an awkward moment, he realized he still had his hand wrapped around hers. He let go. She cocked her head, squinted a little, "I hear you're looking for crew," shifting what could only be her sea-bag from one shoulder to the other.

"Yeah actually, that's right. I'm heading to Alaska and don't want to solo it. It's a long way and I've already got a late start, I need someone to help me get there."

"I'd like to join up. I'm set on getting to Alaska myself and I can't think of a better way to get there than a sailboat..."

***

A loud sound of wood knocking on wood startled him out of his reverie. He popped his head up, heart thumping in his ears, fingers tingling. One knock, two knocks, a third and then silence.

Amy was moving too. “Ian, what was that?”

“I don’t know. It was loud though. Could it be a woodpecker?” He felt stupid even as he was saying it.

“At night?” She sounded dubious, “I don’t think woodpeckers are active at night.”

“Shhh, listen!” He was talking in a whisper now.

“I don’t hear anything,” she was whispering too.

That was what caught his attention. The complete absence of sound. There was no longer any wind. The silence was absolute. There were no scuffling noises, no insects or birds, absolutely no sound except a slight ringing in his ears that pulsed and faded into the darkness.

She started to move again. “Shhhh!” he said and put his hand on her shoulder to keep her still. He thought he heard something, faintly. His senses completely alert, his ears straining and suddenly overwhelmed by a loud reverberating thwack, like the world’s largest stick slamming hard into a tree trunk and then fading, swallowed by the darkness. They both nearly jumped out of their skins, Ian letting out an undignified yelp and Amy a muffled shriek into his shoulder, her head buried deep, arms grabbing hard.

They stayed that way long enough for Ian’s feet to fall asleep, tingling from the unnatural position of his legs. He shifted slowly, ears pricking and thought he heard, maybe had heard, another thwack as if in response, from much further away, the sound pushing its way through all the intervening trees and leaves and brush.

CHAPTER 3

Morning found them stiff and sore, tired and crusty eyed, blinking as the light edged its way into their sanctuary. Ian sat up and rubbed his neck. He could feel a headache edging in, the need for caffeine starting to make itself known. Amy was next to him, back arched, stretching, arms up over her head as she yawned. Her hoodie rose up and he saw the swell of hips, a flash of belly button, and his eyes darted away, embarrassed.

"Well? Shall we go out and see where we are?" he asked, turning toward the entrance and starting to crawl out.

"Ian?"

He paused and looked back.

"What do you think that noise was last night?" She was looking at him, her eyes wide, arms wrapped around her knees.

He swallowed back a spike of fear, "Maybe it was a big branch breaking off a tree?"

She didn't look convinced. For that matter, neither was he. What kind of a branch makes that kind of noise and what kind of branch gets a response from another tree?

He pushed himself the rest of the way out and stood up with a grateful groan, stretching to his full height and looking around. He could hear Amy pushing her way out behind him and standing up as well. The immediate surroundings were as he remembered them. Rock wall to one side, swampy ground to the other, dappled sunlight filtering down through a cathedral-like space, trees reaching to the sky like columns, the forest canopy an intricate roof above. This morning held all the noises of a living forest. He could hear the birds talking to each other, flitting and hopping, their small claws skittering and scratching against rough wood. He could sense insects pushing their way through the litter below and there was the light rustle of leaves as bits of breeze pushed past the beach break.

He was thirsty and his stomach growled. It had been almost twenty-four hours since his last meal. He'd eaten a hearty breakfast the previous morning but they'd skipped lunch because of the rough conditions, then they'd hit the rocks and dinner had no longer been an option.

"Amy, we should get going if we want to get to the lodge by evening. I don't know about you, but I'm hungry."

She nodded, "Yeah I'm hungry. Pretty thirsty too. Let's go."

They put their backs to the sea and started walking. The ground they were on sloped upwards, but it was solid and easy to walk on. After a while the open spaces began to close around them, making progress more difficult. Ian was in front, pushing through branches and brushing spider webs away from his face with increasing frequency. Large spiders, abdomens bloated, perched in their webs waiting for prey. As they felt his human presence, they would drop to the ground, trailing silk, and scuttle away. The instincts of a smaller predator avoiding a much larger one.

It was Amy that found it first. She had good eyes and spotted a small break in the salal bushes that Ian would have walked right past. "Ian, it looks easier this way," and she worked her way through. He followed her, and after scratching through a dozen feet of overgrown brush, found himself on a well-groomed trail winding its way vaguely northward.

"I wonder if it's a game trail?"

"Looks too big," Amy said, following the trail with her eyes to where it disappeared around a large maple.

"I suppose this has to lead us toward the lodge. There aren't any other buildings on the island. Who else could have built this other than the owner, right?" He smiled and felt some of the tension ease from his shoulders. Maybe they'd have full stomachs and comfortable beds to sleep in soon.

CHAPTER 4

"Hey Ian, look at this bush, I think we can eat the berries."

He looked back at Amy and saw her a few feet off the trail surrounded by bushes laden with small red berries. She had picked one and was examining it.

"See the star on the bottom?"

She held it up and he walked over to get a closer look. The bushes were like small trees, branches spreading up and out over a six-foot radius. The berry she was holding was the size and shape of a large ball bearing, dark red with a matte surface.

"These are either huckleberries or red blueberries, doesn't really matter. Either way they're edible."

She popped it in her mouth and chewed thoughtfully. A smile lit her face up. "Try it Ian, they're delicious!"

His hunger reared up, his throat tightening in excitement. Food! They fell onto the first bush, ravenously stripping berries off the branches and stuffing them into their mouths. The little berries popped, thin red juice coating their tongues. A little sweet, a little bitter, astringency mixed with ripe pleasure. The taste was wild, not at all like berries from the store.

Fingers stained red, their lips unnaturally dark, the more they ate, the hungrier they became. Like a wall had been breached, their hunger grew beyond normal bounds as they desperately gathered from the bushes, making small noises as they found each new cluster, reaching up to gather and shove the berries into themselves.

Ian looked at Amy, his stomach aching, his mouth raw from the berry's acidic tannins. Her hair was falling out of its braids, face stained red. She looked back at him and grinned wide – a look so feral that he took a step back. He watched in fascination as a droplet of glistening red hung trembling on the point of her chin and then fell free. She wiped a forearm hard across her face and grinned again, teeth big, eyes bright.

He felt a small chill creep up his spine, raising the hairs on the back of his neck, "Ok Amy, I think we should get moving."

CHAPTER 5

"Amy, what do you think, is this fur?"

Ian was looking at a tuft of light brown fiber caught in the trunk of a cedar tree. It was coarse and wiry as Ian pulled it away from the tree in a solid, oily clump.

Amy came over to take a look, "Looks like fur to me, what do you think it's from?"

Ian separated a few pieces to look at them more closely, "Maybe a bear, but I think it's too light in color to be a black bear and it seems unlikely there would be grizzlies on this island. They tend to stay on the mainland. More room to roam." Raising it to his nose, "It does have a distinct smell though, it's definitely from an animal of some sort."

The smell was musky and strong, but not unpleasant. It reminded him of a horse that'd been running hard, stamping and steaming. Amy smelled it too and gave him a hesitant smile. "Smells good, but I hope we don't run into whatever it came from."

They walked a few more minutes and found themselves in a strange open space, the canopy gone, giving them a clear view of the sky. It was almost perfectly round and the ground was covered with long branches, yellowing leaves intact, arranged so that the thickest parts were facing outward and the thinnest were toward the middle. The ground felt springy, the wood flexing under their feet.

"Ian? Look up."

Ian followed Amy's gaze to the trees that surrounded the clearing. The circle they were standing in was enclosed by mid-sized birches. Every one of them had its top cleanly broken off, fifteen feet up, the wood showing white and fresh. He looked down again. What he'd thought were branches were in fact the tops of the trees gathered and arranged carefully on the ground.

Ian looked at how the tops had been placed, felt the soft spring beneath his feet, "Maybe this was built as a tent platform for somebody?" He thought for a moment, "It looks pretty recent. Maybe there's someone nearby."

He thought about yelling for help, but a sense of caution stopped him. He took a few steps into the platform, moving toward the center. The branches' flex deepened and he noticed small bits of fur floating up from below, little brown motes spinning upward on the eddies of air he'd disturbed.

Feeling a little unstable, he stopped moving and the musky smell of the fur came back. It was much stronger now, filling his nose and worming its way into his chest. He looked back at Amy and froze. She was looking at him intently, an expression on her face that he'd never seen before, her eyes drawing him toward her. He was intensely aware of his breathing, his heart beating in his chest. He moved slowly closer, stopping a foot away. Her eyes had never broken from his, had never so much as blinked, one braid over her shoulder, the other thrown back. He could see her breathing too, could see the heat rising in her face.

His hand floated forward to rest lightly on her shirt just above the waist. She continued to look at him, her lips parted, teeth exposed, breath flaring as his fingers curled down, knuckles grazing the hard plane of her stomach. He could feel the beat of her heart as he brushed inside her pants, grabbing a hold of her waistband, heat rising up and washing over him.

Without breaking his gaze she moved slowly backwards, drawing him with her, a slight tug on his hand where they were connected, moving backward until she was pressed up against a tree. Her chin rose up, head tilted to one side, braid swinging slightly with the movement, her breathing faster, cheeks flushed, neck exposed with the slight movement of a pulse in the hollow of her throat.

She was looking past him now, eyes glazed, shoulders

thrown back, breathing hard. He traced the exposed pillar of her neck and a growl rose unbidden in his throat. He bent forward, the desire to bite and to rend, to feel the liquid warmth spreading over him, rose irresistibly.

The sound of a stick knocking hard on a tree broke the spell. It was close. Very close. Another knock answered, further away. A short, syncopation between the two and then silence.

CHAPTER 6

Her eyes snapped down to his hand and then back up to his face, “Ian? Ian! What the hell are you doing?”

Then she reached up and slapped him hard, rocking his head back, neck cracking, cheek on fire, vision white, then black. Coming into focus he found himself a few heavy steps backwards.

“What do you think you’re doing? Touching me, looking at me like that.” A look of revulsion came over her, “What. The. Fuck!”

She was standing tall, arms tight at her sides, hands clenched in fists, face enraged, eyes flashing.

“Goddammit Amy, you sank my fucking boat. You sank it!” The words were driven forcefully out of him against his will, giving voice to his repressed rage and a feeling of overpowering loss.

“Oh and now you want payback, you dirty pervert? Thought you’d take your payment with my body?” She was worked up now, advancing on him, the words spitting out of her like venom. “Thought you could do what you wanted with me you sick little shit?”

Then she turned on her heel and fled into the forest.

“I. Shit. What the hell?” Ian muttered as he watched her disappear, his hand up to his face, eyes watering.

What in the world had possessed him to let her crew on his boat?

He thought back to that day on the docks in Victoria – his boat tied up next to him, hand on the rail.

***

"So then, what's your sailing experience?"

Her eyes flicked to the left, toward shore, and then back to him again, "I've knocked around a bit, you know. Here and there." She gave him her winningest smile, "I know my way around a sailboat if that's what you're asking."

"Have you ever been on a long voyage?"

Her smile faltered a little, "no."

"How about an overnight?"

She looked down at her feet, good solid boat boots, slightly worn, "No, not really."

She looked back up at him, turned on the charm, "Look, I've been in a couple beer-can races. I'm too light to be rail-meat so my boyfriend taught me how to helm. I guess I'm good at it, I have the knack. He taught me how to trim the sails too. I know what I'm doing."

"Your boyfriend, huh?"

She smiled up at him and shifted her weight slightly, one thumb hooked in the strap of her sea bag.

He took a deep breath, "Ok then. Want to come aboard?" and then took a big step up onto the side deck, nicely worn, old growth teak, and down into the cockpit, shining with polished wood, stainless, and bronze. "Watch your step," he called back over his shoulder, but she hopped up without any problem, all grace and agile strength.

He found himself sitting in the cockpit with those green eyes looking at him, the air around them gaining the density and luminosity it sometimes gets when twilight is approaching. The sound of traffic, street music, hawkers of junk, tour guides, and all the other miscellany of the Victorian waterfront skipped across the water and into their domain. Some of the city lights were starting to turn on, getting ready to fend off the encroaching dark. Being tied to the docks meant they were connected to all of it, part of this great collection of people and technology. Floating in a boat meant they were a step apart, slightly out of phase, able to cast off and become their own floating country, free to enter the great wilderness of the sea.

They both felt the change as soon as they stepped aboard. They had crossed a threshold, from one distinct place to another, a decision to walk through a door and see what was on the other side, to leave civilization behind and explore the wild. They could look into the city and see normal people, doing what normal people did, but they felt the difference – their freedom, their remove from the ordinary. It wasn't like looking through a window in a Christmas story, orphan noses pressed against cold glass, looking at a table laden with glistening food. Instead it was like being at the zoo, looking into a habitat, looking at the animals in their self-contained world. Everything they needed was provided for them, but they were surrounded by walls that they could never escape. While you might envy that safety, you would never trade your freedom for it. You would always choose to turn around, always choose to walk back out into the harsh, beautiful reality of the wild.

They both felt it and it lightened their moods, started the bond forming. He looked out toward the city, then back at her, "Hey, do you want a beer?"

They found themselves in the salon, down below, each on one side of the long table that ran down the middle of the boat. He was sitting easy, legs comfortable, arm thrown over the back of the settee, beer in hand, laughing. She was laughing too, leaning forward, elbows on the table, intently telling a story. "So that's when the preacher noticed a chicken in the pews. My crazy brother had been told to take care of the chickens but he couldn't get them all fed in time. He knew he couldn't miss church, so he had brought some with him and was trying to feed them in the closet. When old Mrs. Davis went to get her scarf, one of the chickens ran out clucking like mad!" She threw her head back and laughed. A sound of pure joy, full and deep, filling the space around them.

She was from Iowa, as far from the sea as you could get. Had grown up looking at seas of corn instead of saltwater and had spent her adolescence dreaming of getting away. Her family was religious and she was raised with the judgement of God resting on her shoulders. When she was old enough she went to school at the University of Washington, with her parents' blessings. They knew she wasn't made for Iowa, knew that she needed to see more of the world before they could begin to hope that she might find her way back home. She studied hard, got an engineering degree, met a boy, learned to sail. But she wasn't satisfied. The call to adventure was getting louder and the easy path into work and adulthood felt like a trap instead of a gift.

"I believe in God too you know," he said with a mischievous glint in his eyes, "Gods actually. Lots of 'em. A landscape of little gods all jostling for position, clamoring for our attention, each with their own agenda." He paused to see her reaction, kept going, "some are troublemakers, some might be helpful. I think they surround us but they are quiet and hard to notice. Sometimes when I'm at sea, by myself, I think I can hear them rustling around, trying to get me to notice."

The mood had changed, more serious now, "No Ian, you're wrong. There is one God, just one" she said, holding up a finger. "Some people think he is all powerful, all loving. Good." Her brow tightened, eyes intense, leaning forward, "I'm sorry Ian, but that's fucking naïve. Wishful thinking for people who aren't strong enough to see the truth." Her eyes had dropped to the table, like she was seeing more than she was saying, "There is one God and I think he's horrifying. I don't want his attention." Quieter now, looking back up at him, "I've learned to hide."

It was a little bit the beer, a little bit her natural charm, and a little bit a feeling of sorrow that was creeping up from the pit of his soul. That human feeling of loneliness that can turn to despair, the realization of your separateness and alienation. A sense that no one can truly help you. For all of these reasons he looked up from his beer and said, "You still want to go to Alaska?" She nodded and he smiled, "It looks like you've got yourself a ship."

CHAPTER 7

Ian walked back through the trees, following where Amy had disappeared. He was back on the trail, but there was no sign of her. Reasoning that she probably would have pressed on rather than turn toward the beach, he walked north, still thinking about how he'd gotten himself into this predicament.

***

The first few days with her on the boat had passed pleasantly and they had quickly settled into a routine. He slept in the v-berth forward and she was in the quarter-berth aft. They woke up together, ate their breakfast together, their mornings spent on the preparations and provisioning necessary before they could depart. In the afternoons he would familiarize her with the ship, teach her what each control did, and what combination of sails worked best in various combinations of wind and sea state.

The night before they started their voyage she helped him change the engine oil and filters, taking to the mechanical work naturally and without hesitation. Tightening the oil-filler cap after pouring in the last quart, she grinned up at him – forehead smudged and a dark stripe of oil on her chin. Her smile was contagious and Ian laughed out loud, seeing her at the base of the companionway, disheveled, dirty, and happy. All the work was done – the boat was ready and so were they. Ian replaced the companionway stairs, covering the engine back up, "We're ready to go tomorrow. I'm going to clean up and then let's celebrate."

Ian scrubbed his face clean, washed his hands, and

changed his shirt. Wanting to give Amy some privacy, he opened the foredeck hatch, propped himself out, closed it carefully behind him, and stood on the foredeck, one hand shading his eyes from the setting sun. Victoria Harbor is always a busy place and that night was no exception. A moderate breeze was blowing in from the west, originating in the Strait of Juan de Fuca and funneling through the harbor entrance. Seaplanes were circling in from the east, using the headwind to reduce their speed on descent. Each plane would circle over the city, line up, and then fall improbably over the Empress Hotel to pass over the forest of masts crowding the head of the harbor, the next plane lining up and ready to land as soon as the waterway was clear again. The planes were drifting down over the ferries and sea kayaks to land in the middle harbor as pleasure yachts motored in from the Strait to seek shelter for the night. As each plane touched down, the air would relinquish its hold and the floats would settle deeply into the water so that it could taxi slowly to the docks like the world's clumsiest bird.

Surrounded by the sound of people – the smell of aviation fuel and frying food lingering in the air, watching the planes land and the water taxis scurrying around and the yachts nestling into dock – Ian felt deeply satisfied. He heard Amy emerge and turned to look at her. Resplendent in clean clothes, freshly scrubbed skin, brushed hair and a hint of makeup, she was glowing and lovely. As they walked up the dock, they saw a cluster of people near the entrance ramp, looking at something and talking excitedly. Amy hurried forward to see, while Ian hung back amused.

"Look Ian, it's the most adorable baby seal!"

"Yeah, they like to hang out there. Don't worry, by the end of this trip you'll have seen so many seals you won't know what to do with yourself. Where we're going, they're everywhere."

"I don't think I could ever get tired of seeing them, look how cute that little guy is!"

The baby seal lay on the docks like an emissary from a wilder world. A world most people had never experienced and hardly knew existed. These people were like animals, looking out through the glass of their zoo habitat, unable to grasp the meaning of what they saw. Let them have their excitement. He was leaving tomorrow. North to the wilds of Alaska.

CHAPTER 8

The following morning, before dawn, they threw off their lines and left Victoria for good, plotting a course along the Inside Passage, north toward Alaska. As the days passed they became increasingly comfortable with each other, and Amy became increasingly proficient on the boat. True to her word, she was good at the helm and had a working knowledge of sail shape. She knew how to set sails for the most power and lift, and how to de-power when it was needed. They sailed day and night, making as much progress as possible. Ian knew that they were fighting the seasons – it was Fall and the North Pacific high was destabilizing, storms tumbling intermittently across Vancouver Island to pummel them. When the weather was bad, they'd stop for the night, trying to find anchorages that were both convenient and secure.

One day, sailing across the Strait of Georgia, they got to talking. The winds were fair, twenty knots from the southeast, allowing them to broad reach in a nice easy motion across the Strait, the boat loping along. The wind-driven waves were getting larger, but the period was long, the tide flooding north, wind behind it, helping to flatten the waves and keep them docile. The water was a lovely grey, shimmering like quicksilver under cloudy skies that threatened rain. The wind was forecast to rise, a storm on the way, but for now all was well. They were on their way to Bowen Island for the night, planning to wait out the worst of it there before continuing north.

"Ian, how long have you been sailing? I haven't heard your story yet." Her green eyes were on him, tucked under her hood, radiating curiosity.

"I guess I've always known I wanted to sail. Growing up in

Vancouver, the ocean was at my doorstep. If I wasn't in school, I was on the shoreline exploring or in the water swimming. If I wasn't on the beach, I was in a boat. When I was ten my dad bought a little sailboat. I helped him fix her up and we sailed her every day we could in the summer. Some days in the winter too. She was an ugly little thing, but we loved her and she took good care of us. When I was in college at U Vic I always found a boat I could sail somehow. I guess it's in my blood.

"This boat is a real beauty. She was built in 1939, an early Sparkman and Stephens design, you can see her racing heritage in the long overhangs and narrow beam. That's why she cuts through the water so well and sails so beautifully. She may not be as fast as a modern design, but she makes up for it in grace and sea-kindliness."

"She was actually built in Maine in a small yard that's long gone now. Built from the finest cedar over a white oak frame, mast and boom of Sitka spruce. Wooden boats have soul and she's stacked full of it. She has a life of her own, her own moods, likes and dislikes. She's alive to me."

Amy was entranced, chin in hands.

"Well, she was owned by gentleman sailors at first. Not many people could afford to own a pleasure yacht in those days. She was taken out in the summers, hauled and wrapped up on land in the winters. Stayed in Maine, on Mount Desert Island, anchored in front of a rich man's 'cottage' until the start of the war. During the war years she cruised Penobscot Bay and kept a lookout for German submarines. Never saw one, thank the gods, who knows what would have happened. What chance does a sailboat have if it comes up against an enemy sub?"

Amy chuckled briefly, urging him to go on.

"After that she had a succession of owners, fell down a little on maintenance and got a little scruffy. I've seen pictures of her from that time, she's definitely down at the heels, doesn't look nearly as good as she does now. Keeping a wooden boat in good shape is hard work, believe me."

Another good-natured chuckle.

"Then she was bought by a hippie couple who'd read a magazine article about sailing the South Pacific. They sold everything, packed their kids up and sailed away, dreams of an island paradise running on repeat in their heads. They were obsessed. Well, he was anyway. The wife made it as far as Florida before she got fed up and left, took the kids with her. I think his decision to round the outer banks of North Carolina on a rough day instead of going inside may have sealed the deal. They don't call it the Graveyard of the Atlantic for nothing!

"Newly single, he was stuck in Port St. Lucie for a while, but I'll be damned if he didn't keep going solo. He made a real go of it, sailing through the Bahamas, then down the Thorny Path to the Caribbean, hopping through the Windwards and Leewards, touching Colombia and then through the Canal to the Pacific. He actually made it to the fabled islands of the South Pacific, but I don't know if he found what he was looking for because a year later he sailed to Victoria by way of Hawaii and the boat's been here ever since.

"When I found her, she was in rough shape. Really rough. I spent ten years and every penny I had bringing her back to life. I know every inch of this boat, every fastener, every plank, and every detail. Stern to bow, she's my boat now. I made her what she is."

Amy let out a big sigh, the romance of it almost too much for her to handle.

"I've always dreamed of Alaska, always wanted to go there, it's the wildest place I can imagine. Huge. Untouched. Wild seas and mountains. There are places where glaciers fall right into the water and if you get too close the waves will swamp you. There are places where you can see mountains over twenty thousand feet tall, right from the deck of your boat. There is room to spread out, room to be who you want to be, room to be free."

***

The sound of a terrified scream pierced his thoughts, brought him back to the present, back into the forest. Without thinking, he ran up the trail as fast as he could, ran toward the scream. A scream that could only have come from Amy.

CHAPTER 9

He rounded a corner, breathing hard. Amy cowered next to the trail, head in hands, shaking.

"Amy, what is it? Are you ok?" Thoughts of her hitting him almost forgotten for the moment.

"There was something there, just behind those bushes. I saw it, Ian, I saw it!"

"Saw what? What did you see? You aren't making sense."

He bent down and tried to help her stand. She wasn't budging though, so he knelt down and put his hand on her arm. She looked at his hand and frowned. A moment of tension and then she looked at him sheepishly, "Ian, about before. I don't know... I don't know what happened to me."

Her head sunk back into her arms and she shook with sobs. That makes two of us, Ian was thinking. What the hell had happened? He didn't have long to think about that before she looked back up at him, eyes red, cheeks streaked with tears. "Ian, I'm sorry."

"Forget about it, ok?" He shuddered a little with the effort of repressing his memories – the memory of the bloodlust that had come over him. An apology of his own was on the tip of his tongue but she spoke first.

"Ian, I saw something. I was pissed, moving fast, not watching where I was going when I heard something big in those bushes. I got scared, I thought it was the bear we were talking about earlier. I froze, I didn't know what to do. I was still angry, really angry, but at that moment I wished you were here with me." A sudden warmth bloomed in Ian's chest. Happiness.

"The movement got closer and I saw... Ian, I saw a hand."

Ian felt a shiver start in his legs and work progressively up his body, waves of chills moving up his spine, into the base of his neck and back down again.

"A hand?"

"Something was moving in there and when I looked to see what it was, I saw a hand through the leaves. Then I screamed... maybe I startled it... whatever it was, it ran away." She paused. "I don't think it was human."

Ian's chills redoubled their efforts, threatening to knock him over with their intensity. "What do you mean it wasn't human?"

She looked at him, truly scared, the fear showing plainly, "It was completely covered in brown fur."

CHAPTER 10

They walked quickly, newly motivated to find civilization, fear pushing them forward, pushing them into exhaustion. There was no talking now, just movement and labored breathing. They followed the trail until it reached a steep section of hillside, the path clearly leading up the slope, a narrow defile splitting a cliff, up ledges and system of roots, a hand over hand obstacle course to the top.

Amy went first, her small size and agility helping her grab roots, feet pushing against rocks as she pulled herself up to the first ledge. She ducked her head under a large root, big enough that it had been easier for her to squeeze under it than try to climb over, and looked at Ian encouragingly. He followed her up, choosing to go over the root instead of under and just when he had both feet up, his hand steadying him on the rock face, his feet slipped out from under him. The root was wet, covered in algal growth and as slippery as ice, all the ridges and grooves doing nothing to help his feet find traction. He went down hard on his stomach, knocked the wind out of himself and found his feet scrabbling feebly below him, his hands scratching forward for something to hold onto, gravity inexorably pulling him downwards. It was Amy's quick thinking that saved him from falling. She ducked under the root, fitting neatly in the small space, grabbed his legs and gave him the stability he needed to find his balance again.

After that they moved more carefully, Amy still leading, up and further up until they emerged on the top of a high hill, sparsely vegetated, clearly wind-blasted, large slabs of granite interspersed with coarse, low-growing plants twisted by the wind. They stood on one of the pieces of granite, catching their breath and looking around in awe. The sun was settling low in the sky, shadows lengthening. From where they stood they could see the entirety of the island. All the ground they had covered lay at their feet to the south, clear to the beach they'd washed up on yesterday. To the north they could see the ocean and a few small coves. One of those coves had to be their destination, the logical place for a lodge to be.

The northern shore looked close, close enough that they gained some confidence, felt that it was within reach. But the path they were on didn't continue north, instead it led east, winding down the hillside, across a broad, thickly forested valley with a large, oddly symmetrical, cone-shaped hill dominating the skyline. They both looked at the trail, at the valley, at the distant hill and came to the same conclusion. They didn't want to go that way. Not one little bit. They didn't even need to talk about it. That direction was off-limits. That trail would no longer take them where they needed to go.

Farther to the north lay the open end of Queen Charlotte Strait, beyond that Queen Charlotte Sound, Cape Caution, and Egg Island, famous for its lighthouse. There was a thick bank of fog out there, white in the sunlight, contrasting brightly against the deep blue water, waves visible but tiny and stationary from their high vantage point.

The fog rolled in quickly. They saw it consume the lighthouse, consume the islands scattered below them, march across Queen Charlotte Sound, and roll right up Queen Charlotte Strait until it was below them, having successfully swallowed all the ocean to the north. Then it reared straight up the island, up their hill, and was upon them. The wind blew it in wisps and streamers at first, only obscuring their vision in scraps before thickening until everything around them was covered in a blanket of moving, scurrying white. Their faces were getting wet, their clothes beading up with it. Growing cold, they ducked behind a rock to wait it out. Slightly warmer, out of the wind, they sat next to each other and stared into the mesmerizing, ever-changing patterns of white.

Staring trancelike into the depths of fog, Ian became aware that there was something solid coming toward them. At first only visible as a disturbance in the eddies, it came closer, becoming more obviously visible, as if the fog was coalescing into a denser object. The color shifted so that the object became less white, a darker smudge in the field of white and still it was coming toward them. Ian nudged Amy's shoulder and pointed at the disturbance, "Amy, look."

Suddenly it broke free from the fog, it was clearly a figure walking up the trail they'd been on earlier. It was coming toward them at an oblique angle, covering the ground with long, steady strides. It walked past their rock, one hundred feet away, face obscured, head turned – was it looking at them? They could see that it was completely covered with a thick, shaggy coat of brown fur. Rooted to the spot, they could do nothing other than watch it disappear into the fog behind them as it continued walking east.

They sat stock-still, the instincts of a smaller predator avoiding a much larger one. Their noses flared, unconsciously trying to catch a scent, anything to prove that what they were seeing was real, but they didn't smell a thing and the figure was gone, the fog swirling and cutting off all visibility.

CHAPTER 11

Unwilling to keep moving while they couldn't see where they were going, blind to any movement around them, they had waited for the fog to blow itself out. When it was finally gone and they could see again, they stood up silently and moved off the hilltop, working their way north toward the series of coves, one of which they felt must contain the lodge they were looking for.

They were both deeply tired now, the constant battle with the forest wearing them down. The ache was bone deep, lancing through joints, settling in thigh bones, reaching up to the hips and lower back. Not as sure of their footing, feeling unbalanced and unsettled, they stumbled down a steep-sided ravine that led toward the shore and from the shore, perhaps the lodge.

Finding the lodge had seemed like a simple thing that morning when they'd set out. Walk north, keep walking until they found buildings and they'd be back in touch with civilization. But the island and the forest were anything but simple and they hadn't given up their secrets easily. Feeling out of place, like they were bumbling and fumbling through darkness, they walked through a forest that was constantly changing, yet somehow always the same. Rock, earth, tree, fern, bird, and bug on infinite repeat. It was like walking through a huge room, the size of a city, able to see no more than twenty feet in any direction, how long would it take to find what they were looking for? Days? Weeks? Months?

They walked on, stumbling downwards, into deeper dark, slippery roots, larger trees, outcroppings of moss-covered rock, huge logs that they climbed over or levered themselves under.

No easy steps, no such thing as an easy path. There was nothing linear here, no straight lines, no square edges – everything a profusion of curves and points, soft piled upon hard piled upon soft.

At one point Amy was walking on a carpet of moss so thick and soft that she had to fight an irrational urge to kick off her shoes and sink her weary toes into the cloud of green. As she walked down the emerald sheet, it began to move under her, an entire section breaking free from the smooth rock that held it, her feet suddenly moving faster than her body. Gravity took hold, no choices left. She landed hard on her side, accelerating on the carpet of moss toward a steep drop, helpless to stop. She rolled onto her stomach, hands thrown forward, fingernails driving inwards to grab a hold of... what?

Ian was unable to do anything as he watched Amy disappear over the edge in a waterfall of green, clods of dirt thrown skyward as the trailing edge whipped past and followed her down. He rushed across the newly bare slope of granite, feeling sick, and poked his head over the edge to see Amy in a heap, prone, twenty feet down.

"Amy! Amy! Are you ok?"

She looked up at him and started to laugh. Huge, uncontrolled laughter until tears came to her eyes and she was shaking, helpless with it, hiccupping and struggling for breath. Ian was at first confused and then he understood. She had landed on top of the moss, a pile several feet thick that had cushioned her fall and spared her from harm. Shaken, but grateful, he picked his way down and sat next to her.

"Are you ok?"

"Yeah, I'm fine. I wasn't even scared. I was surrounded by green all the way down, I think some of the moss wrapped itself around me. I feel safe now. Like everything is going to be ok."

She looked so comfortable there, so at peace, he didn't want to disturb her, but a moment later she was up and had started walking again. Ian roused himself and followed her down the ravine.

Their first hint was a small piece of surveyor's tape tied to a branch, standing out orange and unnatural. It was their first sign of humanity since they'd been delivered on the beach cold and wet the day before. Ian pinched the tape between thumb and forefinger, a bright, slippery piece of nylon that proved without a doubt that another person had stood in this very place. He looked around and saw another piece of tape down the slope, just far enough away that it was barely visible.

They followed the tape, segment by segment, until they came to a narrow trail hacked into the side of a steep slope. It was tricky footing but clearly made by human hands and therefore it must lead them to some human place. They immediately saw the difference from the trail they'd walked earlier in the day. The other trail had flowed through the landscape, almost as if it had been laid down first and the plants had chosen to grow around it, to uphold its sovereignty. This trail was carved into the landscape, a fight against nature, rough around the edges, holes where rocks had been pulled out, rough wood where roots had been cut, bushes encroaching inward, downed limbs that would need to be cut and cleared. A human effort that required ongoing human maintenance or it would be consumed and then subsumed back into the wild.

It wasn't much longer before they found the shore. Steep and rocky, the slope dove straight down into water so clear they could see undersea plants waving their fronds up at them, reaching toward the sunlight that fed them. The water was heaving up and down slightly, as slow as breathing, washing the limpets and barnacles and other sea life that clustered at the tide line. There was a multitude of snaps and crackles, ever present popping noises as water ran in and out of a million tiny cavities. They could smell the iodine of seaweed as well as the inevitable decomposition and rot from dead creatures that had not yet been scavenged by crab or gull or raven.

The trail followed the shoreline, fifty feet up, high enough to give them nerves when the going got tough, stepping over a crevice or crack in the rock that led straight down to the sea below. Rounding a corner, they finally saw what they'd been searching for. At the head of a small cove, perched smartly above the water, the lodge hove into view. There was a main building, flanked by several small storage sheds. To the left, lining the cove for several hundred feet were a dozen small cottages, painted various bright colors, orange, purple and pink. The cottages looked like they'd been transplanted from a Bahamian island; the colors spoke of good cheer, human company and safety. The contrast between these cheery cottages and the wild, dark green of the British Columbia forest couldn't have been greater. They stared at this wilderness outpost for several long moments, feeling an odd sense of dislocation. Then they began to move again, picking their way toward the buildings.

When they got to the lodge they found themselves on a boardwalk fronting the cottages. Each cottage had a colored door, a small, brightly colored table and an Adirondack chair out front. The boardwalk was cantilevered over the shore so that they could look down to see wet rock and tiny crabs scuttling in the dark beneath their feet. Just past the cottages was an outdoor sitting area with rough hewn wooden benches, lounging chairs and a round fire pit filled with ash and charcoaled bits of wood. The main lodge building lay just beyond.

They walked up to the front of the lodge building, right up to a nice wooden door, a sign to the right reading 'Welcome to God's Pocket' with mischievous gnomes, cartoon style, below the letters. Looking left there was a trail that led past a few outbuildings and on into the woods. To the right was a large deck overlooking a floating dock, no boats tied up unfortunately. But there were a pile of yellow sea kayaks pulled up onto a wider part of the dock, upside down and snugged together. The deck wrapped around the edge of the building and another trail started on the far side, rock steps climbing toward a gated wooden fence with a bladed turbine poking over the top.

Ian tried the door, the knob turned easily, and the door swung open revealing a tidy room with a kitchen on one end, a long table flanked by benches, a pair of couches in the corner, and a small library of books. The walls were covered with pictures of sea life, nautical charts, and informational posters. In one corner was a table with what looked like a radio and some other electronic gear. On the far wall were two doors that opened into small bedrooms with utilitarian single beds on metal frames. It felt empty. Like no one had been there for a while.

Ian looked at Amy with a tremulous smile and stepped through the door.

"Hello, is anybody here?"

CHAPTER 12

Amy followed him in and flipped the light switch. It's not that the room was dark, there were windows over the kitchen that were letting light in, it was just that the idea of electricity was so tied into her concepts of civilization and comfort and safety that she reached for it as unconsciously as a toddler would reach for a safety blanket. The switch was old fashioned, flipping up with a solid thunk but the lights didn't come on. The expected feeling of safety didn't materialize. The technology letting her down and leaving a small pit of doubt in her belly.

"No electricity Ian."

"Hmm, that means the radio probably won't work. I'll check on that. Do you want to look for food and water?"

While Ian worked on the radio, Amy walked to the fridge. She opened it and found it as dark and warm as she'd expected. There was nothing in there but the stale smell of what once was cold. With further exploration, she found a door that looked like a pantry and opened it to find shelves laden with cans and boxes of food.

She looked back over her shoulder at Ian, "Jackpot!" grabbing an armful of chili and beef stew. She dumped it on the counter and rummaged for pots, silverware, and bowls to eat out of. Catching sight of the sink she realized how thirsty she was and turned the knob, anticipating the flow of cool, refreshing water. There was nothing, the tap bone dry. The pit in her belly grew.

Resigning herself to thirst and reasoning that the canned food would provide them some liquid, she bent herself to opening cans and pouring their content into the pots to heat up. Ian came over to join her, "No luck, the radio won't turn on. Nothing is working without power. I guess it was worth trying though." He sounded disappointed and was drooping with weariness.

Amy put the pots on the stove and tried to get the gas burners lit. She pushed the knob to 'light' and waited for the whoosh of flame, but nothing happened. No click of igniter, no hiss of fuel, nothing. She placed her hands on either side of the stove and took a couple of deep breaths, wanting to steady herself, wanting to hide the trembling that was creeping up on her.

"Amy, it's ok, let's just eat it cold."

And that's how they found themselves sitting on opposite sides of the table, heads down, eating cold canned food.

CHAPTER 13

After the meal, they both felt a little better. It was starting to get dark and they could feel the cold creeping in, but the fresh infusion of calories had cleared their heads and had given them some energy to think.

Ian started, "So, I was thinking about the power. It's probably off because they closed the lodge up for the winter. They must have a caretaker, probably just hasn't shown up yet. If that's the case there has be a way to turn the power on, we just need to figure out how."

Amy nodded, "Way out here, they'd have to be self-sufficient. I didn't see any solar, too cloudy around here to count on that anyway. There was that turbine, but it looks kind of small, can't generate much power with that. Plus it would only work when the wind is blowing."

"Yeah, I agree. Let's poke around and see what else we can find."

The room was getting pretty dark but when they stepped outside there was still enough light to see where they were going. They walked up the path to an outbuilding that looked promising and stepped into the darkened space. By habit, Ian flipped the light switch, knowing as it clicked that nothing would happen, but he was discomfited anyway.

Once inside he found himself face to face with what could only be a generator. He could make out the word Honda in white letters with small red starter button next to it. With a quick glance back at Amy, standing silhouetted in the doorway, he held his breath and pushed the starter. The mechanism spun smoothly and the generator kicked to life, quiet and powerful, promising warmth and light and safety. The light in the room immediately kicked on, orange spilling in a long rectangle along the ground outside the door, Amy's shadow distorting wildly across the natural undulations of earth.

With big smiles they walked arm-in-arm back to the lodge, the light in the generator room still on, neither willing to turn it off and plunge their world back into darkness.

CHAPTER 14

Amy walked into the main building, flipping the light switch first thing. This time the thunk of the switch resulted in light flooding the room, filling every nook and cranny, pushing the darkness out the windows and the door, reaching past the fire pit to brush up against the cottages, their colors muted in the dim edge of light.

Ian went straight to the radio, turned it on and picked up the mic. It felt good and solid in his hand. He checked to ensure it was set to channel 16 and started transmitting, "Pan-pan, pan-pan, pan-pan this is sailing vessel..." he stumbled, swallowing back a swell of grief for what he'd lost, "um this is Ian hailing from God's Pocket Resort, anyone read?"

He heard nothing but static so he worked the squelch dial a little, adjusting it just under the static threshold and tried again, "Pan-pan, pan-pan, pan-pan, this is Ian at God's Pocket, do you read?" He waited for a few long moments and then looked at Amy, seeing his disappointment mirrored in her eyes.

"Maybe there's something wrong with the antenna?" she suggested.

"Or maybe there's nobody out there? Maybe there was a zombie apocalypse while we've been stuck here." A lame attempt at humor that felt a little too real sitting on the edge of the world in an empty lodge, the wilderness spreading around them for miles in every direction. Primeval forest on one side, wild ocean on the other, with nothing but the drone of the generator, the lights in this room and the brightly colored cottages to remind them of their tenuous links back to the rest of humanity.

"I've got an idea!" Amy walked over to a stereo sitting

next to the couches, selected a CD and pressed play. She turned around just as the first notes of 'Unchained Melody' emanated from the speakers and then, turning on the charm, smiling, swaying toward him, warmth in her eyes, she reached out to cross the distance between them. They gently, oh so gently, held each other in a tender embrace, dancing slowly in the brightly lit space between the long wooden table and the faded fabric couches. Dancing like they could forget where they were, forget what had happened, forget everything and just sway in sweet little circles forever and ever, amen.

Then the lights went out.

CHAPTER 15

They stood in shock, drowning in the sudden black silence, their slow dance frozen in place. The drone of the generator had stopped, the electricity gone. After a few moments, their eyes adjusted to the moonlight that was shining through the windows and illuminating the room, bathing it in silver. They separated like two people who have just woken and can't seem to understand where they've found themselves. Without light, without music, the room seemed empty and they felt empty now too.

Ian knew he could go to the generator and try to figure out what was wrong. It had probably run out of fuel, but it was late and he was suddenly very tired. Everything was catching up with him, the whole long day piling up and pressing him down toward sleep. With a brief look at Amy, he headed toward the small room in the corner where he knew a bed was waiting. Amy padded softly to the other room, claimed her own bed and collapsed onto it. They were separated by mere feet, but there was a wall between them that allowed no sight or feeling to pass through.

As soon as he lay down, Ian felt strange. Restless and overtired, he rolled back and forth trying to get comfortable. Nothing seemed to fit right, the corners were too square, the walls were too smooth, the bed was too level. He settled onto his back, blankets wrapped around him, pillow crushed under his head, feeling alone and anxious.

He stared at the ceiling for a long time, settling slowly into something that wasn't quite sleep. He found himself pulled back toward the forest, his mind wandering paths he had wandered on foot during the day. The walls were shimmering around him, translucent, insubstantial, unable to hold him in, unable to hold the wild out, the building like a fragile shell around him. Through the walls he could see the trees pushing in, their roots pressing deep below his room, cradling it in their quest for sustenance. He could see creatures moving through the foundation, permeable to them, unable to block their searching.

He felt afraid and clung to the safety of the roof above, wanting the walls to cut him off from the creatures below and the blankets to protect him. The wild was pressing in against this thin membrane of civilization that he'd thought would keep him safe. He was afraid. Afraid that the wild would consume him, afraid that he would lose himself to it, afraid to feel it all around him, pressing against his flesh and pushing into his mind. It was too big, too confusing, too alien, too dangerous. He was drawn to the wild but needed to hold himself separate to feel safe. Separate from the ferocity, the unpredictability, the danger and the mystery of it. Separated by the power of technology, human knowledge, clothing, roofs, and walls.

Restless and feverish, he knew there was something missing. He felt an emptiness inside, a hole that he didn't know how to fill. As he sank deeper into these thoughts, he was aware of a ravening desire, the same need that had driven him this far north toward Alaska, and would continue to drive him further than he knew how to go. It would drive him to the end of his life and beyond. A desire that was indistinguishable from despair. On this island he had felt intensely alive, focused on the need to survive, deeply connected to Amy, no longer alone, driven to get them to safety, senses alert, the wild entering him, acting through him, an intensity of experience that he couldn't let go of, the rest of his life like a shadow in comparison.

He must have fallen asleep because the next thing he was aware of was the sensation of something sitting on the end of his bed. It was a comfortable, solid presence. It stood, his bed creaking as it rose.

He got out of bed and followed it out of the room, everything clear, sight coming effortlessly, the smallest details crisp, silver light throwing sharp edged shadows and washing out color. He followed it out of the building and into the open air, the sky as clear as glass, a million pinpricks of light above him, everything luminous and solid. He felt the grass beneath his feet and realized he was barefoot, yet he was warm and comfortable. Safe and at peace. Content. He was holding Amy's hand now. He could see her face but she didn't notice him, she was looking straight ahead, out to sea.

Following her gaze, his breathing stopped, the breath hitching in his chest. The cove fronting the lodge was completely filled with luminescence. Phosphorescence glowed on the tip of every wavelet, moving in graceful arcs toward them, glowing briefly brighter and then fading as the water lapped and receded on the shoreline. Within the cove, fish showed themselves as pressure waves of phosphorescence preceding their path and blasts of glowing light left behind by their fin-strokes through the water.

Further out, in the middle of the cove, was the most marvelous thing of all. A mother humpback whale and her calf reclined in the tranquil cove, resting magnificently. The top of their bodies floated out of the water, their skin speckled with living, glowing dots of phytoplankton. Phosphorescent. Their limbs stirred the water, shimmering waves of light radiating away in concentric circles. The calf made a small grunting noise, content and protected. The mother made an answering noise, a deep growling muffled bark and then she blew out her breath in one long stream of air and water that hung above them, hung in a glowing double-lobed cloud, before slowly settling back down upon their bodies and the surrounding water like a glistening, jewel encrusted blanket.

Ian was quite simply in awe. He had never seen anything so beautiful. Had never imagined the possibility of such wonder. The love of mother for child had never felt so encompassing, so all-consuming and protective, so luminescent. He stood hand in hand with Amy, enraptured for a very long time before he realized that there was another presence standing with them. Had been with them the whole time. Had led them out to this place to see this sight. Much larger than either of them, it reeked of a wild and oily musk, unwashed and untamed. It stood beside them breathing, blowing steam, taking in the scene, immobile.

Almost against his will, fighting against a fear that welled from deep within, he turned his head to look at the creature standing next to him. His eyes saw but his mind failed him. He simply couldn't take it in, couldn't make sense of this thing he was seeing; twice as tall as a normal man, brown and shaggy, breathing in steam-bellow blasts from its large, leathery nostrils. His fears rushed back over him, he couldn't stop them, they bowled him over.

He saw himself in an alpine wilderness, surrounded by snow and ice, an avalanche bearing down. He tried to turn and run but he was too slow. A shockwave of air knocked him flat and then the snow was on him, tumbling and spinning him down the slope, completely out of control. The snow like air in his lungs, chilling him, collecting in his hair, packing into his face, pouring down his jacket and into his pants. The tumbling slowed down and it grew dark as the snow settled around him, harder than cement and he could no longer move. Muscles trembling, hyperventilating, claustrophobic, fighting his end with every ounce of his being, lights sparking and popping in his eyes until his breathing slowed and his heart fluttered to a stop. He was consumed by the mountain. Entombed.

He saw himself on his boat, waves growing larger, the wind pressing with unnatural force. Lightning a startling white against the dark sky, thunder cracking and rumbling across the watery void, the chaotic seascape of a world gone mad. Monstrous waves to the horizon, tumbling and frothing, each one deadly, the sound rumbling and throbbing through his chest. He struggled with the wheel, struggled with the sails, but he knew he was being overpowered. He couldn't stand against forces so much larger than himself and his tiny boat. The waves pummeled them and the boat groaned, the wheel breaking from his grip as they fell off a wave that dwarfed human scale. He screamed his frustration, his rage and fury, his desire to live, his failure to dominate that which could not be dominated. The boat rolled beneath him, cutting off sound, tossing him into the water and wrapping him in icy cold. He was fighting the urge to gasp, to fill his lungs with the sea, when his tether snapped, releasing him into the depths, the roiling currents pulling him down. He looked up to see the boat slowly right itself, the surface of the water frothing in turmoil, and he stretched his arms upward toward life. He sank down, his lungs filling with liquid cold. So cold. He was consumed by the sea. Lost.

He saw himself tired, his strength failing, deep in the forest. He could walk no further and there was no-one who could help. He sat with has back to a giant tree, nestled in an enormous root structure, closed his eyes and gave up. He watched as the insects and the animals ate him. The roots grew around his bones, embracing him. He was consumed by the forest. Decomposed.

He saw himself old. Unimaginably old and frail, his skin paper thin, his eyes clouded. He was surrounded by his family, they were holding his hand as the light faded from his eyes and he gasped out his last breaths. They embraced him and cried for him and later with great ceremony and preparation they lowered him into the ground, alone. He was consumed by the earth. Consumed and resting in peace.

CHAPTER 16

Something woke Ian up. He was curled up on the dock, Amy beside him. He saw an aluminum fishing boat approaching, fenders down, engines rumbling, idling forward. On the boat were three men, short and stocky with the dark skin and distinctive features of First Nations people. One at the helm, carefully steering them in, two on the side tipping the boat slightly with their weight, each with a line in hand ready to jump onto the dock and tie them up. Competent, efficient, they had the look of men who knew what they were doing and had done it a thousand times. All three of them looked at him with interest, the skipper giving a tip of the head, one eyebrow slightly raised, the other two looking at him intently, but without expression, giving nothing away.

The boat drifted up alongside the dock, bow nudging forward, and then with a quick blast of reverse to kick the stern in, two men jumped off to tie lines to the dock cleats, holding the boat securely while the skipper shut the engines off. Ian could feel the dock rock slightly, from the boat's wake and from the weight of the men jumping off the boat. He stood, Amy stirring nearby, and looked at the three men, still feeling groggy and not quite believing what he was seeing.

The skipper leaned forward, pushing the windscreen in front of him so that it folded up and out of the way and then stepped forward onto the flat, non-skid bow to take Ian and Amy in. His men had moved to the back of the boat, busying themselves securing the lines and stowing gear.

"Hey-o, what you doing here? You lost?"

Ian had no words.

"Grandfather said there'd be some people here needing

help. Guess you're it. I'm your knight in shining armor, ya?" He laughed, slapping the top of his metal boat hard, the ring on his finger making a resounding clang.

Ian startled, the noise seeming out of place, harsh. Amy was standing now, slightly behind him, looking at the man too.

"So? What happened to you two then? Oh sorry. My manners. I'm Richard, that misfit back there is Tmustsa." He said this last word with a slight hitch between the syllables.

"Traditional parents, you know? You can call him Tum. That's what we all call him, just look at him eh-o, he likes to eat, yeah?" Jerking his thumb back over his shoulder as if to indicate the men in back.

Tum waved lazily in their direction at the sound of his name. The other man poked his head out to introduce himself, "Hey there, I'm Norm," and then his head disappeared as he went back to work.

His voice had a nice lilt to it, a cadence that was a little bit of exotic mixed with the familiar, civilized sounds of British Columbia. Ian began to relax.

"I'm Ian. This is Amy."

Amy stepped forward, reaching her hand out, "Hi Richard, it's nice to meet you."

Richard stepped easily off the boat and onto the dock, the bow bobbing up and down as his weight came off of it.

"Hi Amy, good to meet you too. Do you kids need some help? What are you doing out here? I don't see a boat. Those kayaks belong to the lodge. Someone drop you off and forget to come back? Didn't know the lodge was closed, huh?" His brown eyes squinted in amusement, as if to acknowledge their incompetence, like babes in the woods, but good natured too as if he was happy to help and would set them straight.

"Yeah we could use some help. Wrecked our boat on the rocks on the south shore."

"Wait. You what? You landed down on the south shore, did ya?" Deadly serious now. The sounds from the back of the boat stopped and Ian saw two brown faces poke out, looking at him.

"We hit the rocks just off the beach. We were lucky to get off the boat with our lives. We have our clothes and that's it. Had to walk across the island to get here and found the lodge last night. I'm really happy to see you, not sure what we would have done."

The two other men walked up to flank Richard, one on each side, still silent.

"You say you walked across this island? Walked from the south shore?" Richard's deep brown eyes looked troubled and he seemed less sure of himself than a minute ago, his fingers fumbling in his pocket for a cigarette. He lit it and took a drag. "Sorry. You mind?" he waved the cigarette in from of them, a small trail of smoke looping up.

Norm and Tum stood there, implacable, their faces giving nothing away.

"What you two have done. Well. I don't know what to say." Another drag, looking straight at Ian now, "You serious? You aren't messing with an old man are you? You walked across the island did ya?"

Ian just stared at him and nodded slightly, "yeah, that's right."

Richard let out his breath in a big sigh, shoulders slumping a little, "Did you see anything? Anything, um, strange?"

Ian and Amy looked at each other. A small understanding passed between them. What they'd experienced was for themselves only. Not to be shared. No one would believe them anyway. They needed to look normal, not crazy.

Ian looked back at Richard, "No, not really. Took a little while, had a few falls, but mostly uneventful. Beautiful woods aren't they?" and he swept his hand to take in the cove, trying to act normal. As normal as you can act when you are stranded and need rescue.

"You two couldn't have known this. If you had... Well, I guess you couldn't help it, what with the problems with your boat. Hey, is the boat ok? Can we help you pull it off the beach or something?"

"No. She sank. At least I think she did, she was filling up with water when we jumped off, then she was gone. We were hard up on the rocks. But that was two days ago, during the storm."

"Oh yeah. Ok. I'm sorry to hear it. Hate to lose a boat. Worst thing. Can't imagine losing this one. But she's tough, would take a lot to bring her down." Proud now, gesturing back at the solid little work boat behind him.

"Anyways, guess you couldn't help it. Guess not. It's just that we don't go near that place. No-one in my tribe has been there in two generations. No-one in any of the tribes. We just don't go there. Not anymore."

Ian raised his eyebrows at that. Risked a glance at Amy. Her face impassive, looking blandly interested.

"Sasahevas lives over there. Grandfather says there's a family of them. He's been living there a long time, but we don't go there. Not any more."

"Sasahevas?"

"Yeah, that's Coast Salish for Wild Man. Wild Man of the Woods." Norm and Tum looked down involuntarily, they'd both heard this story before.

"He's on our totems. He's a guide for us. For our tribe. For our young people. He used to show us the way. Show us what was real, pull back the veil you know?" Another drag on the cigarette. Drawn out slower this time.

"Not anymore though. I've just heard the stories, like how they'll bang on trees to talk across the island, how they'll build their nests, snapping the tops off of trees. Hey, I think I might have heard one once when I was out fishing, at least I thought I did.

"Grandfather says we've lost our way, that Sasahevas won't help us anymore. It's not safe for us. He told me the stories of how great grandfather went to vision quest on the men's hill and great grandmother had her visions on the women's hill. They went alone and came back changed, full members of the tribe. Trusted. They had passed the Sasahevas's test."

His eyes looked inward, considering what had been lost.

"Around the time of our last potlatch it stopped. We were no longer welcome. We'd entered the modern world. Now we have gasoline boats, watch TV, drive to jobs just like the white folks. Just like them. But we remember. Some of us anyway." Norm and Tum nodding behind him.

"We still do things for our kids though, you know? I've got some cousins camping out for a month. They have tents and stuff, but they still seine-fish for Salmon. Tastes better than Dinty Moore, eh-ya? They've got canoes, even if they are Coleman. But it's not the same, you know? They aren't really tested, but they do get something out of it, come out better because of it."

He dropped his cigarette, ground it out with the toe of his boot and looked up at them with a crooked smile, "Well? You want to get out of this place or what? Ready to leave or would you rather meet the Wild Man tonight?"

They loaded onto his boat and pushed off, retrieving lines, pulling up fenders, and then Richard motored them out of the cove, watching the depth, careful around obstacles. Tum handed them each a water bottle and Ian realized how very thirsty he was.

"I can take you to Port McNeill and you can take a bus down-island from there. It leaves in the morning. If you need a place to stay, the wife and I would be happy to have you two for dinner tonight."

Ian looked behind them, watching the lodge getting smaller, the brightly colored cottages disappearing behind a screen of trees one at a time, until the last one was visible and then it too slid out of view.

Richard nailed the throttle forward and with a roar the boat leapt up, plowing into its own bow wave, digging deeper and deeper until it had climbed up and out, achieving a solid plane and arcing away down the channel toward the open sound.

Ian found himself sitting on a hard seat in the boat's boxy, aluminum cabin, Richard, Norm and Tum in front of him, Amy to the side. Surrounded by windows, he could see the water speeding by in a steady, solid froth, islands sliding past, sharp bow cutting through the waves. He knew the tide was running, probably four knots or stronger, but for this boat, running steady at forty knots, the tide was nothing. Inside the box he couldn't feel the wind or the spray and he felt cut off from the outside world. The roaring of the engines filled his head and blocked the sounds of the ocean and its creatures. The smell of gasoline and oil filled his nose, overpowering the smell of the sea. A feeling grew in him, a feeling of dislocation and loss. Devastating loss. It became too much for him. It was hard to breathe. Everything felt unreal. He was floating outside of himself. He was stuck inside his head. He was throbbing with pain.

Ian stood up to escape, Amy watching him. She looked concerned. Holding tightly to the rails on the top of each seat he worked himself unsteadily rearward, out the back door and onto the aft deck. It was quieter here, in the open, exposed to the wind and spray. He sat down and closed his eyes, tilting his head back, feeling the sun on his face.

He felt Amy wedge herself next to him, hip pressed hard against hip. Connected. Barely enough room for two. He opened his eyes and looked at her.

Her face was close to his, serious, searching his eyes for something. "Did that all happen? Was that real?"

Ian nodded. "Yeah. I think it was. Real I mean."

"I've got something for you, I thought you might want some," and she opened her hand to reveal a small pile of berries nestled in her palm. Perfect little spheres, glowing in the sunlight, filled with delectable juice, protected by a thin membrane as if to keep the world, the real world, at bay.

PART 2: THE ISLAND

CHAPTER 17

Amy was wedged up against Ian, the vibration of the boat working its way into her feet and legs. The sun, the drone of the motors, and the solid feeling of Ian's body next to her conspired to make her feel lazy and slow, muscles warm and loose, mind pleasantly fuzzy. She was heading back to civilization. Port McNeill, then Victoria and then who knows where, maybe home? She closed her eyes and let her mind relax. She didn't want to move, didn't want to stir from this place, it was her first true comfort in days. She leaned her head on Ian's shoulder, closed her eyes and let the boat's motion lull her.

Her mind began replaying events of the previous days, settling on the accident and the sinking of Ian's boat. She hadn't had time to think about it yet, to deal with it and truly come to terms with her feelings of guilt. He hadn't said anything to her about it, not since yesterday morning when they'd both been out of their minds yelling at each other. What had caused him to act like that? Caused her to act like that? She felt ashamed, embarrassed, and if she was honest with herself, a little curious. The feelings hadn't all been unpleasant, not really. Not all of them.

Her thoughts returned to the boat. How had she managed to run Ian's boat into a fucking island? It didn't seem possible to her. What the hell had happened?

The sailing had been good, ten to fifteen knot winds from the west, a perfect beams-reach up Queen Charlotte Sound toward the open ocean of the mid-coast. The marine forecast had been calling for the wind to build to twenty knots with one meter seas predicted at the West Sea Otter buoy. It was a good forecast, they'd have to keep an eye on conditions, but it wasn't anything they couldn't handle.

It was late in the afternoon, there had been a light drizzle earlier in the day, but the sun was peeking through the clouds now and it was warm enough to take her foulies off, leaving her in quick-dry pants, several layers of wool and her favorite hoodie – the comfort food of clothing. The decks were constantly wet, spray from the bow washing over the front of the boat, running down the side decks and into the cockpit to the drains at her feet.

Ian had broken the silence. "Amy, I'm feeling pretty tired. Last night must be catching up with me. Is it ok if I head below and get some rest?"

"Yeah that's fine, I'm in a groove here. I'll yell down if I need any help."

"Sounds good. Keep an eye on the wind and don't hesitate to wake me if it gets stronger. I can help you put in a reef."

With a smile and a wink, "You got it captain. Sweet dreams!"

Ian clambered down the companionway stairs to lay in the quarter-berth. Since it was furthest bunk aft, it had the least amount of motion making it their best sea-berth while underway. Ian's foulies were already off, so he peeled back the top blanket and dropped into the bunk, the rest of his clothes still on, and within seconds he was snoring.

Amy looked at him fondly. He was the reason she was on this adventure, without him none of this would have been possible. Before meeting him, she'd been walking the docks for weeks looking for a boat, losing hope that anyone would let her join as crew. He'd been the first one willing to take a chance on her. She took a quick glance at the instruments, checking on wind speed and heading, then she pulled out her phone, plugged in her earbuds and pressed 'play'. Her tunes were thumping, the boat was sailing free and easy, so obviously in its element that Amy could imagine it grinning with satisfaction. Water was pearling down her sides in steady streams, sails and rigging creaking rhythmically under the load as they plunged up and over the regular ocean swells.

Amy felt satisfied too. All was right in her world, everything fitting neatly in place. Here upon the ocean wilderness, so inhospitable to human life that falling in was almost certain death, she was being borne north by a perfect synthesis of man and nature, a wooden sailboat of character and soul, its only purpose to keep her safe and convey her where the wind and tide allowed.

Her mind fell into the steady daze of long-distance travel, not fully conscious, but still aware – eating hours and gobbling miles. She was in the groove, working the helm with precision, easing the sails or tightening them as needed, the boat responding perfectly. She was in her element, doing what she had been made for. She felt timeless. Limitless. Her awareness expanding out toward the horizon, ranging north, as she imagined what it would be like as the seas grew wilder, the mountains taller, the settlements spreading ever further apart, pinpricks in a vast wilderness.

The fog entered her awareness as a faint line to the north, the horizon changing in consistency, becoming softer and less defined. They had seen fog several times in the past week but it had never reached them, never coming close enough to be a factor in their navigation or sailing. Along the way, Ian had taught her how to sail in fog safely, showing her how to use the radar, the ship's bell and the air-horn, just in case.

She ignored the distant fog, watching for dolphins and whales, until she noticed that the fog was getting noticeably closer, the upper portion crawling higher in the sky. As it came toward her it obscured more of her vision, swallowing large portions of the horizon and surrounding waters, swirling layers reaching forward and falling back with variations in temperature, humidity, and wind.

Focused as she was on the fog, she heard the spouts before she saw them. Suddenly surrounding the boat, encircling it in all directions, were Pacific white-sided dolphins, torpedo shapes moving effortless through the water, driving rhythmically to the surface to breathe in a spume of air and spray. They were playing at the bow-wave, diving under, crossing from side to side and front to back, the wind blowing puffs of their breath to leeward where they dissipated into the air.

Wind! Immediately, she was awake and aware. The wind was from behind, the fog in front and yet it was coming closer. The fog should be blowing back, it couldn't possibly push forward against prevailing wind. She sat up, peering over the metal frame of the dodger to get a better look. The fog was much closer now, the bank towering over the boat and wrapping the entire horizon in front of them. Behind her was sea and islands, trees and rocks, sharply defined, solid and real. In front was white, billowing nothingness.

She looked up to find the top of it, craning her neck until she was looking almost straight up, well past the second spreader on the mast. The top of the fogbank was clearly defined, white against blue, a line drawn hard and sharp against the sky. She was starting to feel worried. Something didn't seem right. Fog shouldn't be so dense, so well defined. So solid. She brought her focus back down, staring straight into the wall of it. Now it seemed like it was floating directly in front of the boat, hovering just before the bow, keeping pace with them, the distance unchanging. The dolphins continued to swim around them, surrounding the boat with the sound of their breathing, their breath merging with the fog, guiding her forward into it.

Staring into that swirling mass, her eyes widened and her pupils dilated. She was frozen in place as a large arm of fog reached out, swallowed the boat whole and wrapped them in utter silence. They were floating in a sea of endless white. The fog eased its way down the decks, over the cabin top and into the cockpit, brushing up against Amy. She was powerless to move as a tendril of fog reached out, caressing her cheeks, her forehead and finally her eyes. Her eyelids fluttered closed as her body slumped to the floor and her hand slid down and off the wheel.

CHAPTER 18

A sudden impact shocked her back into awareness, forcing her into a world of chaos. Wind blowing, waves crashing, the sailboat tilting precariously as barnacle covered rocks punched through the wooden hull.

"Oh shit, oh shit, oh shit!"

She was in shock. Everything had been right in her world, the sailing perfect, islands and ocean sparkling in the sun. Then the fog. That unnatural fog. Now this shocking new reality. Over the sound of sea and spray, wind singing through the rigging, sails flapping angrily, through all this she could still hear her music thumping away in one ear, the other earbud hanging down, swinging wildly with the boat's motion.

Ian flung himself up the companionway stairs, hands wet, knees dripping water, eyes staring wildly into her own.

"Oh shit Ian, what just happened? I think I'm..."

Then Amy felt her consciousness leave once more, lifting straight up, right through the top of her head and away as her body fell to the cockpit floor. A sensation of flying, neither up nor down, a tunnel of swirling colors, all senses disjointed, and then with a sickening shock, a reverberating thunk that she felt from the tip of her toes to the top of her skull, she was conscious of her body once more.

Feeling dizzy, bracing her feet to counter the expected motion of the boat, she opened her eyes to find she was in a sun-dappled forest, surrounded by trees and bushes, the sound of birdsong, and the chirp of squirrels. She was spinning in place, trying to make sense of what was happening to her, trying to understand where she was. A whirl of green leaves, yellow sun, grey rock, orange lichen, her world tilting, the ground rising up to meet her. She fell hard, the world sideways, trees stretching upwards to infinity. The last things she saw before her eyes closed were her hands. They were no longer freckled, her fingers no longer slender and white. As blackness overtook her, she saw strong brown hands, tattooed, and most definitely not her own.

When consciousness returned she was in the same body, walking on a trail through the forest. The day was warm and she could feel a trickle of sweat run down her forehead and into her brows. Leather moccasins covered her feet, her legs were bare and she wore a shirt woven out of a fibrous material that smelled like cedar. Stopping mid-stride she looked around to get her bearings.

The forest was composed of closely-spaced trees and thick underbrush. She could smell the sea but she couldn't see it, a profusion of leaves and branches blocked her view in all directions. The sea. That tickled a memory for her. She felt like she was missing something. Something important.

She shook her head and took a deep breath. Dreaming, that's what this must be. A dream. She'd had lucid dreams before. Her old boyfriend had taught her how to do it. He'd been interested in all that kind of stuff. Meditation, incense, dreams... yoga even. All of his ideas had been new to her, fresh from Iowa and her midwestern corn-fed family.

She'd never had a dream this powerful though. It was extraordinarily clear, like she was living inside it, every detail perfect, sights and sounds coming through without distortion. She could smell the forest around her, see dappled light on the forest floor, feel the movement of air around her and the solid presence of her own body. All her previous lucid dreaming had been vague, confusing and quick to dissipate as soon as she had gained any awareness that she was in a dream. Her boyfriend had told her that once she was completely aware inside a dream she could manipulate her environment, fly if she wanted. But she'd never gotten that far.

She smiled wryly, he'd be so proud of her if he could see her now! He even believed that you could visit real places in your dreams, see real people and interact with them. She could believe in the basic idea of lucid dreaming. Maintaining consciousness while in a dream state wasn't too big of a stretch for her, but sending her spirit out into the real world? That was too much. She couldn't believe in that. Maybe that's why they hadn't stayed together. His beliefs were too close to the occult for her taste. He'd made her nervous. She grimaced at the memories she'd stirred up.

Here she was though, in the mother of all lucid dreams. What was she going to do with herself? With a little giggle she stretched her arms straight up into the sky, willing herself up. Fly!

Nothing happened. She was standing on her tiptoes, arms up, face pointed to the sky, eyes closed, waiting. Still nothing. She opened her eyes and found herself looking into the face of a very quizzical squirrel in the branch above her. He blinked at her, let out a chirping noise and twitched his nose. She sighed, dropped her arms and settled back onto her heels. The squirrel, surprised by the sudden movement, let out a series of chirping complaints and retreated up the branch, heading for the safety of the trunk.

It hadn't worked. Damn. She'd always wanted to fly and had been hoping this was her chance. Then she thought about her hands. She distinctly remembered being taught that looking at her hands was the best way to tell if she was in a lucid dream. Some dreams could feel so real that you wouldn't know if you were dreaming or in the real world, so there had to be a way to distinguish the difference. In lucid dreaming, you didn't have a real body so if you looked at your hands they'd be distorted in some way. Misshapen. Missing fingers. Stuff like that.

She raised her hands and looked at them. They were perfect little hands, nothing wrong with them at all. Except for the fact that they weren't hers.

Then she was moving, she felt like something had grabbed her by the top of the skull again, was pulling her straight up and out of her body. She had a sensation of flying, swirling colors surrounded her once more and then she was cold and wet and she could feel someone touching her arm, "Amy, wake up."

She was dazed. Like she was stuck between worlds, the forest scene still imprinted strongly in her mind. She could feel the touch of sunshine on her face and see the trees swaying gently above her.

Ian shook her hard, "Amy!"

She blinked once slowly. A few more fast blinks and she was back. The whole situation returning to her with shocking clarity. Running the boat up on the rocks, the sound of wood splintering and tearing, Ian's panicked expression as he bolted up the companionway stairs to see what she had done. Now she was on a beach, bruised and battered, no sight of the boat, realizing it must be lost and it was her fault. All her fault. She found herself falling into him, hugging him hard, shuddering, and making incoherent noises that might have been words.

CHAPTER 19

Ian could still feel Amy wedged beside him on the aft deck of the boat. He had savored the berries she had given him and then had closed his eyes in an attempt to get some rest. Through his closed eyes he noticed it was getting darker and it was getting colder too. The air felt moist and the sun was losing its power. He opened his eyes and to his surprise he saw that the sky was white, the sun no longer shining down on them, moisture condensing on all the exposed surfaces of the boat as they approached a thick bank of fog.

The fog had extended itself up and over them, blocking the sun and plunging them into a wet gloom. He stood up to get a better look forward, the mariner's natural fear of fog kicking in. Richard must have been feeling the same way up on the helm, because Ian could hear the engines throttling down as the boat settled into a slower pace. Amy stood up too, a worried look on her face. Ian opened the cabin door and walked in, holding it open as Amy followed him.

Richard glanced over his shoulder, "Sorry kids, looks like we've run into a bit of weather. Wasn't expecting fog, but it can happen at any time I guess. Don't worry, I've been fishing around here for forty years and I know these waters like the back of my hand. Might take us a little longer to get to Port McNeill, but we'll still get there before dark."

Ian sat down behind Richard so he could see the instruments and maintain a good view out the front windshield. As far as he could tell, all looked well. The GPS showed them making steady progress, motoring south in over a thousand feet of water. Richard was steering a course to keep Vancouver Island about a mile to the west, the mainland ten miles to the east across Queen Charlotte Strait. As they motored south, the fog continued to thicken, the color changing to a slate grey, the cabin darkening as the sun became increasingly obscured.

Ian was starting to feel anxious. The fog was so dense that Richard had to use the wipers to drive excess moisture off the windshield. Glancing at Amy, Ian noticed that her face looked pale, hands gripping the seat in front of her hard enough to whiten her knuckles, ropy muscle standing out on her forearms, head thrust forward as if she was urging them forward and out of this infernal fog.

Richard slowed down further. "Getting hard to see, no point in us blundering into a dead-head. This boat can take a hit but I'd prefer not to add any more dents to the collection." He gave them a grin, clearly hoping a little humor would help to lighten the mood.

Ian took a deep breath, trying to force himself to relax, and sat back to look out the side window. He let his eyes lose their focus, willing the time to pass. The water was mostly flat, the wind having died away once they'd entered the fog. They were moving at eight knots, slow for this boat, but close to the speeds he was used to while sailing. The cabin was relatively quiet, engines purring along at little more than idle, the water easing by in a steady stream. Looking out the window he could imagine himself on the bank of a wide river, the water inexorably sliding past him.

With his eyes unfocused, he began to notice patterns in the fog. He let his mind wander, still trying to relax, letting his mind pull fantastic objects out of the fog. Was that a bear? Maybe a bear chasing a rabbit with huge ears? No, it was a hunter. A hunter with a headdress, running pell-mell with the bear on his tail. Ian smiled, urging the hunter on, hoping he would make it to safety, losing sight of them both as they fell behind the boat.

A tall figure appeared in the patterns of the fog. She was wearing a traditional dress and had long hair that floated in a wild halo around her head. Her large mouth gaped, unnaturally round, lighter around the edges and pitch black toward the middle. She had something on her back. A basket of some sort? Was that a head sticking out? Her arms reached forward, toward a small figure crouched below – a child gathering something from the ground, unaware of the danger looming behind.

Ian shook his head and let his eyes snap back into focus. “Not really helping me relax, is it?” He thought. Ian looked at the water beading on the side window, each drop distinct, reflecting the whole world in a distorted sphere. The water flowed together from the boat’s movement, forming a bird, then a fish, then it was blown off the side of the window and into the sea. Glancing around the boat he noticed Norm looking at him. As soon as he noticed that he had Ian’s attention, he give him a thumbs up and a warm smile. Ian felt a little better, Norm’s good spirits were contagious.

He brought his gaze forward again, looking out the front of the boat past Richard, and saw that the fog was lightening. It was starting to break up, the ocean sparkling around them in a broad circle, the fog still out there, but backing away, giving them space. He glanced at the instruments and noted that they were moving a little faster now, nearly twelve knots, the GPS showing only blue water, no land in view.

He could see Richard’s shoulders relaxing and could tell he was feeling better about the situation, the fog visibly improving, a break apparent in front of them. Richard pushed the throttle forward and the boat surged ahead, gaining speed, noise swelling in a crescendo of engine, wind and water as they broke through into bright sunshine, perfect visibility forward, the fog bank hanging solidly behind them.

Richard jumped, startled, lunging for the throttle and pulling it back to neutral. The boat settled into the water, speed bleeding off, the engines no longer pushing them forward, Richard looking forward in disbelief. Ian couldn’t believe what he was seeing either. He looked at the GPS map. It showed them in a small cove, the map perfectly matching what he could see out the windows. They were back in God’s Pocket, the brightly colored cottages perched above the water cheerfully, as if they were welcoming them back.

CHAPTER 20

The boat was dead in the water, moving gently up and down on the wavelets within the cove. Richard turned off the engines. Silence.

Amy was the first to talk, "Are we back at the island? How is that even possible?"

Richard shook his head, looking alternately out the window and then down at his instruments as if he couldn't believe what his senses were telling him. It was clear they were back at the island, but he had no idea how it had happened. His mental map put them near Port Hardy, on their way to Port McNeill, well on their way home. Now they were at Hurst island, right back where they had started. Sunlight in front, thick fog behind.

"Well... Um... I don't know what happened. I've never gotten lost like this before. Not that we are really lost, but I guess I must have gotten turned around in the fog. I don't see how it could have happened. I was watching the GPS and we were following the correct compass heading..." Richard's voice trailed off, the question left hanging in the air. He knew he sounded nervous.

He was turned around, confused and unsure. He'd been fishing these waters since he was ten years old and nothing like this had ever happened. He'd never even heard of anything like this happening, not since the advent of GPS. There were stories of people who had gotten well and truly lost in the old days, but not now. Sure, the fog had been thick. Almost unnaturally thick, but that wouldn't have impacted his GPS. Satellite signals don't care about fog. This shouldn't have happened. Ever.

Richard looked back at the group to judge their mood. Tum looked stoic as usual, waiting to see what he'd do next.

They'd spent many years together and the trust he'd built up over that time was paying off now. He looked at the kids he'd rescued and winced. They looked nervous. Very nervous. They were his responsibility now. He'd told them he'd get them home and dammit that's what was going to happen.

Jaw set, face resolute, he turned the engines back on, cranked the wheel over and sped back out of the cove, fog swallowing the boat whole.

Several hours later they were back in the cove again, but now they were low on fuel and running out of daylight. Richard's shoulders slumped in defeat. He'd spent the last few hours navigating through the fog, eyes straining, glancing back and forth between the outside world and his GPS chart, doubting himself, unsure where they really were. His stomach had been tied in knots and he'd felt a constant weight on his shoulders. The weight of failure. Having gotten lost once, he'd been determined not to let it happen again. Yet here he was, back in the same damned place. When they'd broken out of the fog and into the cove for a second time, he'd let out a grunt of shock. What was going on? He couldn't wrap his mind around it.

Richard took a moment to collect himself. There was no point fighting it. Undoubtedly, they were back in the cove and that's just the way it was. Now he needed to take stock – do what was necessary to understand their situation and figure out a plan that would get them home safely.

He looked around once more, noting the now familiar bank of fog in the channel behind them. The sun was hanging low in the sky, nearly behind the western arm of the cove and the surrounding forest was gaining depth, the angle of the light casting long shadows, the trees nearly glowing. He looked down at his fuel gauge. Not nearly enough to left get them back home, even if he had felt confident that he could navigate through the fog. There wasn't even enough to get them to Port Hardy, the closest town.

He didn't like the idea of floating around the Strait of Georgia without engines, it was not a body of water to underestimate. They needed to get some help or find some fuel or both, and they definitely needed to wait until the fog lifted before he'd be willing to try leaving again.

Richard sighed and nudged the throttles, moving the boat forward.

"Prepare the boat to dock. I'm taking us in."

His crew sprang into action, moving more quickly than normal, nervousness obvious to his eyes. He nodded at Tum, standing ready on the aft deck, stern line in hand.

Once they were safely on the dock, Richard addressed the group, "We're low on fuel and running out of daylight. It looks like we're stuck here for the night, so let's head up to the lodge and figure out our next steps."

Ian and Amy looked downright spooked. Ian spoke first, "Is there any way we could cross over to Vancouver Island? Isn't there anywhere else we can go? I really don't like the idea of spending another night here."

Amy was nodding as Ian spoke, "Richard, we may not have been totally honest with you before. There's something really strange going on here..." She glanced at Ian, gathering her courage, then back to Richard, "I think we may have seen Sasahevas."

Richard responded sharply, "Wait, you what? You think you saw Sasahevas? Both of you?"

Ian cut in, "Yeah, we both saw him. A couple times. Even before we saw him, we both felt... um... not right."

Richard was stunned, "What do you mean you saw him a couple times? Nobody has seen Sasahevas since before I was born. The stories are frightening." He paused for a moment. "Did you feel or act differently than normal? I've heard stories of people acting strangely when he is near."

Amy looked questioningly at Ian for a moment, as if she was wondering how much they should share. She seemed to come to a decision and started talking, spilling it out. "I think I know what you're talking about. We were in the forest and there were these berries and I was so hungry. Not just hungry for food, it was something else, I can't describe it, but I felt it. It was an appetite like I've never had before. At first it felt good, I had all this energy. I could see better and smell better, the experience was so vivid. I felt so alive...

"Then we entered this strange clearing. I think maybe it was one of the nests you told us about? I felt like I was losing control of myself. I was still hungry, but it was as if I was feeling somebody else's hunger, and it was a hunger that was directed at me. I was scared but also felt ready, like it was natural that something else would feel that kind of hunger toward me. Like I was outside and looking at myself with... with an appetite... and I wanted it to happen. Then I woke from it and I saw Ian looking at me like that, like he had that hunger too, and it didn't feel good anymore. It was terrifying so I started yelling at him, and then I ran."

Ian had stood up and was pacing while Amy talked. He looked upset as he turned toward them, "I know what you mean, Amy. I was feeling it too. Like I wasn't myself. I don't know why I was looking at you like that, but I was feeling things I shouldn't have felt. It was unnatural. Unnatural and dangerous...

"I followed her up the trail and found her crying. She was totally unhinged. She'd heard something big moving around and then she saw a hand in the bushes. It wasn't a human hand though... it was covered in brown fur, just like the fur we saw on the tree and in the nest. I think the fur is what affected us. Once we entered the nest, the smell became really intense. That's when I lost control of myself until I heard knocking on a tree nearby. They were knocking back and forth and that's what woke us up from whatever it was that was wrong with us."

Amy spoke up again, "Then we actually saw it. Up on the hill behind the lodge. The fog was rolling in so we stopped to rest. We were sitting up there, waiting for better visibility and it walked right past us. It was walking up the trail we had just been on. It went over the top of the hill and kept walking until we lost sight of it. Once the fog lifted, we hiked through the forest until we found the lodge. And then..."

She was looking at Ian now, a question in her eyes, "Ian? Did you have a strange dream last night? A dream that took you outside the lodge and… there were whales?"

Ian looked like he'd seen a ghost. "Yes I did." That's all he said and then he shut up.

Amy looked to Richard again, "We dreamed about it last night too. It came to my bed and woke me up. It took me outside, or I followed it anyway. I chose to. Then I noticed that Ian was there and everything was so clear and it was so beautiful." Her eyes were welling up with tears, forced out by the intensity of her emotions, "I was standing there, I was holding Ian's hand. Sasahevas was there too, but he didn't feel like a threat anymore, he was just … just waiting there. I wasn't paying attention to him because the entire cove was glowing and there were these two whales and they were glowing too and I've never seen anything so wonderful in my life. It was more amazing than I deserve, I never should have been shown anything like that, I don't deserve it, I just don't." She blinked hard, a tear rolling down her cheek and falling to the ground at her feet.

Richard didn't know what to make of it. Not entirely. But he was starting to get some ideas and he wasn't sure if he liked them. Actually, he was pretty sure he didn't like what was going on, but he also knew that it didn't matter one whit what he thought. They were all here now and they were going to have to deal with the consequences.

Richard sighed, gathering his confidence around him like a cloak and faced Amy squarely, "Thanks for sharing that with me. I'm sure it wasn't easy. I've never seen Sasahevas, but I've been hearing about him all my life. I may have some ideas about what's going on."

Talking to Ian now, "Let's collect some supplies off the boat and then get ourselves set up at the lodge. We are definitely going to be here overnight. Maybe longer." He sighed, "What you saw yesterday and what we experienced today in the fog… It's not a coincidence. I think someone, or something, is forcing us into this place, limiting our actions, blocking us from leaving. I hope their motives are to our liking, but right now I'm feeling a lot like prey."

CHAPTER 21

Richard sent Ian and Amy up to the lodge to find beds for everyone while he and his crew organized the supplies. In addition to coolers filled with food and water, he had backpacks, flashlights, foul weather gear, knives, compasses, hand-held radios, and their personal cell phones. Once past Port Hardy, cell service died out, but it was possible they could find a high point with a clear shot to a cell tower on Vancouver Island.

When he made it to the lodge, Ian and Amy had opened up a few of the cottages and were letting them air out. They also had the lodge opened up, but none of the lights were on.

"Hey Ian, is the electricity working?"

"It was earlier, when we had the generator running, but it stopped and we didn't have a chance to fix it."

Ian pointed up to the generator shed and Richard walked in to take a look. He saw a Honda generator pulling gasoline from a 50 gallon barrel. He grabbed the barrel and wiggled it to see how full it was. Based on how much it weighed, he figured it must be at least half full. Enough gas to last for weeks if not months. Too bad it wasn't diesel. Gasoline wouldn't work in his boat's engines.

He pushed the starter button and the generator turned over but didn't start. He spoke softly to himself, thinking aloud, "Hmm, wonder what's stopping it from running. Gasoline engine..." He checked the air intake first, finding it clear of debris and the air filter seemed fresh. He couldn't pull a spark plug without returning to his boat for tools, so he took a look at the fuel feed next. The fuel pump looked fine from the outside, no obvious signs of leaking, and the fuel hose looked fresh without any obvious problems. As he visually traced the hose from the generator toward the fuel barrel he saw the problem. There was a shutoff valve near the barrel and it appeared to be closed. When Ian started the generator, it must have run for a while on residual fuel and once that was gone, it had stopped.

He opened the valve, pressed the starter, and after turning over for a few seconds the generator started right up. As soon as electricity started flowing, the light in the generator room lit up. Richard shook his head, a little bemused that the kids had left it on, then he left the shed turning off the light and closing the door behind him. As he walked away, he could hear the sound of the generator, muffled behind the door, a comforting drone.

He joined the rest of the group where he found everyone picking which cottage they wanted to sleep in. Ian and Amy had picked the first two, side by side, then an empty cottage followed by Tum. Richard thought about taking the cottage on the far side, past Tum, but then thought better of it, selecting the one next to Amy. If anything odd happened in the middle of the night he wanted to be able to hear it and take action if necessary.

After selecting where they would sleep and placing all of their supplies in the main lodge building, the group gathered, disconsolate, around the fire pit between the lodge and the cottages. Richard took control of the situation, "Hey Tum, run on down to the boat and grab the fire starting kit. I have some hot dogs we can roast and a bit of beer. It'll be a regular camp out." He kept the rest of his thoughts to himself – forest creatures don't much like fire, maybe the flames will provide some protection.

By the time they had gathered everything and started the fire, the sun was well and truly down. They piled on the wood, probably more than they needed. The flames were leaping high, shadows dancing and flickering behind them, some of them recognizable as human in shape, others grossly distorted. Richard had hoped to improve morale, make things a little festive, but they ate in silence. He chewed on his hotdog and took sips of his beer, not really tasting anything. He was considering what they'd shared with him and what he wanted to say in return, trying to decide how much he wanted to tell. He looked up and judged the mood. Tum was done eating and on his third beer, sucking it down, on a mission. Ian and Amy were still eating, chewing slowly, each with a beer in one hand, a hotdog in the other, staring into the flames, lost in thought.

Richard made up his mind, "Hey kids, I should tell you more of what I know. More about Sasahevas... and Tsonoquah. The Wild Woman."

They looked at him immediately, both of their heads popping up. If he had been anywhere else he might have chuckled at their reaction, but not here. Not now. He continued on, speaking earnestly, "The stories I'm going to tell you are old. Old as my tribe. Some even older. As old as the first humans who came to this place.

"You have to understand that my people have been here a very long time. We came to this continent during the last ice age, that's over sixteen thousand years ago. Think about that... sixteen thousand years. Your ancestors were still in the stone age, your Christian religion was fourteen thousand years away from even starting. No-one had agriculture or industry or towns, they were all living simple hunter-gatherer lives, with rocks and sticks as their only tools.

"My ancestors were travelers, nomadic. They'd settled on the Bering land bridge when it emerged from the sea, and as the glaciers melted they followed the land as it opened up to the south of them. It was a huge migration, one of the largest and longest in the history of the world, and the land they discovered was absolutely new. No humans had ever been there, hardly any animals or plants had taken root yet either. The land they settled had been under ice for thousands of years and was newly free from that burden when they found it. It was the definition of virgin land, an incredible saga of exploration and discovery. A huge migration of plants and animals and humans, together they colonized a new world.

"When my people came down this coast, the great forests

didn't exist yet. They found a land entirely composed of rock and grass and brush. The trees hadn't had a chance to get started. Think about that for a moment – my people have been here longer than these forests. My bloodline is older than these trees.

"The glaciers had more impact than just clearing the land. They were extremely heavy, so heavy that the land sank under their weight. When my people were settling here, the coastline was very different than what you see today. As the glaciers melted, the sea levels rose and with the land still depressed from the weight that had been on them, the coastline was far to the east of where it is today. Then the land rebounded and the coastline moved far to the west, pushing the sea before it. Most of the coastal fjords were above water at that point. The reason they are fjords now is that they used to be river valleys, high and dry, with people living there for many years. When the land finally settled back down to where it rests today, the waters flooded back, submerging mountains and valleys, covering villages under hundreds of feet of water.

"My point is that we've been here a very long time. I'm sure you've seen middens on your voyage up here and recognized them as ancient village sites, but in the grand sweep of time, those middens are modern. Village sites that currently sit above water are new compared to the many millennia that my people have been living here. All of the smaller islands you've sailed past were once populated, even Vancouver Island was filled with my people. The waters were our highways, boats filled with people working and socializing.

"Just imagine that, imagine what it was like when my people numbered in the hundreds of thousands and this was an interconnected oceanic empire. Before we met your ancestors we had many thousands of years of history. Stories of tragedy, comedy, and heroism, all the culture you would expect from a large and diverse civilization.

"I'm telling you this, trying to impress you with it, because I want you to know that Sasahevas was here even before we were. Nobody knows how he got here, but we do know that our stories of Sasahevas are extraordinarily ancient. The first people have stories of meeting him, and the stories of contact with him have continued down the ages into modern times. We've lived side by side, sometimes in peace, sometimes at war, and eventually we became symbiotic. He has became an important part of our tapestry of legends, a critical part of our spiritual landscape, and along the way we became something important to him as well.

"Tribute. Sacrifice. There are no good ways to put it. We became his prey and in turn we figured out how to manage his impact, minimize the risk to the tribes and organize our culture so we had some control over how and when it happened. If we could offer up what he needed, offer up what he was hungry for, he wouldn't come to our villages and wreak destruction. It was a rational arrangement that was built over the centuries and had been stable for a very long time.

"I told you earlier that our contact with Sasahevas stopped several generations ago and that's a fact. Our culture changed rapidly after the Europeans appeared. Disease killed the majority of our people and then trade made the survivors dependent. When the conquest came, we didn't have the strength to resist. We were far too diminished, far too spread apart. We almost welcomed it at first, we needed the help to recover from what had been done to us. Eventually we were integrated, our culture outlawed, our children enslaved in the residential school system, our people forced to dress, act, and think like white people.

"Our contact with Sasahevas was cut off at that point, our traditions were broken and our people no longer knew the old forms. We don't know how to communicate with him, how to make offerings to him, how to give him what he hungers for or how to take from him what we need in return. The old stories are still told but they've lost their power, our people have turned to jobs and fast food, cars and computer screens.

"We know that Sasahevas has been here all along. He may have been pushed deeper into the forest but he's still around.

Especially on this island. On this island he never left. Our Elders think he may have been on this continent for over one hundred thousand years. All I know for certain is that he's been living in this area with us for at least ten thousand.

"We've never found a body or bones or any other sign of a Sasahevas that has died. As far as we know he's immortal, and that's exactly what our oldest legends imply. He is not just Sasahevas, he is also known as the Ancient One. The Sasahevas that my people found on this island over ten thousand years ago, the Sasahevas that we've been feeding for all of these years, is very likely the same Sasahevas that you saw yesterday and the same creature that stood with you in this cove last night. My tribe has been separated from him for less than a hundred years. For him, that's the blink of an eye, it's like no time has passed at all. I think perhaps he is just now noticing the change. Noticing the lack of sacrifice. I think maybe he is just starting to get hungry again."

CHAPTER 22

Richard had been staring into the fire as he talked, images from the stories dancing before his eyes, but now he looked up at his audience to see their reaction. Tum was deep into beer five, he knew the stories and was taking advantage of the free drinks. Ian and Amy were enraptured, looking for all the world like he'd cast a spell on them, their beer and hotdogs forgotten.

"This creature that we saw, Sasahevas, you think he has been around since before your people came here over the land bridge?" Amy was trying to make sense of it. "He's been *eating* your people? Actually eating them?"

Staring back into the flames, "In a manner of speaking."

"What? Why? How have I never heard of this before?"

"The last time it happened was before the Europeans came. So much was lost when our civilization was destroyed. Some of the fragments are just now getting put back together again by our Elders. And why would we share it? Your people wouldn't believe us. You wouldn't understand it. Even to us it seems unreal, something from another time, a lost age that won't be coming back. But now... now you. You've seen him and he's communicated with you. You say he's touched your minds. These are things that are spoken of in the stories, and I'm afraid they may lead us to a dark place. A very dark place."

"But why us? Why now? What does he want with us?" Amy was starting to look panicked, the words coming out a little too fast and a little too loud.

"I don't know. But we need to figure it out. The more we know and the more we understand, the better our odds are of escaping this island and surviving this."

"What did your people get out of it?" Ian was looking intently at Richard.

"What?"

"You said you'd get something back from Sasahevas, something in exchange for your sacrifice. What did you get?"

"We were given visions. Visions of what was coming, visions of the future. Visions that helped the tribe survive. Visions that our Elders could interpret and our chiefs could use to make decisions. Visions of power. Each tribe collected their visions as a sacred cache and passed them down from Elder to Elder, memorized by our holy men.

"Our potlatches were used to give physical gifts, but that wasn't the most important reason for them. You may have been taught that the holder of a potlatch would gain power by giving away all his possessions and this is true, but it leaves something important out. The important thing is what he got in exchange, that which would motivate him to give everything away he'd accumulated in a lifetime of hunting, fishing, and raiding other tribes.

"He gave away all of his worldly possessions in exchange for visions from the other tribes. Coming to a potlatch to exchange visions was a sacred duty. The visions would give the receiver power and the more visions he accumulated, the more power he would have. These visions were the true currency of our people and their circulation was our most important trade.

Ian nodded, "Ok, that makes sense. I've never understood the potlatch ceremony, I've always felt like I was missing something. This vision exchange, that was the hidden piece I didn't know about." He looked thoughtful, "You also mentioned Tsonoqua. How does she play into all of this?"

Richard paused, looking at Ian and chewing the inside of his cheek. The fire was very quiet, burned down to embers, just a few small flames licking up from the glowing orange core. Tum was paying attention now too, curious to see what he would say.

"Tsonoqua. She's... well... she's a real piece of work." Richard paused again. Thinking. Trying to find the right words.

"There are a few stories of her bringing bounty to the

tribes, but those are rare. For the most part she is fear itself, the uncaring wilderness, personified as an ogress of immense strength, power, and appetite.

"She is the reason, maybe the excuse, for why my people never went far inland. We were coastal people, the ocean was our front yard and gathering place. You might imagine us spending our time on land, gathering in the forests and clearings, but that's not how it was. We lived our lives in our boats, the sea is where we felt safe. We slept on land, but we crowded our longhouses onto the beaches as close to the water as we could get them. We spent our days in our canoes. The forest is where people went to disappear. Most of my ancestors would never have been more than a few miles inland. The snow covered peaks might as well have been on the Moon, that's how inaccessible they were. Nobody would have dreamed of going that far.

"Tsonoqua is huge, at least twice as tall as a human, with protruding brows and sunken eyes, wild hair in a tangled pile around her head. Her mouth is unnaturally large and round and red. No-one has ever seen teeth, just a deep black hole taking up the lower half of her face. She wears a basket on her back that she uses to hold the people she scoops up so she can eat them later. Our stories tell mostly of her taking children but I think that's because these stories were told primarily to children as a warning. I imagine that Tsonoqua would take anyone she could get. But if you could teach your children how to stay safe, they would remember those stories when they grew into adults. They would remember to stick to the beach, close to the water, and avoid the forests."

The fire was burning very low now and Richard was having trouble seeing the other's faces. They looked like disembodied heads, orange and flickering, staring at him silently with wide eyes. He shook his head. There was one more thing he had to tell, one more thing to get out before he was done, "That's not all... She would also consume those who drowned. They were her favorites. People say that when you see her at twilight you can also see the spirits of the drowned clustered around her.

They are drawn to her in their death, unable to break free and move into their afterlife. You can see them hovering around her shoulders, lost and bereft.

"Sometimes a wife or a mother, a husband or a father would be so grief stricken after losing a loved one to the sea that they would seek Tsonoqua out. They would lose their minds, enter the forests alone, walking through the shadows until they found her. They would receive one last sight of their beloved before they too were swallowed whole.

"The tribe would watch the doomed one walk into the forest, they wouldn't try to interfere. They understood that this was a necessary process, as natural as any other death. They would watch the back of the departed as they made their final walk into the gloom, and then they would retire to the long house and wait for the sound of Tsonoqua's 'Uh, huu, uu, uu' ululation. They would hear that horrible sound, the sigh of wind through cedar and the rattling of a final breath. When the tribe would hear that noise, then hear a final 'hu!' they knew it was over. That was when they would begin the chanting and wailing that would last through the night, ending only after the sun had risen once more."

With the conclusion of that ghastly fireside ghost story, Richard stood up and walked to his cottage.

CHAPTER 23

Ian hadn't slept well and was up early the next morning. Richard's stories about Sasahevas and Tsonoqua had haunted his dreams. Having already met Sasahevas, he had absolutely no desire to meet this other creature. She sounded like something to avoid. Seriously avoid.

He'd tossed and turned, memories of Sasahevas playing through his head. He felt afraid and alone and wanted to be anywhere except for where he was, on this godforsaken island. Every time he thought about the stories of Tsonoqua he cringed. He couldn't quite believe what he'd heard, but he was unable to dismiss his dread. He'd simmered in a soup of anxiety and fear for hours before finally slipping into a fitful sleep, well after midnight. He startled awake at dawn, the fading memories of a dream sliding away, unable to recall anything other than a vague sense of unease.

Ian joined the rest of the group in the lodge for a breakfast of smoked salmon from the boat and dried cereal from the pantry. Someone had figured out how to turn on the water and he drank heartily with his food, trying to rehydrate.

Once he had food in his belly he started to wonder, what was the plan? He had no idea, so he turned to Richard, trusting in his competency, "Richard, what do you think we should do next?"

"Well... I was thinking about that. As long as we stay here we are safe. This lodge has been here for years and Sasahevas seems to have accepted it. As soon as we venture into their territory we run the risk of a nasty encounter. That said, we can't just sit around and wait either. We need to find a way off the island.

"The VHF radio doesn't seem like it's working, so I think

our cell phones are the best chance of reaching someone off island. Our first goal should be to spread out, find some high points on the island and see if we can capture a signal."

Amy looked up from her breakfast, "I don't think splitting up is a good idea. Wouldn't it be better to stick together?"

"I have enough handheld radios for all of us, so we can stay in touch with each other. Look... We've lived in this area all our lives and we have a lot of experience in these forests, we know how to keep you safe. We'll have to be careful and keep an eye out for anything that seems *off*, but I feel confident we can find our way to a couple of hilltops without getting lost. Splitting up allows us to cover as much territory as possible and might get us off the island before evening, so we don't have to spend another night here."

Amy nodded at that and Richard continued, "Ian, you go with Tum, he can tell you more of the stories from this island. Amy, you should come with me, I can teach you what I know as well. Once we get to the top of the hills, one of us should be able to get a call through."

Richard looked and sounded more optimistic than Ian felt, but he held his tongue. He felt nervous about leaving the lodge, but he knew it was their best chance to avoid spending another night here. He had grown to like Richard and he trusted him. He knew that if anyone could get them safely off the island it would be this man. "Ok Richard, that sounds like a reasonable plan. When do you want to get started?"

"As soon as everyone's done eating. But first let's figure out where we're going." Richard stood up and pulled a topographic map off the wall from where it had been tacked between a poster of The Common Mushrooms of British Columbia and an identification chart for cetaceans. He placed the map on the table where everyone could see it.

The first thing Ian noticed were markings for a cluster of buildings and a dock in a small cove on the northern shore. That's where they were. He put his finger on it and noticed that a series of trails had been drawn on the map in various colors of ink. Each trail originated at the lodge, led about a mile into the forest before stopping. There was an orange trail that traced along the eastern shore of the cove before terminating in a larger bay. The color was the same as the surveyor's tape they had followed yesterday when they'd been lost.

"Richard, do you see the different colors for each trail?"

"Yeah, someone was having fun with their colored pens."

"No, I think they mean something. The trail we found was marked with orange tape. This trail on the map is orange as well. I think the colors on the map may correspond to the color of tape used to mark the trail in the forest. It's just a guess but maybe it'll help us once we're out there."

"Ok, good thinking. We have five different trails leading away from the lodge: Orange, Purple, Green, Red, and Yellow. There are also a set of connecting trail segments, all marked in blue. So if your theory is right, we should follow the trail that takes us closest to our goal, while keeping in mind that if we see blue tape we can use that to move onto another trail in the network."

Ian nodded, "Seems right to me."

"Ok, let's see where we need to go." Richard pointed to a hilltop that was southeast of the orange trail. "So this must be the hill that the two of you were on yesterday. That's high point number one. We can use the orange trail to get close and then hike through the forest up to the summit."

He swept his hand further east to another hill, clearly cone-shaped on the topo map. "This is high point number two. We can use the purple trail until it ends and then use a compass heading to find the hilltop."

Amy interjected, "When we were on top of the first hill, we noticed that the trail we'd been walking on continued east toward the second hill. Should we use that instead? It might be faster."

"I don't think so. From your description it sounds like you were on a trail used by Sasahevas. While we have no guarantee we can avoid them on our own trails, or while cutting cross-country, I think using his trails would be looking for trouble."

"Ok. Yeah. I guess you're right."

Richard then moved his hand to a finger of land on the southwest corner of the island, "This is our final possible target. It's not a high point but it has the clearest view south and west to Port Hardy and we might be able to pick up one of the cell towers from there. Looks like the yellow trail goes closest to that one."

"Ian, you and Tum can head to the hill you were on yesterday. Amy and I will head to the second hill, further east."

Norm interjected, "I'm comfortable hiking on my own. I'll go to the southwest..."

Richard cut him off, "Any questions?"

Nobody had anything to add.

"Ok. Remember we need to travel quickly to get there and back before nightfall. We need to be quiet and we need to be respectful so we don't stir up any trouble with the... um... inhabitants of this island. If you see or feel anything strange, back off and stay safe. We all have radios so if you need help or don't know what to do, radio in. We'll talk it through."

Richard looked each of them in the eyes, "Job number one is to stay safe. Don't take any unnecessary chances. We have a couple shots at making a connection, so don't be a hero. If you can't get through, it's ok, one of the others will do it. Between all of us, this should work."

After the plan was made, they sprang into action. Richard handed out radios, compasses, knives, rain jackets, and backpacks. Each of them loaded a pack with these supplies as well as food and water and then they assembled near the fire pit.

"Amy and I have the furthest to go, so we'll take the map with us. Let's shut our phones down until we get to our target areas – we need to conserve our batteries."

Ian turned on his radio, "Hey Richard can we do a radio check, make sure these all work?"

"Sure, that's a good idea. Everyone power up and let's check 'em out."

After making sure the radios worked as expected, there was nothing left to do but leave. Everyone shouldered their packs and then stood looking into the forest, eyeing where they needed to go in order to find their trail.

Ian was reminded of summers as a kid when his family would spend weeks at a time at their cabin on Harrison Lake. He'd stand on the edge of the water, dipping his toes and feeling the cold creep up through his body. He'd want to swim, he really would, but finding the will to jump was so difficult. Some days he'd return to the cabin, never having gotten wet past his ankles.

Standing at the fire pit, surrounded by the others about to return into the forest, he felt that familiar lack of will pass over him. He knew he had to take a first step, knew he needed to get back out there, but damned if it was going to be easy.

CHAPTER 24

Ian and Tum said their goodbyes to the rest of the group and started walking on the orange trail. Tum was characteristically quiet and Ian followed suit, feeling nervous about leaving the lodge and being separated from the rest of the group. He was happy he had someone to keep him company though, unlike Norm who he knew was walking alone.

After about a mile he recognized the gully that he and Amy had taken from the top of the hill. "Hey Tum, I think this is the way. I remember it from when Amy and I were here yesterday."

Tum nodded and they turned off the trail, heading uphill toward the summit. Part way up, close to where Amy had taken her fall, Ian decided it was time to ask some questions. "Tum, what do you know about this island? Richard said you could fill me in."

Tum stopped walking, forcing Ian to stop too.

"Yeah. I know about this island. Everyone in the tribe knows something about it. My parents taught me what they had learned from their parents and from their grandparents. My parents told me that my great grandparents had a vision quest here, so they heard the stories."

Tum started walking again and Ian fell in next to him.

"Can you tell me about the vision quest? What was that like? What did they do?"

"I can only tell you what I know. Every year, when the young people of the tribe were nearing adulthood they would be sent to this island. Not all at once. Two at a time. A boy and a girl. Each was given three days to complete their quest. If they didn't come back in that time, the tribe knew that the child had been taken by Sasahevas. They wouldn't be seen again. Whether they returned or not, after one week the next pair was sent.

"Every youth was tested by Sasahevas. Those that passed the test would come back with new wisdom. When they returned to the tribe, they would share the visions they had seen with the chief and the medicine man and then they were forbidden to tell anyone else. The chiefs held these visions close. They saw them as a source of power and I think they felt there was a disrespect in sharing the visions outside of a potlatch.

"I was never told what the test was or the details of any visions. So I don't know exactly what used to happened here. I only know that at least one in ten failed and the rest came back changed. The youth who came to this island, they arrived as children, but they returned as adults. They would always pass or fail as a pair. They both came back, or neither one returned.

"The hill we are climbing now, this was the men's hill. This is where the boys came to complete their visions quest. The other hill to the east is the women's hill. That's where the girls would go. I think Richard had a reason for sending you to this hill and taking Amy to the other one. He knows what the purpose of each hill is. It's no coincidence that you are going here and she is going there. I think he has a plan that he has not shared with us." Tum lapsed back into silence.

Ian wasn't sure what to think of what he'd heard. He'd been up this hill once and while he hadn't had anything like a vision quest, the experience had been decidedly odd. Regardless of what else Richard was planning, Ian knew that trying to use the cell phones was their best chance. As for the rest... he'd have to keep his eyes peeled and be ready for whatever came.

Deep in thought, he almost didn't notice when the trees started to thin and the distinctive slab-rock of the summit came into view. Then they broke into open ground and they were walking over smooth granite past twisted, wind-blown bushes and stunted trees. They continued to the middle of the hilltop and climbed onto a large block, putting them several feet off the ground. Spinning in place, Ian could once more see a

360 degree view of the island and the surrounding ocean.

But instead of the panoramic view of scattered islands, flanked on one side by the tall mountains of the mainland and on the other by the rolling hills of Vancouver Island, the island was now completely surrounded by a wall of white fog, blocking the view on all sides. He could see the beaches far below, surrounded by a fringe of ocean, and directly off the island in every direction lay the thick fog. It was a white featureless wall, a sharp line along the water far below, rearing up above them to a height at least twice as tall as the hill they were standing on. Looking way up, to the upper limit of the fog, he could see a grey, overcast sky like a roof over the top of them.

He had the strangest feeling that he was inside a giant room large enough to encompass the entire island. After a time, he could discern some details in the fog, swirls and eddies that showed up as light and dark streaks. As he watched, the patterns formed into shapes and images similar to what he'd seen on the boat. Not wanting to repeat that experience, he averted his eyes, looking toward the ground and trying to shake the impression that he'd seen the shape of a giant, hairy creature looming within the wall of fog, head turned to look at him.

He darted his eyes back up to where the shape of the creature had been. He couldn't help himself, he had to know if it was really there, but all he saw were random eddies swirling and dancing around each other. Feeling slightly better, he turned away to find Tum staring into the fog, mesmerized.

"Hey Tum, should we check the phone?"

"Yeah. Yeah, that's what we should do..." He shook his head and pulled off his pack. "Hold on, let me get it out."

While Tum was busy with his pack, Ian decided he wanted to hear a friendly voice, so he pulled out his radio and keyed the mic, "Hey Amy, how are you guys doing?"

He heard a burst of static and then, "Hey Ian! Yeah we are doing fine so far. No problems. We just made it off the trail and we're following a compass heading toward the other hill. I think we are in the valley we saw from that hilltop yesterday. How about you? Where are you?"

He smiled and keyed the mic again, "Tum and I have made good progress. We are on top of the hill and he's going to test the cell signal now. If we get through to someone I'll let you know and you can head back to the lodge to meet us."

A slight pause and then, "Yeah ok, that sounds good. It feels a little strange here. Darker than I remember it. I think maybe the trees are bigger or closer together or something. Hey Ian, did Tum tell you anything about these hills and what they were used for?"

"Uh huh, yeah he did. I guess I'm on the men's hill and you are headed toward the women's hill. Funny coincidence, right?"

There was a slight pause and then, "Well... I don't think it's a coincidence. Richard told me about the hills and about the vision quests. I don't think he believes the cell phones are going to work. I think he is taking us up these hills as part of a backup plan. He told me there might be something more we need to do. I don't know for sure what he means but I have some ideas and I'm not sure I like it."

"Hmm, Tum said something similar to me. Whatever you do, be careful, ok? You don't have to do anything you feel uncomfortable with."

"Yeah, I know that. Ian, have you seen anything weird up there. You know, like last time?"

"Not like last time, but yeah, it's kind of weird up here. Do you remember how the fog came in before?"

"Yeah, I remember."

"Well, there's fog again, but it's not like it was last time. There's no fog on the hill, but it's completely surrounding the island, like a big wall holding us in. I've never seen fog do anything like that before."

"Huh. That is weird. I can't see it from here, but I'll tell you as soon as we're up on the hill and let you know what I think. I'd better concentrate on walking now, it's getting kind of rough."

"Ok. Talk to you soon."

Ian thought for a moment and then held the radio up

again. "Norm, you there?"

Ian waited for a few moments, but there was no response.

"Norm? Norm, come in."

Still nothing.

"Norm, this is Ian. Can you hear me?"

He must be in a dead zone. Hopefully everything was ok. Feeling worried, Ian lowered the radio and called over to Tum. "Hey Tum, how's it going? Do you have anything?"

Tum was on his toes, holding his phone straight up in the air and the look on his face wasn't good, "No. It isn't working. I've found a few places where I can get a little bit of signal but it doesn't last. I haven't been able to get any calls or texts through. I can keep trying but I don't think it's going to do any good. Here, you take a look."

Ian walked over and took the phone, handing the radio to Tum, who held it up and keyed the mic. "Richard, you there?"

"Yeah, Richard here."

"No luck with the cell phone, I can't get a good signal."

"Ok, thanks for letting me know. Radio again if anything changes."

Ian looked up from the phone. "I'm not getting anything either... still no signal." He handed the phone back to Tum. "What now?"

"Now, we wait.

CHAPTER 25

They had been sitting on the rock for about an hour when the radio crackled to life. Ian was staring studiously at the ground, at the bushes, anywhere except for that strange wall of fog.

"Tum, you there?"

"Yeah Richard, this is Tum."

"We are on top of the second hill and we aren't getting a signal here either. We should have picked something up by now, we have a clear shot to the towers near Port Hardy."

"I agree."

"What do you think of the fog?"

"I don't really know. It's been stable for as long as we've been up here. It's not acting like anything I've seen before. Do you think it could be blocking the signal?"

A pause and then Richard's voice again, "Yeah I was thinking the same thing. It doesn't make sense, fog shouldn't block the cell phones, but nothing about this is normal. I don't think we can rule anything out at this point."

"Ok, what do you want to do?"

There was a moment of silence and then a burst of static, loud and prolonged. The static worked its way up and down the registers randomly, Ian's ears straining against it, searching for a pattern. In the hissing and swirling noises he thought he could make out a voice. It was very faint, but if he cocked his head just right he could make out something... what was it?

He noticed Tum had his eyes closed and his face was the picture of concentration, head tilted, straining to hear. Ian closed his eyes too, maybe it would help him to hear better. The static swelled into a crescendo of hissing, louder and louder until his eardrums were throbbing with the power of it. Then there was a loud crack, a yelp from Tum and as Ian opened his eyes he saw the radio hit the ground, clattering across the rocks. Ian looked on in shock as Tum shoved his finger into his mouth, trailing a small puff of smoke.

Ian shot up, still looking at Tum, feeling truly frightened now. "What in the hell was that?"

Tum looked back at him with bewildered eyes, nursing his injured finger. Ian walked over to the radio and nudged it cautiously with his foot. It squawked to life, startling him so badly that he jumped back several feet, waving his arms around in what would have been a comical display if the situation hadn't already been so strange.

"Tum? Ian? Are you two ok?"

Ian edged closer to the radio.

"Tum! Ian! Come in! Can you hear me?"

Richard sounded well and truly panicked and his tone of voice was enough to overcome most of Ian's reluctance. He bent over, carefully touching the radio with the end of his finger and then jerked back. When nothing happened, Ian, feeling extremely nervous, reached down and picked the radio up. He looked at it for a few moments and then he keyed the mic to answer Richard.

"Hey Richard, we're ok. A bit shaken up but all in one piece."

"Did your radio malfunction like ours? We heard a lot of static and then the radio shot out sparks. I'd set it down, so we got lucky and neither of us is hurt. "

"Um... yeah, our radio did the same thing. Unfortunately, it hit Tum's finger. I think he'll be ok, but it looks like it hurts." Ian looked at Tum sympathetically, seeing that he had the finger out of his mouth now and was examining it intently.

"Ok, glad to hear there weren't any serious injuries. Right now we have more important things to worry about."

"Um... Richard, what kind of important things?"

"Hand me back to Tum, I'll explain."

Ian shook his head. He wasn't feeling good about any of this, but what choice did he have? Head back to the lodge on his own? And then what?

He offered the radio to Tum, who looked at it like a snake about to bite, involuntarily backing away a few steps.

"Take it Tum. It's ok now and Richard needs to talk to you. I think we are about to hear about his backup plan."

Tum reached out tentatively, touched the radio, and when it didn't shock him he took it and keyed the mic, "Hey Richard, I'm here." His voice was a little shaky, but not too bad considering what had just happened.

"Ok Tum, do you remember the sweat lodge ceremony we performed last summer?"

"Yeah, I remember."

"I'm convinced that Sasahevas is forcing us into a vision quest, and I think he expects Amy and Ian to be the ones to do it."

"Wait? What? Why not one of us? We should be the ones to do what needs to be done!"

"I know, but we don't get to choose. Let me ask you something. When was the last time someone landed on the south shore?"

"As far as I know, no-one has landed there since the last vision quest three generations ago."

"Exactly. The south shore is where our ancestors would land to start their quest. Right where Ian and Amy were shipwrecked."

"Oh... Oh shit."

"Yeah. My thoughts exactly. Sasahevas doesn't care about ancestry or race, he probably doesn't know there is such a thing. As far as he's concerned we are all humans and that's about as much distinction as he's likely to make. He's been on this island for a hundred years, waiting for the next vision quest pair to show up, maybe starting to wonder why it's taking so long. Suddenly Ian and Amy wash up and as far as he's concerned he has a pair of new participants, ready to be tested."

"This is bad. So, so bad."

Ian was paying close attention. He didn't like what he'd heard so far.

Richard continued, "I think Sasahevas has been confused. Ian and Amy weren't acting as they expected, so Sasahevas has been trying to remind them of what they need to do, giving them nudges to get them to come to these hills and start the vision quests. But Ian and Amy didn't know what was going on. Everything they saw pushed them further and faster toward the safety of the lodge and eventually off the island with us."

"Yes, I see it. It makes sense."

"Sasahevas couldn't allow them to leave, the test hadn't begun yet. When we tried to take them off the island, that was a clear violation of the rules. Once you arrive for a vision quest, you need to see it through. We're lucky we aren't all dead right now. There hasn't been such a serious breach of etiquette for ... well probably for at least ten thousand years."

Ian found that his legs had given out and he was back on the ground. This couldn't be happening could it? This wasn't real.

"Tum, we need to get the visions started. If we don't do that we won't be getting off this island and time is running out. The clock started ticking as soon as Ian and Amy showed up. I think Sasahevas is running out of patience."

Tum looked sideways over at Ian and then keyed the radio again, "What do you need me to do?"

"We don't know for sure what the vision quest ceremony was like but we do know how to do the sweat lodge ceremony. Hopefully that will be close enough. It's another path to the spirit world, so I think it might work. Either way, it's all we've got."

Ian could hear Amy on the radio, in the background. "Richard, what are you talking about? We need to do what?!" and then the sound cut out.

Tum spoke one more time, "Alright, I'll try it. I know what to do." He looked at Ian thoughtfully.

After a busy thirty minutes of gathering what they needed from the forest around them, Ian found himself sitting cross legged in the middle of a circle of stones, each topped with a different type of leaf, a pile of fragrant vegetation directly in front of him.

Tum stepped out of the circle and rummaged in his pack. "Ian are you ready?"

"Um."

"Good enough."

"Uh... urk. What do I do?"

"Close your eyes. Use your nose to smell what's around you. Use your ears to listen. Focus on your third eye. Use your spiritual focus and when you are ready, let yourself fall in."

"Um..."

"Right. Let's get started... Close your eyes."

As Ian closed his eyes, he saw Tum reach into the circle and light the vegetation mounded up in front of him. He was aware of Tum walking around the circle. He circled once clockwise, once counter-clockwise and then three more times in each direction. The hilltop was otherwise silent, not a breath of air, not a single sound from animal or insect, just the sound of his own heartbeat, his breathing, and Tum's footsteps.

A smell like incense worked its way into his nose, growing steadily more powerful until he felt dizzy with it. He opened his mouth to get some air and felt the smoke work its way in past his tongue and down his throat. The smoke was uncomfortable at first, he felt a cough working its way up, but then it eased and he relaxed into it.

Tum began to chant. Ian focused on the wordless sounds, rising and falling, Tum's feet stamping in time. The sound and beat weren't like anything Ian had heard before. His mind had a hard time following it, the tonality and rhythm changing in unexpected ways, it sounded random and unnatural to his ears, but he found himself relaxing further. Relaxing until he was no longer aware of his body. He couldn't feel the rock pressed against his legs, couldn't feel his head on his neck, couldn't feel his hands in his lap. He felt like he was floating free, smell and sound his only anchors.

He remembered what Tum had said about a third eye and searched inside himself for it. He didn't know exactly what he was looking for but he felt himself journeying upward and inward until he found the center of his awareness. In that center he became aware of a sharp focal point, a piece of his inner landscape that he'd never been aware of before. As the sound of chanting and stamping faded, as the smell of smoke left his awareness, he concentrated hard and in that moment he opened his inner, third eye. He found himself standing on an endless ledge, staring over a dark precipice. With his arms hanging loose by his sides he tipped forward and let himself fall into the void.

The next thing Ian heard was the creaking of rope and wood. Then he was aware of the smell of tar and over that the smell of the sea. Next he was aware of color and shape, brown and tan, blue and cream, the picture swimming into focus just as he began to hear the sound of voices.

"King Maquinna, on behalf of John Salter, Captain of the merchant ship *Boston* I accept your gifts and I invite you to dine with us." The voice had the clipped, nasal tones that you might hear in New England.

Ian found himself on a square-rigged ship with cannons on the foredeck, a group of sailors hard at work on the aft deck and directly in front of him, five natives wearing pale yellow cedar-bark shirts, one of whom was magnificently cloaked in dark fur with white feather-down spread like snow upon his hair.

Ian looked around in shock. Where in the world was he?

CHAPTER 26

After leaving the lodge, Amy and Richard walked on the purple trail until they hit its end. The trail was distinct and easy to follow at first, so they had made easy progress, walking with long strides, packs swinging on their backs. As they walked further, the trail became imperceptibly rougher, forcing them to slow down and pick their way across the ever present roots and rocks. Eventually there was no trail left and they found themselves following purple tape markers tied to branches, while pushing through waist high brush and ducking low under hanging limbs.

Richard spoke up, "I should fill you in about this island and explain where we are headed."

"Ok, sounds good" she said, stepping over a root.

"I told you last night how this island was used for vision quests. How the youth would be sent here every year in pairs."

"Yeah, I remember."

"The tribe would always land the pair on the south shore, probably close to where you and Ian washed up. Then they would make their way to these two hilltops. The boy would go to the men's hill, where I sent Ian and Tum. The girl would go to the women's hill. That's where we are going." He looked back to see if there was any reaction.

Amy raised an eyebrow quizzically. "Is there a reason for that? Are you taking me to the women's hill for a specific purpose?"

Richard started walking again, "Maybe."

Amy wasn't sure how she felt about that. She wasn't particularly fond of mysteries. Especially now. Especially here. "Richard, what aren't you telling me?"

"I'm not sure yet. I could be wrong. Let's give it some time and see what happens. If we can get the cell phones to work, none of it will matter."

"What? What won't matter?"

"Not now, we'll talk about it later. If necessary."

Amy chewed on that for a while and then lost herself in the rhythm of walking. Let her mind go still, focused on breathing and keeping pace with Richard as he moved quickly in front of her.

Amy was watching her feet, taking care not to trip, when she noticed that Richard had stopped. "What's up? Time to take a break?" She shifted her pack to pull out a water bottle.

"No, we need to keep moving. But I'm not seeing the next piece of tape. Can you see it anywhere?" He walked forward a few more paces, scanning the trees in front of them.

Amy capped her water bottle and wiped her face before responding, "no, sorry I don't see it either. Must be the end of the line."

Richard squatted down and took out his map while Amy shouldered her pack and walked over to join him. He had his finger on the map and was tracing from the lodge along the purple line to its end.

"I don't know how accurate this trail marking is, so I'm not sure if we are at the end here or somewhere slightly off. What do you think?"

Amy squatted down and looked at the part of the map he was pointing at. The purple line set out straight from the lodge and then meandered back and forth to follow the easiest terrain before plunging into what looked like a steep-sided gully just before the line stopped. "We walked through that gully just a few minutes ago. Remember we had trouble finding the next tape as soon as we came out? Then we found it off to the right, which would be... south I guess?"

"Good thinking, yeah I think you're right. So that would put us right about... here." his hand traced past the purple, veered south and then stopped about an inch further on.

Amy looked at the topo lines on the map, then glanced around and decided it was a pretty close match. "Yup, looks right to me. So which way do you want to go now?"

Richard laid his compass on the map, marking a straight line from their current location to the top of the second hill. Looks like we need to go nearly due east, ninety-five degrees true." He was talking to himself now, speaking softly under his breath as he fiddled with his compass. "Let's see, the compass declination needs to be plus seventeen degrees, twelve minutes." A little more fiddling and then, "Got it! Let's go." He stood up and started walking, compass held in front of him to check the course, the map folded in his other hand.

They had to walk slower without a trail, but they continued to make reasonable progress until the forest grew thicker and closed in around them. Amy sensed that they had been steadily losing altitude and were now in what constituted a low-land for this island. The size of the trees and ferns was positively Jurassic and she wouldn't have been surprised to see the snout of a velociraptor poke out from behind one of the massive leaves. The amount and variety of vegetation was astounding, such a proliferation of life that her eyes had trouble taking it all in, there was just too much to process.

The air was becoming humid, thick and stagnant, water dripping off of every exposed edge as if the moist respiration of the entire forest was settling in around them. She had long since given up trying to avoid the mud and her feet were wet, socks sloshing in her shoes, the front of her legs soaked from brushing up against wet leaves and fronds.

Suddenly her radio crackled to life, "Hey Amy, how are you guys doing?" The unexpected sound startled her but she broke into a smile as soon as she realized it was Ian's voice.

"Hey Ian! Yeah we are doing fine so far. No problems. We just made it off the trail and we're following a compass heading toward the other hill. I think we are in the valley we saw from that hilltop yesterday. How about you? Where are you?"

She was still walking, holding the radio up as she brushed

branches and leaves out of the way with her other hand, doing her best not to fall behind.

Ian responded, "Tum and I have made good progress, we are on top of the hill and he's going to test the cell signal now. If we get through I'll let you know and you can head back to the lodge to meet us."

She looked up as she walked, trying to figure out how to explain her experience, "Yeah ok, that sounds good. It feels a little strange here. Darker than I remember it. I think maybe the trees are bigger or closer together or something. Hey Ian, did Tum tell you anything about these hills and what they were used for?"

Ian came back right away, "Uh huh, yeah he did. I guess I'm on the men's hill and you are headed toward the women's hill. Funny coincidence, right?"

Amy winced a little at that and glanced toward Richard, trying to gauge if he could hear their conversation. She let herself fall back a bit more, adjusted the radio volume down and then held it close to her mouth so she could talk more quietly. "Well... I don't think it's a coincidence. Richard told me about the hills and about the vision quests. I don't think he believes the cell phones are going to work. I think he is taking us up these hills as part of a backup plan. He told me there might be something more we need to do. I don't know exactly what he means but I have some ideas and I'm not sure I like it."

It was true. She was feeling increasingly uncomfortable with what they were doing. Not that she'd felt good about it before, but the oppressive atmosphere they were walking through along with the knowledge of how far they were getting from the lodge was weighing on her. There was something strange about the forest now. It was... familiar. She couldn't put her finger on it, but it felt like there was something she was missing. Something important.

She could feel a nervous pressure building in the pit of her stomach and she focused on trying to relax... take a few deep breaths, drop the shoulders, ease the tension... Richard was getting further ahead, so she picked up the pace. She definitely did not want to lose sight of him in these trees.

Ian on the radio again, “Hmm, Tum said something similar to me. Whatever you do, be careful, ok? You don’t have to do anything you feel uncomfortable with.”

That goes without saying right? Men. She almost rolled her eyes, but keyed the mic and tried to respond as kindly as possible, “Yeah, I know that. Ian, have you seen anything weird up there. You know, like last time?”

“Not like last time, but yeah, it's kind of weird up here. Do you remember how the fog came in before?”

That got her attention. She had never been a big fan of fog, but it was very low on her list of favorite things at this point. She keyed the mic again, “Yeah, I remember.”

“Well, there’s fog again, but it’s not like it was last time. There’s no fog on the hill, but it’s completely surrounding the island, like a big wall holding us in. I’ve never seen fog do anything like that before.”

She swallowed painfully, trying to keep her fear in check, and hurried up a bit more, being closer to Richard sounded really good about now. Trying to sound nonchalant, not wanting to let Ian know how she was feeling, she spoke into the radio again, “Huh. That is weird. I can’t see it from here, but I’ll tell you as soon as we’re up on the hill and let you know what I think. I’d better concentrate on walking now, it’s getting kind of rough.”

“Ok. Talk to you soon.”

It was reassuring to talk to Ian but the conversation hadn’t helped her nerves. She wanted this trip to be over. She was looking forward to getting to the top of the hill so they could turn around and hurry back to the lodge. There was something about this forest… something eerie. She was finding it increasingly hard to keep walking, her breathing was racing beyond her conscious control, speeding up beyond her will, flooding her body with too much oxygen, making her light headed and woozy.

“Richard, can we stop for a moment. I’m not feeling very

good."

Richard turned toward her, his face red and sweaty from exertion, pants and shoes soaked. "Yeah, I guess we could use it. Let's keep it short though, we need to give ourselves enough time up top." He looked at her more closely, looking concerned, "What's going on, how are you feeling?"

"Have you noticed anything strange? Does this part of the forest seem odd to you?"

"No, not really. Not any stranger than all the other parts of the forest we've been walking through."

"It seems familiar to me… I can't put my finger on it. I know Ian and I didn't pass through here on our way to the lodge yesterday… I can't figure it out." The last part came out a bit strained, frustration and worry leaking into the tone of her voice.

She looked up, willing herself to think clearly, staring at a large branch above her head. Her mind suddenly flashed to a tree branch very much like this. A tree branch with a curious little squirrel looking down at her. The memory came flooding back to her. Memory of a sunny day, walking through this forest, on a trail, wearing a body that was not her own. It was cloudy today, but all the other details matched up: the distribution and size of the trees, the thickness of the vegetation, even the smells were as she remembered them.

This was the forest from her dream. The dream she'd had during the shipwreck. But how was that even possible?

CHAPTER 27

Involuntarily she looked at her shoes and then at her hands. No moccasins. Hands were her own. She felt like herself. It wasn't another dream. Probably.

Richard was looking at her funny, "Amy? What are you doing?"

"I've been here before. I had a dream. It was a lucid dream, just before the shipwreck. I dreamed I was here, but I wasn't myself. I was a native I think. I was wearing moccasins and my hands were different. Brown. Tattooed. I was here, in this part of the forest, I know I was."

Richard took a step closer, "That is interesting." He stared into the trees for a moment, contemplating something, and then back to her, "What do you remember? Tell me everything."

Amy started at the beginning. She told him about the day of sailing, Ian going below to rest, her feelings of peace and well being and then the strange fog that had come upon them so rapidly and had such strange effects.

"I saw the fog coming toward me, like it was... like it was reaching out to touch me." She shuddered, "and then I think I lost consciousness. The next thing I knew I was on the floor and we had hit the rocks." She looked away, unable to bear looking him in the eyes as she re-lived that horrible moment.

"Go on. What happened next?"

She explained the feeling of being pulled from her body and finding herself in the forest. How she had thought it was a lucid dream. While she was in the dream she had felt fully herself, except now that didn't make any sense. She had been inside a different body, hadn't had any memories or awareness of what was happening on the boat. Meanwhile Ian's boat was sinking and he had saved her life, kept her from drowning. How did any of that make sense?

Richard had a different impression. “This is starting to make sense to me. I think you've given me the information I needed in order to understand what's going on here.” He paused a moment, “You said there was a trail you were walking on?”

“Yes. What do you mean it's making sense to you? None of this makes any sense. Not at all!” She was close to hysterics but she didn't care. The world was going mad and she was sick of it.

Richard was infuriatingly calm, obviously trying to soothe her. “I'll explain when we get to the top of the hill. Maybe I'm wrong. We'll know soon. Let's see if we can find this trail of yours.”

Richard reasoned that the trail was probably heading toward their hill and then used the map to find the most-likely location for it. After a bit of searching they pushed through some brush to find it just as Amy remembered. Seeing the trail before her, solid and inexplicably real was terrifying.

Richard smiled with satisfaction and started walking. Amy stepped on it tentatively, unsure if any additional strange events would ensue. When nothing happened, she started walking as well, following Richard uphill and to the east.

The trail allowed them to make good progress and within an hour they were at the top of the women's hill. The last section had been steep and so they paused to rest and drink water, letting their hearts and breathing settle back into a normal rhythm. The exercise had steadied Amy and she felt better than she had before. She found that the hilltop was lush with soft green moss and stately, well-spaced cedar trees – an army of gentle giants standing sentinel over them. The ground beneath each tree was springy with a thick mat of needles that had fallen, creating a perfect mat for laying down and resting. She felt good here. It felt protected. Sacred ground.

Amy let out a big sigh, dropped her pack and sat down, making herself comfortable. She took another moment to admire the beauty of the setting. Unfortunately, the trees blocked the view off the island, so she couldn't see the fog that Ian had mentioned. On second thought, maybe that was for the best.

While Amy rested, Richard had taken out his cell phone and was walking around the hilltop, trying to find a signal. He shook his head, pulled out his radio and spoke into it, "Tum, you there?"

"Yeah Richard, this is Tum."

Amy tuned the voices out, relaxing further into the soft ground. This was the best she'd felt for days. Weeks maybe. All of her anxiety and fear seemed to fall away. She lay back, closed her eyes and smiled.

She must have fallen asleep because she was startled awake by a hissing sound, a loud crack and the sudden smell of ozone. She startled up and saw Richard staring in disbelief at the radio. He picked it up off the ground, and turned it over, looking puzzled. It must have seemed ok, because he held it up and keyed the mic, "Tum? Ian? Are you two ok?"

He waited a few moments, looking increasingly worried, "Tum! Ian! Come in! Can you hear me?"

Amy found herself next to Richard, having crossed the distance without fully realizing it.

Richard was lowering the radio, hands shaking, when it burst back to life, "Hey Richard, we are ok. A bit shaken up but all in one piece."

It was Ian's voice. Thank God.

Richard continued to talk back and forth on the radio as Amy stood there feeling shaky. What had happened? She would ask Richard as soon as he was done talking. Then she heard Richard say the word Sasahevas and she turned her full attention back to the conversation. Something about a vision quest? That the creature expected them to take a test? What!?

Amy burst in, interrupting the radio conversation, "Richard, what are you talking about? We need to do what?!"

Richard looked at her meaningfully as she heard Tum's final words on the radio, "Alright, I'll try it. I know what to do."

Richard put the radio away and sat down, motioning for

Amy to do the same. "Amy, it's time I explained some things. I was hoping it wouldn't be necessary, was hoping that I'd been wrong about what's going on, but... well, we are in uncharted territory, and it's only fair that I tell you what I know."

Richard paused for a few moments, collecting his thoughts. "As you know, this was the island where my ancestors used to perform their vision quest ceremonies. You know that we had a trade, of sorts, with Sasahevas. We would get our visions, and he would get something in return. You know that this is the hill for the women and Ian is on the hill for the men. None of that is an accident. I've been setting things up to follow through on what Sasahevas may want from us before he will let us leave.

"What you told me before was helpful. Your experience while sailing through the fog, and your vision, that was what allowed me to put all the pieces together. It's been several generations since anyone has arrived on this island for a vision quest, and I think Sasahevas is feeling that absence acutely. Then the two of you show up, sailing, no engines... similarly enough to how our ancestors would have arrived in their canoes. The fog you experienced, that we've experienced. It can't be a coincidence."

Amy wasn't feeling right about this. In fact, she was starting to feel a bit like bait being held up to satisfy a monster. "If he is hungry for something, hungry enough to sink Ian's boat... Well, I'm not so sure I want to give him what he wants. What is your plan? Feed me to him? Feed Ian to him too? Did you think to ask us what we wanted to do?"

Richard sighed, "I understand what you're saying. But I don't think we have a choice. We need to complete the vision quests. Anything less will result in greater danger to all of us and then I don't think any of us will be getting off this island. Try the vision quest. He isn't going to eat you. Not in the way you're thinking. It's... well, it's hard to explain."

Amy gave him a flat stare, "Try me."

"Ok, let's see... When you experienced your vision before,

how did it feel?"

"How did it feel? It felt like I was transported to another time and place and into another body. I was no long on the boat, only aware of being in the forest. It was like a dream, but not really. It was too real for that. I guess I was really there, wasn't I? I mean we found the trail, so it wasn't a dream."

"The visions feel real, but they aren't. Sasahevas is showing you what he wants you to see. That forest, the trail, that girl, those were all formed within the mind of Sasahevas."

Amy looked at Richard blankly, "I was inside that creature's mind?"

"I think it's more like he is projecting into your mind. Maybe you are projecting into each other's mind. I don't know. But I think that's what he is hungry for. He wants to be in a shared experience with you. We don't know why, but it's something he needs."

Richard looked thoughtful. "Maybe it's simply the result of having lived so long. Maybe he needs to see the world through our eyes in order to renew himself. Just like we need to connect with nature and the wilderness to renew ourselves."

"I guess that doesn't sound so bad. He doesn't plan to eat me? Like chomp on my flesh?"

"I have heard stories of him attacking humans, but it's rare. And that doesn't seem to be the purpose of the vision quest."

Amy was feeling relieved, but then she remembered something he'd said last night, "Some of them don't come back."

"What?"

"You said that some of the boys and girls that went on vision quest never returned. What happened to them?"

"Oh... I don't know. I can give you my theories. One possibility is that the participant may come to harm in the vision quest and that keeps them from returning. Maybe a vision death is a real death?"

"Like the Matrix?"

"Yeah, I guess so... Another possibility is that Sasahevas

keeps some participants from leaving. Sasahevas might continue to feed upon their experiences for as long as the body stays alive."

"Neither of those possibilities sounds very appealing."

"I agree. They don't. But we can minimize the risks. I'm here with you, so I'll keep your body safe while you're away."

"Wait, how long do you think I'll be gone?"

"I don't know. Time might flow differently once you're in the vision. You could feel like you're gone for weeks, while very little time passes here. Stay safe, stay well, and don't allow yourself to be injured or killed. Most people return from their vision quest safely. You'll get through this, I know you can do it. When you're done, we can all leave this island and go home."

Amy was digesting this new information when she saw a towering, hairy figure in the trees behind Richard. It was standing very still and it was quite clearly looking in her direction. Fog was roiling behind it, tendrils reaching forward, wrapping over its shoulders and pushing their way toward where she was sitting.

She looked to Richard in a panic, wanting to tell him what she was seeing but she couldn't get it to come out, she couldn't say a word. She saw Richard's mouth opening, she could tell he was speaking, but she couldn't hear anything over a sudden rushing noise in her ears. It filled her head, obliterating all else, and she felt a familiar tugging, straight up, pulling her out of her body into a sea of swirling colors, end over end and then with a reverberating thunk and a sudden shock her senses came back to her again.

The first thing she saw was a window. In the window she saw the reflection of a woman of average height, with a slim build, nice clothes, hair falling over her shoulders. Her forehead tickled, a loose piece of hair was curling down, moving in the slight breeze. In a daze, she reached her hand up, brushed the hair back and saw the reflection do the same. The sounds of a city slowly filtered into her ears – cars and people, voices and footsteps, doors opening and closing. Harsh. Grating. Starkly different than the sounds of the forest that she had grown used to.

"Honey, are you ready to go?"

She turned her head and saw an attractive young man with dark hair and warm brown eyes standing on the side of a city street, bounded on both sides by tall buildings, glass storefronts on the bottom floors, windows reaching upwards, story after story toward the sky.

He was looking at her. Reaching toward her. Waiting for her to take his hand and walk away with him.

She looked again at her reflection, marveling at herself. Who was this man? Where in the world was she?

She reached out and took his hand.

PART 3: THE VISION

CHAPTER 28

Ian was standing on the deck of a mid-sized ship, staring at his feet. He noticed that his shoes were different. Instead of boots, he was wearing thin leather shoes adorned with metal buckles. His clothes were different too. Roughspun cotton pants reached to mid-calf, and a grey woolen jacket over a course canvas shirt covered his chest, itching uncomfortably where his skin touched the unaccustomed fabric.

Beneath his feet, the wooden boards were scarred – dented with age and use, the taffrail behind him, a large wooden mast in front. He looked up the length of the mast and into the rigging, his gaze following a maze of lines overhead to where they held the masts and sails in place against the force of the wind. The sails were stowed at the moment, bundled neatly at the base of each of the cross-braced yards. He turned in place, trying to take everything in.

The ship was a hive of activity, crowded with sailors mending lines, climbing in the rigging, sewing sails, cleaning and performing various other tasks. He was standing just behind a small group of sailors talking with a tall First Nations man clothed magnificently in a dark fur cloak. The man was well built with a handsome face and a straight roman nose, striking to behold, his hair collected in a knot on the top of his head and dusted liberally with white, downy feathers. He held himself with the grace and pride of a King, unquestionably the leader of the native men standing behind him.

Tearing his eyes from the King, Ian examined the sailors on board. They were dressed simply, in rough clothing, many barefoot, giving them better traction on deck and to make climbing easier. Most had long hair, braided in back, holding it out of the way while they worked. On the whole, they appeared dirty, many were missing teeth and they smelled horribly. Two of the sailors, leading the discussion with the natives, appeared to be better groomed. Probably the Captain and Mate.

The man who appeared to be the Captain took a step forward and spoke, "Maquinna, will you join us for supper? I would be honored to have you as my guest and would be most grateful to have your companionship at my table."

The Mate continued, "We have prepared your favorite meal of ship's bread dipped in molasses, as well as sweet tea and coffee. Just follow me if you will."

Ian heard someone behind him speak under his breath, "Captain just wants to see if those monkeys can use a chair. They don't know a table from their arse. They'll be on the floor, mark my words on that one mate," followed by a few sniggers.

The King didn't seem like he'd heard the whispered insult. He dipped his head and spoke in heavily accented, frequently halting English, "Thank you Captain Salter and Mate Delouisa, I would be happy to join you." And with that, the Captain and the Mate, followed by the King and his entourage proceeded through a door leading into the ship's interior.

A hand fell heavily on Ian's shoulder, causing him to nearly jump out of his skin. "John, we have some muskets that need cleaning and there are a couple of belaying pins found bent and needing fixing. Go on below and get these taken care of." The man nodded toward a hatch located midship, dumped a couple of heavy metal objects in Ian's arms and then stumped away to join the other sailors.

John? Who was John? Ian, feeling bewildered, looked down at the bent pieces of metal in his arms, over at the open hatch and then at the burly man walking away. The man seemed to have sensed Ian's eyes on his back because he stopped and turned to look. When he saw Ian hadn't moved, he widened his eyes, waggled his bushy black eyebrows up and down a few times and nodded his head once more toward the hatch. "Go on then. Time's a wastin you lazy dog. Get to work, will ya!" Seeming pleased with his outburst and confident in its effect, he continued on his way.

Ian turned toward the hatch, noticing that the ship was anchored in a small bay, trees and rocks surrounding them. It looked like many of the anchorages he had visited while exploring British Columbia in his own boat. He continued to the hatch and found a ladder leading down to the hold below. He tucked the belaying pins under an arm and gingerly climbed down.

Once his eyes had adjusted to the dark, he saw a table in the corner, surrounded by muskets, a vice on one side and a collection of tools arranged both below the table and hanging on the wall behind it. There was a young man, no older than seventeen, working on a partially disassembled musket, rubbing parts with a rag and occasionally dipping them into a bucket that smelled strongly of alcohol spirits.

As Ian walked over to place the belaying pins on the table, the young man looked up at him, "Good day, Mr. Jewitt! It looks like you have some bent pins. Do you want me to straighten them while you work on the muskets? I think I can do it this time, I've learned from what I did wrong last time."

"Well, yes... sure, you can take them."

"Thank you, Mr. Jewitt. Thank you! You won't regret this!" He took up both pins and hurried further aft, disappearing behind a bulkhead.

Mr. Jewitt? Why did that name sound so familiar? Then it came to him. He'd learned about a Mr. John Jewitt in school, many years ago. He was an English sailor who'd signed aboard an American merchant vessel trading along the Pacific coast of Canada. He was well educated and had kept a journal of his entire adventure which he later turned into a book that every high-schooler in British Columbia had to read.

Could he be living John Jewitt's life? The dress and language of the sailors matched his expectations of what American sailors would have been like in the early 19th century. And the ship seemed like a merchant vessel from that era. It certainly wasn't a modern ship, and it didn't have the look of a naval ship either. The sailors were too lax and the armaments too scarce; he'd noticed a few cannons on the foredeck, and he'd seen a few pistols, but nothing like what he would have expected to see on a true man-of-war.

This was exciting! His vision quest had placed him in a historical sailing ship. But where could they be?

The view from above-decks seemed very much like they were in the Pacific Northwest. The trees and terrain didn't have the look of the South Pacific, South America or anywhere else he knew the American's would have been actively trading. And the natives he'd seen were dressed in traditional Coast Salish clothing, just like he remembered from an exhibit at the Royal BC Museum in Victoria.

Based on what he'd seen, he must still be in British Columbia somewhere.

Racking his brain he tried to recall details of what he'd read so long ago. He remembered that Mr. Jewitt had arrived on the west coast of Vancouver Island after a long voyage around Cape Horn, stopping in Nootka Sound after months at sea.

The state of the ship and the weariness of the sailors indicated a long sea voyage. The buzz of activity indicated a refit using both ship's stores and local materials. They must be in Nootka Sound!

This was wonderful! Nootka Sound was one of the most historic locations on the coast. It was where Captain Cook had landed, initiating first contact with the natives. It was where Captain Vancouver had negotiated with Captain Valdez for transfer of Vancouver Island from Spain to England. He was reliving history!

He had been transported back into the age of sail. This was the most interesting and exciting time for a sailor to be alive. Incredible ships. Courageous men. Huge adventures. He'd read extensively about this era, devouring seafaring tales voraciously. It was why he loved wooden sailboats so much, why he'd taken up sailing himself. But he'd never dreamed he'd get to experience it for himself. Wow!

He took stock of himself and his surroundings. As far as he could tell, this experience was as rich and detailed as real life. His body was fully present, his thoughts and memories clear, and his senses seemed normal – he could hear the creaking of wood, smell the musty interior of the ship, and the solid boards beneath his feet.

Ian looked at the workbench, the musket laying in pieces where his 'apprentice' had left it. In order to avoid suspicion, he should probably try to get the job done. He picked up the stock and barrel of the musket and tried to figure out how they fit together. He could see how the pieces fit but not how to attach them. He pushed them together a few times, but of course, they fell apart again. He looked at the other parts arrayed on the workbench, complicated bits of wood and iron in various shapes and sizes, and then decided that the job was beyond him. Hopefully, he'd be done with this vision before anyone noticed that he didn't know what he was doing.

A head poked down the hatch, "Hey John, you're off duty. Get some sleep if you can," and then it disappeared as its owner stood up and walked away on deck. Ian had noticed a hammock hanging in the corner next to his workbench. Some time alone to think, no-one disturbing him... that sounded like a good idea, so he settled himself into the hammock and closed his eyes, reflecting further on what he knew so far and what he needed to do next.

With his eyes closed, his other senses became more focused. He concentrated on what he could hear and smell. Like most ships, this one stunk. He could smell wood and tar, pungent in his nose, but mostly he smelled sweat and mold and the methane stink of stagnant seawater rising from the bilge.

As he settled further into his hammock, he noticed the sound of voices. Sailors shouting instructions, yelling insults, and laughing. Footsteps as men walked overhead. As his mind filtered through the various noises, he could make out the quieter sounds of the officers dining – clinking dishes and muted conversation. Underlying all of these human sounds was the soft slap of water against the hull and the creaking of rigging holding the masts in tension as the ship rocked back and forth in the gentle swell.

The movement of the ship, the soporific effect of adrenaline leaving his system, and his overall state of exhaustion overtook him as he drifted into sleep.

CHAPTER 29

Amy was walking down the street of a modern looking city, holding hands with a handsome, dark-haired stranger. The vision quest had worked! She wondered where she was and what she was supposed to be doing. The experience was similar to the last time when she'd been in the body of a native girl in the forest, but now she was surrounded by buildings instead of trees. The sound of humans encircled her instead of birdsong, and unlike last time her body felt like her own, red hair drifting into her face, arms white and freckled. She looked at her hands, they seemed normal as well. Long slender fingers, and a small scar on her right thumb where she'd cut herself years ago.

She looked around, willing herself to take in the details. Sleek buildings, unlike any she had seen before, rose on either side of the street, ground floors housing various types of stores and shops, the upper levels apartments. There were cars, all the same rounded shape rather than the variety of vehicles she was used to seeing. She was surrounded by a mix of clothing stores, art galleries, and restaurants – in the retail district of some strange city.

The handsome man was in front of her, tugging gently on her hand, trying to hurry her along. She wanted to look around but wasn't sure how she'd explain herself, so she picked up the pace, concentrating more on walking than on sightseeing. She couldn't help but notice that the clothing on everyone, including herself, was not of a style she'd seen before. It was a synthetic fabric and lighter-weight than she was used to, shimmering in the sunlight and draping beautifully over her. She was very comfortable, neither too hot nor too cold, though she could tell the air was warm where it touched exposed skin.

They passed into a small park with brilliant, green grass. There was a fountain spraying water in the air, benches with people sitting and talking, some sharing a meal. Children were running amongst the trees, mostly cedar, with a few madronas and a magnolia or two. She loved magnolia trees and felt a little bubble of happiness in her chest when she saw them. They reminded her of good times in Seattle, walking the cliffs in Discovery Park, enjoying lazy summer afternoons and admiring the views over Puget Sound toward the Olympic Mountains.

Distracted, not watching where she was going, her foot struck something solid. She would have fallen face first if she hadn't been holding Mr. Handsome's hand. The object she had kicked grunted and moved a little, peering up at her with bleary eyes. It was a person! A homeless man? She steadied herself, pulling her hand away from Mr. Handsome and leaned over to apologize. "I am so sorry! I didn't see you there. Are you okay?"

The homeless man sat up and crossed his legs, a blanket falling off his shoulders, leaves and other debris from the ground stuck in his hair. "Hmmph!" he said, his face set in a scowl.

"I'm sorry, I..." she felt someone grab her elbow and pull her back to standing. The handsome man's face was uncomfortably close to hers.

"Allison, let's go! Why are you talking to him?" He looked angry.

"Let go of me!" she said, pulling her arm out of his grasp. Nobody, no matter how handsome, was going to manhandle her like that. She turned her back on Mr. Handsome, leaving him to fume, and squatted down so she was face to face with the homeless man. "I'm... ," she'd almost said Amy, but that wasn't her name here was it? "I'm, um... Allison," and she held her hand out, wanting to treat him like an equal.

The homeless man stared at her as if he'd never seen a hand before. His eyes traced up her arm to her face, a look of disbelief replacing his earlier scowl. "Hi?" And then he took her hand, giving it a solid shake. His voice was gravelly and it sounded like it hadn't had much use recently.

Amy smiled at him, hoping to break through his reserve. She wanted to show him that she was truly sorry for kicking him, that she saw him as a human, not a piece of garbage on the street. She'd never felt comfortable around homeless people. Not because she thought they were bad people or feared for her safety, but because she couldn't stand to see their suffering. When she'd first arrived in Seattle, she'd tried to give money to every homeless person she saw. After a week of giving, her cash was running low, and she'd realized that the scale of the problem was too large for her. She'd learned to ignore the homeless like everyone else did, but her heart broke every time she had to walk by someone and pretend they didn't exist.

But kicking someone while they were down, that was too much. She had to help. She just had to!

She let go of the homeless man's hand and tried again, "I'm Allison. What's your name?" She could hear Mr. Handsome huffing and pacing a few feet behind her, but for now he was keeping his distance, so she ignored him.

"I'm Norman."

"That's a nice name. I know someone named Norm and he's a very nice guy. I'm sure you are too," she said, still smiling.

That got a little smile from him, and he sat up straighter. Looking closer, she noticed that the dark color of his face wasn't entirely due to dirt and grime. He looked a little like Norm, now that she thought about it. Brown hair and brown eyes, a high forehead and proud cheekbones. He had the skin and facial features of a First Nations tribe member.

"Why are you sleeping in this park Norman? Don't you have a place to go?"

"I'm fine. Don't worry yourself any. Just taking a little nap. I live... over there," and he waved his hand vaguely over his shoulder.

She looked past his hand but could only see more park and more trees. "Ok... I guess. Well, take care of yourself Norman, and I hope to see you again." She stood up and looked for Mr.

Handsome. Since he was the only person that seemed to know who she was, she probably shouldn't lose him.

As they walked out of the park, he kept a firm grip on her hand as if he was worried that she would run away or do something crazy. As soon as they were well away and around a corner, he stopped and turned toward her. "What was that about? We walk by that vagrant every day, and you've never so much as glanced at him. Now you're best friends?"

Wow, he was angry! She racked her brain, trying to figure out how to diffuse the situation. It was hard since she didn't know who this man was or who she herself was supposed to be for that matter.

"Um... I felt bad about kicking him. Do you think I should have walked away without saying anything?"

"Yes, that's exactly what you should have done. Look Allison, You can't trust homeless people, you know that. And you especially can't trust anyone from the Tribes. It's sad what's happened to them. I get that. It's tragic. But there's nothing you can do. It's best to ignore them and hope they go away. You have a soft heart. Too soft."

"What do you mean? What's happened to the Tribes?"

He gave her a long steady look as if he was trying to gauge if she was pulling his leg. Then he started walking again, towing her behind him, a bit less gently than before.

CHAPTER 30

Ian awoke with a start. He wasn't sure how much time had passed. The sun was slanting gently across the hold, illuminating the far wall with a glowing impression of the hatch above. He could hear chairs moving as people stood up in the captain's quarters. Supper must be over and the sounds of the party breaking up had woken him. He rolled himself out of the hammock, stood up, and pulled his clothing straight on his body, again noticing the coarse feel of the rough-spun cloth. His body was stiff from sleeping in the hammock, but he was otherwise well-rested and alert. He looked at the work table and noticed the belaying pins were straightened and polished – cleaned, fixed, and ready for use again.

He grabbed the pins, tucked them under his arm, and climbed up the ladder to the main deck. It was a lovely evening, the sunlight golden, the air a perfect temperature, the wind light and refreshing. Small ripples were standing out on the water below, the boat riding atop a very slight swell that was making its way into the cove from the open ocean a few miles away. Beside the sound of the crew working, he could hear gulls overhead, the occasional cry of an eagle from the surrounding trees, and the noise of seals as they'd poke their heads up, take a few breaths, and then dive back down with a slap and a splash.

After looking around the ship for a few minutes, feeling awkward, he caught sight of the burly man who had given him the pins earlier in the day. He was sitting amidships with a group of other men, surrounded by piles of white sail fabric. They were working with stout needles and thread to repair tears in the sails and to reinforce existing stitching.

As Ian approached he heard one of them addressing the

burly man. “Thompson, I don’t care what you say, I think Maquinna could take the Captain in a fight. He’s got the look of a brawler, that one, and he’s got reach. Have you put your eyes on those arms?”

“Jarvis, you watch what yer saying. Captain won’t be none too happy if he hears you saying such things. We won’t never be getting into a fight with them heathens anyhow. That’s what our muskets are for. A fair fight is for fools or madmen. I ain't neither fool nor mad, and neither is our captain. You mark my words, if it comes to a fight it’ll be our cannons and swivel guns against their knives and arrows.”

“Come on, man. I’m just trying to pass the time. We can’t be talking about those native girls all the time. They got funny lookin’ faces and twisted legs. I gotta squint real hard to pretend they’re real lasses. Only thing they’re good for is bringing us salmon. They smell like salmon too. How their men can stand them, I don’t know - ha, ha, ha!”

Thompson looked at Jarvis and frowned, deep grooves cutting into his forehead and between his bushy brows. He turned his head and glowered at Ian. “What you wanting then?”

Ian held out the belaying pins and Thompson’s expression softened. He reached out and took them, they looked like toys in his massive hands. “I’ll be thanking you for this. That was fast work and well done. Don’t think it makes up for earlier, you hear? You still owe me a whole heap for the trouble you caused me. A whole heap.” With one more deep glower in Ian’s direction, he turned back to his work and to the conversation in which Jarvis was extolling the virtues of Shropshire women, comparing them to sheep in order to prove his point.

As Ian turned away from the group, the Captain and Mate, accompanied by Maquinna and his retinue, emerged from the Captain’s quarters and walked toward the side of the ship where ropes had been set to allow the natives access to their canoes.

Maquinna stopped and faced the Captain. “Thank you, Captain Salter, for the sustenance you have shared with us. We have broken bread with you and there is peace between us.”

Maquinna gave a low bow, which the captain returned, carefully stopping so that he bowed less than Maquinna had.

“I thank you Maquinna for the useful information you have provided to us. Your people have been generous in trade and the crew has enjoyed the salmon you have brought us. It is a welcome break after months of salt-pork, I am sure.”

“I hope that you have found the watering place that I showed your Mate?”

“Yes, thank you. We have been in dire need of freshwater. The stream you showed us was perfect for filling the casks.”

“Captain Salter, may I ask? Do you also hunt?”

“Yes, though I have not hunted since we left England. I do appreciate a bit of sport now and again.” He said with a knowing smile and a wink at his Mate.

“Our village is rich in birds. I think you call them fowl? They are the kind that float in water. Some small, some large. Rich meat and good for eating. While you are here as my guest, you may hunt them.”

“Why Maquinna, that is very kind of you. Very kind. I could use a diversion before we leave, and I am sure my cook would not turn down a fresh duck or goose. Very kind indeed.” He was all smiles, nodding his head enthusiastically.

“You tell me when you wish to go. I will show you these fowls. It is not far from our village, you will see.”

The Captain gestured to his Mate, “Do you hear that Delouisa? We must go hunting before we leave. You will come with me.” He stopped talking, turning thoughtful, “Delouisa, we have a spare gun. Fetch that up for the King. I shall make a gift of it to him in recognition of his generosity.” He smiled at the King while Delouisa hurried back to the Captain’s quarters to fetch the gun.

Ian stood transfixed. These were historical figures standing before him. History made real. Flesh and blood, real men, just like him. But somehow it felt like he was watching a play, the actors playing out their parts in deadly earnest, acting for all the world as if their fates were not already determined.

Delouisa soon returned, the gun cradled in his arms. It was a beautiful double-barreled flintlock rifle, engraved metal polished and glowing in the waning light.

The Captain took the gun from Delouisa and handed it beneficently to the King, "Make good use of this fowling piece. It has served me well, and I think you will eat many excellent meals in my honor - ha, ha, ha."

Maquinna took the gun, a look of awe on his face, nearly overcome with emotion. Before speaking, he composed himself and with an obvious effort he restored his regal bearing. "Mr. Salter, this is a good gun and I say to you that I will honor this one with my life. I will use it to provide food for my tribe. The fowls will fear me, yes?"

"Yes, that's right Maquinna, they will fear you - ha, ha, ha." Captain Salter patted him on the shoulder and urged him toward the side of the ship where he could return to his canoes. The King looked once at the Captain's hand on his shoulder and for just a moment his lip curled, a look of naked hostility that passed so quickly Ian wasn't even sure he'd seen it.

The Captain continued, oblivious. "Farewell Maquinna, please pass my kind regards to all of your wives - ha, ha, ha!"

CHAPTER 31

Amy let Mr. Handsome hustle her along the next couple of blocks, away from the park and up a steep hill continuously lined with multi-story buildings tall enough to pierce through the cloud layer above. The light was falling and she noticed that the crowds of people on the streets were diminishing. Street lights, previously hidden flush against the walls, were emerging from the buildings and winking on. Restaurants were lighting up, their storefronts glowing with high definition renderings of food and happy customers.

She didn't have much time to take it all in, Mr. Handsome's grip was tight on her arm, just above the elbow, and she had to concentrate so that she wouldn't lose her footing as he hurried her along, muttering under his breath the entire way. Eventually the hill leveled off and they slowed down in front of a metal door midway along one of the blocks. Mr. Handsome placed his hand on an access panel while looking into a small camera, and the door opened, sliding straight up into the wall above them. He ducked in, pulling her behind him, and the door closed, fast and silent.

Amy found herself in a softly lit corridor, digitized paintings on the walls. She saw pictures of a whale breaching, a lichen-covered rock, a cedar tree, and a snow-capped mountain before she was ushered into a cylinder-shaped elevator. Once the elevator doors closed, the walls flickered to life showing a 360 degree perspective of the buildings and streets around them. The image was flawless, unmarked by lines or buttons, offering a perfect view in every direction. She stood stock still in the middle of the elevator, feeling dizzy, momentarily happy to have the solidity of Mr. Handsome's hand on her arm.

As they moved upwards, the street scene became smaller and the buildings around them proceeded downward at a rapid rate. A cloud bank appeared above, rushing rapidly closer, and then they were surrounded by white for a few long moments before they burst through and were climbing above a sea of clouds, buildings poking up like blades of grass all around them. The elevator slowed to a stop and based on the tops of the buildings around them, Amy guessed they must be near the top of their building as well. As they turned toward the doors she noticed snow-capped mountains rising above the clouds in the distance, a line of bright, jagged teeth brilliant against a vivid blue sky.

The elevator walls flickered back to a soft white glow and the doors opened revealing another corridor. The corridor stretched in both directions, resplendent with thick red carpet, wood paneling, and lustrous wooden beams on the ceiling. Sconces were spaced on the walls every few feet, glowing with a rich, orange light.

Mr. Handsome exited the elevator, paused and looked back at her, perhaps trying to decide if he needed to grab a hold of her again. She gave him a pained look and walked out on her own, following him down the corridor to a softly gleaming copper door with the name 'Steven Josephs' embossed upon it. He placed his hand on an access panel, looked up for the camera, and then they were in. This must be his apartment. Steve. That was his name.

The apartment was beautiful. Richly furnished with beautiful digital art on the walls and a collection of sculptures on pedestals distributed throughout the living area. There was a fireplace, now cold, comfortable-looking overstuffed couches, a tidy kitchen, and a full wall of windows that looked out over the cloud-scape toward the mountains.

Out of the corner of her eye, she caught movement and looked in time to see one of the sculptures move. She was looking at what appeared to be a cat carved from stone, perfectly still. But then it yawned and lifted a paw to lick. Amy stared at it incredulously. The cat gazed back at her, paused what it was doing, and cocked its head in curiosity. Amy looked away and saw that all the other sculptures were making small movements as well. Animals were grooming themselves, a caricature of a woman was boldly staring at her, hands on hips, and a tree was blowing in an imaginary wind, leaves dropping in a tidy pile around its roots.

She reached a hand over to the cat, unable to resist herself, and watched as her fingers passed right through its head. The cat didn't blink as her fingers disappeared into it, it went back to licking its paw, unperturbed. It must be a hologram or something, but she couldn't see any indication it was fake other than the fact that it had no solidity to her touch. Her fingers didn't disrupt the visual in any way, they just vanished as if cut off. She pulled her hand back, suddenly worried, but her fingers emerged unscathed, never having felt a thing.

Something flitted in the corner of her eye. She looked up at it, but it skittered away, just out of the center of her vision. She stopped moving and concentrated on her peripheral vision, willing her eyes to tell her what was there. After a moment, it became brighter and easier to see. It was a little thumbs up icon with the number 34 next to it. Then she saw a laughing face with a 12. In the corner of her other eye, she saw a face, eyes spinning, with a 63 next to it. What? Why was she seeing emoticons?

Steve cleared his throat and Amy startled. The look he gave her was so perplexed she almost laughed out loud. She could only imagine what she had looked like. Putting her hand through his cat, lurching suddenly backward, then spinning, her face twitching as she tried to figure out what was going on with her eyes. She couldn't help but feel a small giggle rising in her throat. Her lips gave a slight twitch trying to hold it in and that must have made her look even more deranged because Steve was starting to look downright worried.

"Allison, are you feeling alright?"

"Yes, I think so. I'm sorry I'm behaving so strangely. It's

just been a strange day, that's all." She hoped that would relieve some of his concerns. She pressed on, hoping to change the subject. "Those are lovely mountains aren't they?"

The look on his face made her realize that she had sounded like an idiot again. Of course. She probably lived here. She probably saw this view every day. Dummy. "I mean the mountains are lovely today, aren't they?"

His face softened a little as he turned to look out the window. "Yes. I love this view. It's worth every penny of the enormous rent I pay to be on this floor. I feel a sense of peace up here, away from it all, separated from the rest of the city." Odd. He sounded like he was giving a speech to an audience. He let out a dramatic sigh and turned toward her, his arms spread wide.

Hmm. He wanted a hug, did he? Guess it couldn't hurt, right? Amy stepped into his embrace and let her head rest comfortably on his chest. She could hear the regular thumping of his heart and his voice sounded rumbly when he spoke again. "It's ok. I've had bad days too. Let's relax a bit, get some food, and I think a good night's sleep will have you feeling better in no time." In her peripheral vision, she saw a face with hearts for eyes, with the number 124 next to it. A green puking face appeared in her other eye, the number 12 next to it.

She stepped away from him and noticed a bureau with picture frames set on top. She walked over to get a closer look and saw that while the frames looked normal, the pictures inside were continually changing. When she looked at one of them closely it froze for a moment so she could see it better. It was a picture of an attractive blond woman with information scrolling around it – likes and dislikes, where she worked, colleges attended, and a small map that appeared to be her current location. As Amy watched, words appeared, like they were being typed in real-time, "Jerome thinks he can trick me into eating seaweed, but I will never fall for it," and then there was a smiley face, a kiss blown into the wind, and the woman flipped her hair back over her shoulder.

She looked at another frame, and it was similar, this time

a thin, sun-bronzed man standing on a surfboard, the ocean curling behind him as he rode a wave of deep blue water. She saw that he liked reading and surfing, disliked okra (who doesn't?), and was currently in Madagascar. Some words appeared, "Never get tired of this wave, I think I could ride it forever," and he gave a satisfied smile.

Amy stood up and looked at Steve in wonder, "What...?" but she stopped herself from going too far with her question. He would expect her to know about all of this. She settled her face and pretended she knew what she was doing.

Steve looked at her, a hint of sadness in his eyes. "This again? You'll get more followers. I know you will. It's hard to get over a hundred million like me, but there's no point in being jealous. Just keep being interesting and you'll get more in no time. You are at what, ten thousand now? The first ten thousand is always the hardest. It gets easier after that. Plus hanging out with me will work miracles for your visibility." He paused for a second. "And quite frankly, just being around me can't help but make you more interesting, right?"

Amy felt a bit like hitting him before she reminded herself that she didn't care one bit about followers or whatever it was he was rambling on about. In the corner of her eye, she saw a pair of boxing fists pumping up and down with 1.2k next to them. Hmm... maybe she was getting more interesting already.

CHAPTER 32

The next few days passed in a blur. Ian shuffled from watch to watch, sleeping in his hammock when he could, pretending to work at his workbench when given jobs, and relying heavily upon his apprentice to give him the appearance of competency. He'd learned a little about the young man over the past few days. He couldn't ask too many questions without seeming suspicious, but he had discovered that the young man's name was Jacob, he'd been born and raised in New Bedford, and had signed onto this voyage in order to learn a trade. He was obviously a quick study because he had done the work well enough so far to save Ian from having to answer difficult questions about his own lack of skills.

The natives were on the boat every day, exchanging salmon and other food for trinkets from the crew, and participating in other types of small trade. Trade-beads were a favorite as was anything made from metal. Even small scraps of iron from his workbench were enough to get him fresh salmon from the excited native women. As the days went by, he saw evidence of the ongoing trade in the form of trade-bead necklaces adorning women's necks and a proliferation of small iron tools carried by the native men.

The crew kept him at arm's reach. They considered him in a different social class. He could read and write, do math in his head, and the fact that John Jewitt had attended college was enough to make him a different type of human in their estimation. Additionally, he was the armorer, an essential position on the ship, therefore not to be trifled with.

The only people he interacted with were his apprentice Jacob, and Thompson, the burly sailmaker. His apprentice was in awe of him and almost overly obsequious. Thompson, on the other hand, looked at him with disdain and only talked to him in order to give him tasks or to cast insults in his direction. The Captain and the Mate never acknowledged his existence, they may as well have been on another planet. Those two spent most of their time walking the quarterdeck, discussing ship's business.

In a way it was convenient. If he'd been part of the fraternization that occurred amongst the rest of the crew, he probably would have been found out long ago. As long as he kept his silence he could continue to pass as John Jewitt. If he had to talk much, he'd probably give himself away. There was just too much he didn't know about the current time and too much he knew, from the future, that they didn't. He was constantly reminding himself to be careful, and as a result he tried to keep to himself as much as he could.

He did have near constant companionship at his workbench, and not just in the form of his Jacob. The natives were intrigued by him and would cluster around as he pretended to work. They would let out sighs and gasps as he fiddled with pieces of metal, banging on them with hammers or using the hand drill and press to cut holes. He wasn't actually getting anything done, but he'd learned how to make a good show of it. The natives looked at him like he was a wizard, capable of magical deeds and possessing of otherworldly knowledge. It was a bit flattering and he could feel himself puffing up with self-importance under their sense of awe, until he would remind himself that he was actually a fraud and had no idea what he was doing.

After several days had passed the mood of the ship changed, energy and anticipation ratcheting up several notches. He learned that the Captain had ordered the crew to make ready for departure, and he felt a spike of anxiety at this news. If they left this bay, would it be harder for him to get home? He had no idea how the vision quest worked nor how long it was supposed to last. Was he stuck here forever? No, that didn't make sense. Richard had mentioned that most people returned unharmed. Then again, some didn't...

He tried to banish the worry from his mind, there wasn't much he could do about it anyway. He could jump ship, but he'd probably be caught and punished. Even if he wasn't caught, what would he do? He didn't know how to survive in a 19th-century wilderness! He just had to bide his time, observe, do his best and trust that at some point the vision would end.

There had been no natives on board the ship all morning and Jacob was getting some much deserved sleep. His work-space was blessedly quiet for the moment. While he was trying to decide what to do with himself, Ian heard a few thumps against the side of the hull and decided to go up on deck to see what was happening.

Emerging into the sunlight, he saw that there were canoes alongside the ship, a group of natives requesting permission to come aboard. The officer on deck granted their request and waited as they tied fast and clambered over the side. Evidently, someone had informed the Captain because he emerged from his quarters, blinking in the bright light, "Hello Maquinna, welcome aboard."

The King looked like he was in a bad mood, his face unusually serious and his chiefs were scowling. He was carrying the beautiful gun that the Captain had given him, cradling it gingerly in both arms. The entire group was wearing sea-otter cloaks as usual, but they no longer had feather-down in their hair. Perhaps, familiarity had removed the need for such formalities?

The officer on deck asked the natives to remove their cloaks, a matter of protocol to ensure no-one came aboard with hidden weapons. Once the cloaks were removed, folded, and placed in a chest on deck, the King and his Chiefs stood in a semi-circle around the Captain and a few of the other sailors. Ian had never been so close to the natives before. He was fascinated as he watched the tense tableau before him, small details jumping out at him as he took it all in. The cedar mantles worn by the chiefs contained a red border painted in a series of fantastic designs of animals, people, and supernatural creatures – the depictions popping with stunning clarity. He felt nervous, his body charged with adrenaline for no reason that he could readily comprehend. He knew something important was happening, but he couldn't put his finger on what it was. He stood still, fingers tingling with latent nerves, uncertain of what to do next, unsure if he should stay to witness what was happening or if he should turn and flee.

The King spoke next, "Captain Salter, I offer you these fowls as a gift." He stated it very formally, speaking sharply, biting off each syllable as it left his mouth. One of the chiefs stepped forward and presented a line of ducks – killed, plucked, and hung upon a string.

The officer on deck took the ducks, nodded formally to the chief, and turned crisply to bring them to the larder. The King looked intently at the Captain. He was waiting for something.

The Captain swallowed visibly and responded, "Maquinna thank you, I'm sure. The ducks will go very well with my port tonight – ha, ha, ha."

Maquinna bowed his head very slightly, without taking his eyes off the Captain. The Captain looked unsure. Typically he would bow back, but it would be impossible to bow less than what Maquinna had already done. So he didn't move his head at all, instead choosing to stare straight ahead and smile nervously. The continuing silence of the King and his Chiefs was evidently affecting the Captain as he began to fidget. He plucked at his collar a few times and shuffled his feet. A small bead of sweat stood on his brow.

The Captain broke the silence. "Well then Maquinna, what can I do for you? As you know, we will be leaving shortly. Sailing north to trade with your neighbors – ha, ha, ha."

Maquinna looked at the gun in his arms then back to the Captain, "This gun. It is not working. It is *peshak*!"

Ian had picked up a few of the native's words in the past days and this was one that he knew. *Peshak* meant 'bad,' but stronger. Intentionally bad. Almost a curse. If someone had purposefully sabotaged your property to cause you harm, you would call that *peshak*.

The Captain evidently knew the meaning because his demeanor changed in an instant. He became rigid and his face turned red. He looked around to see who had witnessed the insult and his humiliation. Most of the crew were watching now, and with this realization his face turned an even deeper shade of red, spreading in waves up his neck from his collar to the roots of his hair. Ian watched, transfixed. He had never seen such a vivid display of anger, never having seen a man of such deeply held honor so deeply insulted.

"Why you... you ungrateful sod. You lying, no good, lazy son of a whore." He seized the gun roughly from Maquinna's hands. "You've broken the lock. I should expect nothing better from a backward, uneducated savage. You are clumsy, you are crude, and you are undeserving of such a fine gift. I'll be happy to be done with you and your entire misbegotten, heathen tribe. Begone!" The captain thrust his head forward, he was deeply enraged now, bellowing directly into Maquinna's face, showering him with a spray of saliva.

Maquinna took the abuse without flinching, but Ian saw his face turn a red to match the Captain's as he suffered the tirade. He may not have understood everything that had been said, but it would have been impossible for him to miss the tone and the insult to his pride. His hand fluttered upward toward his chest where he pressed it flat upon his breastbone. Then his hand moved unsteadily to his throat where he grasped himself just below the chin, squeezing hard, his knuckles whitening. After a long moment he stroked his hand down his throat to his chest, still pressing hard. All the while, his face was like a thunder-head, anger standing out sharply on his proud features. The chiefs gathered close, forming a tight knot around their king, where he stood with his hand pressed upon his breast.

The Captain, oblivious to the native's anger, threw the gun carelessly toward Ian, "John, this fellow has broken this beautiful fowling piece, see if you can mend it."

Ian looked down at the broken gun, up at the Captain's angry face, and over at the group of enraged natives. Outrage had surrounded him, blooming forth like a harbinger of doom to come.

CHAPTER 33

"Well then. What should we eat, hmm?" Steve was looking at her with wide eyes, a smile plastered on his face.

"Umm... what are our options?"

Steve stretched his smile, making it bigger somehow. "Good question! Let's see..." and he started ticking options off on his fingers. He was standing in a power pose, teeth gleaming white. "We could go down to the avenue and eat with the plebes. You know, mix it up!"

What was it with this guy? It was like he was on stage, always playing a part, every movement a little too big, every word a bit too loud. It was getting creepy. She resisted the urge to look over her shoulder to see if he was performing for someone she couldn't see.

"Or we could head over to South Coast for some ethnic fare. If you know what I mean?" And he winked at her. A big theatrical wink as if they were in on some joke together. She definitely was *not* in on the joke. She was becoming increasingly unimpressed. Who did he think he was, anyway?

"Or we could go Uptown to eat at a classy establishment with all the movers and the shakers. Wait, we already are in Uptown - ha, ha, ha!"

Amy clenched her teeth trying hard to resist an overpowering urge to roll her eyes.

"Or... we could stay right here. In this little love-nest. Eat some comfort food, turn on the fire, sip a little wine, enjoy our view from the top of the world? How does that sound my little duckling?" He waggled his eyebrows at her, an expression on his face that he must have thought was sexy. It struck Amy as a half-drugged come-hither, mixed with a heavy dose of conceit.

Ugh. Not that. Anything but that. Amy did *not* want to eat here in his 'little love-nest.' Her mind was racing. How to get out of it? She'd just pick one of the other options. South Coast sounded picturesque. And ethnic food always sounded good to her. "How about South Coast? That would be good tonight, wouldn't it?"

She saw a steaming bowl of noodles in the corner of her right eye with the number 36 next to it. In her other eye, she saw a roaring fire and a cartoon rendition of lingerie with the number 867 flashing red. Amy had no idea what that meant.

"Oh, my little chick-a-dee, are you sure that's what you want?" Again with the eyebrow waggle.

The noodles in her right eye blinked up to 38, and the fire/lingerie combination shot up to 1.4k, still flashing red. "Oh yes, I am quite sure. I think I could use some fresh air." That part was true. She was feeling a bit queasy.

"Well ok. Let's go out then!" and he twirled toward the door, his arms bent upward like the world's worst bullfighter.

Amy waited for him to say Ole' and when it didn't come, she followed in his wake as he sashayed down the corridor and back into the elevator. The noodles rose up to 128, turned a solid green and then winked out. The fire combo deflated like a popped balloon, fading down and out of sight.

To her surprise, they rode the elevator up toward the top of the building. The clouds around them were a brilliant pastel pink, dark purple in the east. The mountains were luminous, alpenglow painting them a golden orange, the snowy peaks reflecting the last light of the day. When she emerged from the elevator, Amy found herself in a glass dome perched on the roof of the building, the view around them as beautiful as anything she'd ever seen. The sky was now deep purple, fading to black in the east, the horizon pin-pricked with stars.

Steve paused in the middle of the dome and used his arm to sweep her dramatically to his side. He blinked rapidly, eyes moving in a strange zig-zag pattern as he muttered under his breath, "Skycar to South Coast, priority zero, clearance code one-oh-three-four-alpha-five. Destination: ethnic of choice. Selection criteria: visibility, trending, vibe, music, presence of other influencers, food quality."

Most of what he said was incomprehensible to Amy, so she was surprised when the top of the dome opened and, with a roar of rotor wash, a quadcopter the size of a small car descended upon them, belly opening like a giant mouth to swallow them up. Amy would have run away, but Steve kept a hold of her. He was somehow both suave and nonchalant while also being utterly off-putting as the quadcopter settled onto the roof, the two of them now firmly ensconced in the middle of it.

Steve released his hold on Amy and sat on the plush bench that lined the back wall. Amy sat next to him, mimicking his movements to secure her seatbelt and shoulder harness. There was no pilot in front of them, just a bubble of glass showing the curve of the dome and the edge of the building beyond that. The quadcopter had another set of benches, both empty, giving a clear view out the windows on either side.

Once they had their feet on a set of molded foot-rests below the bench, the belly of the quadcopter closed, a transparent panel sliding smoothly into place. Steve reclined with a sigh of contentment, gallantly brushed back his hair and put his arm around Amy, draping his hand over her shoulder. Amy tried to shake off his hand and glared at him, but he was oblivious, apparently indifferent to her discomfort. In her right eye, she saw a heart with an arrow through it, 2.3k pulsing next to it.

A female voice evincing a tone of incredible culture and competency filled the space. "Welcome passengers. It is my pleasure to be your conveyance this evening. I hope that you have a wonderful flight to El Sambal Dos Chiquinos, the finest Indonesian, Mexican, Asian ethnic restaurant for those who love living life and are sophisticated enough to show it. It's the perfect dining experience for influencers like yourself. Sit back, relax, and enjoy the ride."

Steve let out another self-satisfied sigh as the quadcopter lifted up and out of the dome, banking and speeding toward the south. They were rushing between tall buildings, each lit with different colors and designs, the clouds glowing below them, pulsing and alive with the reflected light. Amy was terrified at first, the g-forces tugging her down in the seat as they banked hard and then pulling her up toward the ceiling as the quadcopter dropped, rapidly plunging toward the surface of the clouds. Once the quadcopter settled into level flight, she found herself entranced by the view. The clouds flowed beneath them, heaps of billowing, indistinct shape and glowing color.

Eventually, the quadcopter descended into the clouds, water beading on the windshield and blowing backward over the side windows under the pressure of their passage. A moment later they burst into clear air and Amy gasped in wonder. The city spread below her, thousands of lights in every direction organized in lines following the pattern of the streets. Lights moved below them, vehicles of some sort. There were lights moving to their sides and above them, quadcopters carrying passengers to other destinations. There were a multitude of lights on the tips of buildings and towers, the structures shorter here, tops well below the clouds. Thousands of lights combined in a huge, glowing pattern, the city alive beneath her.

A curve of shoreline was in front of them, outlined in the lights lining the beach, a distinct break between the glowing city and the water, sparkling with the reflections of an overflowing humanity. The clouds above were softly aglow, reflecting light back at the city, a luminous roof overhead. The ocean had dozens of lights on its surface, boats both stationary and in movement, tracing lazy arcs as they moved about their business.

The quadcopter continued to descend and the scope of the scene diminished as they flew closer to their destination. The view shrank from thousands of lights to hundreds, to dozens, and then they were on the ground, settling onto a hexagonal pad, the quadcopter rotors spinning down as the engines shut off.

The female voice spoke again. "Thank you for flying with

Volant, a division of Uber Transport. We hope to see you again soon." The belly panel opened to reveal a set of stairs.

Amy untangled herself from the bench and followed Steve down. At the bottom of the stairs was an access panel and a camera that Steve used to get them out into the night. The temperature was lovely, warm enough to be pleasant, cool enough to be refreshing, a soft breeze brushing their cheeks. Amy took a deep breath, reveling in the sensation of the beautiful air in her lungs and looking around to get her bearings.

They were on a concrete strand, a small railing between them and the actual beach. The area around them was lit by the nearby restaurants and shops, the strand filled with happy, well-dressed people. The beach, however, was empty, the sand deserted, water lapping on the shore, a slight phosphorescence visible in the wavelets. The sand looked odd to Amy, almost like it was glowing. She stepped to the railing to get a closer look and saw that it was a very light color, almost white, causing it to reflect the light around her. Walls of dark, blocky rocks formed borders on either side of the crescent beach, reaching seaward and descending into the water. There was something about the beach that seemed very familiar to her.

"Are you coming my sweet little wrenling? Let's eat before you become famished, shall we?" Steve was waiting for her, a dozen paces away, reaching an arm out, willing her toward him.

She ignored him and looked back toward the ocean, focusing, trying to see the details. And then it came to her. That rock on the left side, that's where she and Ian had stood after the shipwreck. The white sand below her was an ancient midden. She could see where she had curled up, insensible and waterlogged, until Ian had roused her. The rocky reef in the distance... that's where the sailboat had foundered and sunk. She knew this beach, this place... she was on Hurst Island.

CHAPTER 34

The natives had been angry but they left peacefully, climbing into their canoes and paddling away without another word. The next day dawned clammy and still, not a breath of air. The sails hung limp and dead. The water lay stagnant, slopping viscously against the hull where the *Boston* sat at anchor. Long strands of algae fringed the ship at the waterline – a greasy green beard giving testament to the time they'd spent stationary. The Captain had the sails ready to catch any wind that came and the crew was prepared to pull the anchor cables at a moment's notice. The air hung motionless over the ship. Everyone knew it was time to leave, but without wind the ship couldn't move. Simple as that.

Feeling discouraged, Ian retired to his workbench in the early afternoon to get some time to himself. Time to think. Time to remember who he was. Ian. Not John. He stared at his tools, a pile of pad eyes that needed work, the never-ending supply of muskets that required cleaning and repair. Maquinna's gun sat in the middle of the workbench. He hadn't attempted to fix it, nor had he asked Jacob to try. He had dropped it on the table after the Captain had thrown it to him and he hadn't touched it since.

Even to his untrained eye the problem was obvious. There was supposed to be a hammer on each side, one per barrel. But the hammer on the right side was broken clean off and there was a small dent in the pan. The dent wasn't the problem, the pan would still hold gunpowder, but the lack of a hammer meant that the barrel wouldn't fire. It was an easy fix. Unscrew the broken hammer, find a replacement, screw it back together again. Might take some time to find a new hammer that would fit, but with his extensive collection of muskets he knew he could find something that would work.

He stopped and marveled for a moment, he was actually gaining some skill. It had sort of slipped up on him. He could perform simple repairs now and he no longer had to fake his way through all the time. Sometimes he was doing real work, acting like a real armorer. Living in this time and this place was affecting him. He needed to hold onto his sense of self, his memories of being Ian. He couldn't lose himself to John. He knew intuitively that if that happened, he'd never make it back. He had a purpose here... he just needed to figure out what it was.

The sound of a whistle being blown roused him from his contemplation. Above his head he heard thumping footsteps and then the whistle sounded again. Curious, he climbed up on deck to see what was going on. The languor that had hung over the ship had been replaced with turmoil and commotion. There was a party of natives on board, cloaks piled on the side deck. They were shirtless, painted red and glistening, stamping their feet on the deck, leaping in the air and letting out loud shouts.

To Ian's complete and utter shock there was a creature standing with the natives. Dominating them. He could see the back of its brown furry head, small black ears poking out, and a wooden whistle in its left hand. It was stomping its feet and blowing short blasts on the whistle in time with the native's dancing. Sasahevas, standing before him, right here on this ship!

The group of natives and the creature were facing each other across the deck, the rest of the crew taking their leisure, laughing and calling encouragement. He looked around, desperate to find the Captain, certain that he would take action against what was happening. But when Ian caught sight of him on the quarterdeck, he was casually leaning up against the rail, watching the dancers, and occasionally passing a remark to the Mate who was standing beside him.

Ian looked at the Captain in disbelief, how could he remain so calm? He turned his gaze back toward the creature. It was intermittently facing him now as it blew on the whistle, stomped its feet and spun in time with the other dancers. Ian took a couple of steps forward, hands outstretched, ready to do... something. He knew not what. Then the scene resolved in front of him. The creature was quite clearly Maquinna in a remarkably crafted wooden mask, fur glued on to give the appearance of Sasahevas. It was intricately carved – crafted cunningly into a striking resemblance of the creature that Ian had encountered on Hurst Island.

Now that he was closer he couldn't understand how he'd mistaken Maquinna for a monster. His size and stature were too small, his arms and legs too distinctly human. Ian had been taken in by the mask. Confused and surprised, his senses had fooled him – filling in the blanks to paint a picture that didn't match reality.

Ian felt woozy, his body weak from the passing shock. The stomping feet were making his head throb, the whistle was piercing his skull. He wanted to be somewhere else, anywhere but here, stuck between the wildly dancing natives and the cheering, carefree crew.

He was making his way back to the hatch, to his workspace, when the dancing stopped. The sudden silence stopped Ian in his tracks and he turned to see what was happening. The dancers held themselves rigidly still for the space of three breaths, locked in strange poses, fierce expressions on their faces, mouths open, tongues out, arms and legs spread wide. Maquinna stood still, his head bobbing, scanning the crew with the visage of Sasahevas, cold and threatening.

Then the moment broke. The dancers returned to normal human poses and Maquinna pulled the mask from his head. He looked up to the quarterdeck and called out, "Captain Salter, did you like our entertainment?"

"Very much Maquinna. Thank you for this display. Very entertaining indeed. Quite diverting." He looked at his Mate, who quickly concurred. "Yes, quite. But what was the purpose of the mask? Were you supposed to be a bear?"

"No, it is not a bear. What would you call it... it is... a wild man. We call it Sasahevas. It is a guide for my people. It helps us to see what has been done and to see what must be done." Maquinna looked from the Captain to Ian, staring into him. "We have learned to pay attention. We are sorry when we don't."

Maquinna glared at Ian for a moment longer, then he turned back to the Captain and Mate. "Captain Salter, you will be leaving soon?"

The Captain conferred briefly with the Mate before responding, "Yes, tomorrow. If the wind and tide be true."

"You like salmon, yes? There is much in Friendly Cove. Why not go to catch some before you leave?"

The Captain smiled, "Very thoughtful of you Maquinna. That's a capital idea. We could use the extra supply."

Maquinna smiled back, eyes never wavering, a feral intensity in that smile that chilled Ian to the bone. Perhaps he had been unduly influenced by the savagery of their dance, because the Captain seemed at ease and no-one else from the crew was disturbed by the exchange.

Ian shook his head. He didn't understand this place. Didn't understand why he felt this way. His thoughts and impressions weren't adding up. His danger-sense was ringing loudly, all his nerves on end, anxiety flooding his veins with the need to do something. But there was nothing to do, nothing to say, nothing he could put his finger on. He didn't have enough standing with the Captain or the crew to raise unwarranted concerns and be taken seriously.

As the crew dropped boats in the water and organized a fishing party, Ian walked back to his hatch. He felt so tired, his were feet dragging on the boards and his heart was heavy. The last thing he heard before he ducked below was the Captain's voice. "I say, Andrew, do take my laundry, will you? Mr. Delouisa and the fishing party will drop you where you can complete the washing. I want it all done before we sail tomorrow..."

Once below, Ian stared listlessly at Maquinna's gun. With a sense of dread he picked it up and worked to unscrew the broken hammer from where it was attached to the stock. After some fiddling he had it out, the small piece dense and heavy in his palm. He bent under his bench to look for a replacement hammer that would fit.

With his head buried, it took awhile for him to hear what was taking place above. Some sound must have alarmed him, because he wrenched his head out and stood up, ears cocked. The usual sounds of the ship had been replaced by something new. Something foreign to his experience.

Ian could hear yells, both from the crew and from the natives, the muted shock of something heavy landing on the wood just above his head, then the unmistakable sound of gunfire – the retort of a pistol shot. Ian startled into movement. Driven by an overpowering need to see what was happening, he rushed to the ladder.

He peeked his head out of the hatch and found pandemonium. Complete chaos. Native bodies entwined with the crew, arms flailing in close-quarter combat. One of them rushed by, his feet at the level of Ian's eyes, teeth bared in a grimace of violent intent, death incarnate.

Ian's closest taste of violence was a fist fight in the fifth grade. Nothing he had experienced prepared him for what lay before him – the brutality was overwhelming. The shadow of death hung over this ship, blackened arms reaching down to take men as they fell under the blows of knife and club and axe.

As if of their own accord, in horrid fascination, his eyes focused on a body lying beside the hatch. The throat was cut, eyes open, face white, shirtfront drenched red with blood that was already drying, forming a crust on the fabric. He felt he was going into shock. Sounds were muted, his ears were going fuzzy.

Snapshots of the battle passed before him. A knife up, plunging down. A body falling. A native whooping in triumph. A knife, slicing sideways, blood spraying in a misty arc. A mortally injured member of the crew groaning and gurgling, grasping at his throat. Struck again in the head with a club, dropping hard to the deck.

The crew was becoming difficult to see, the press of native

bodies thick, few familiar faces remaining. Those that he could see were back to back in a small knot, fighting desperately, the knowledge of impending death evident in their eyes. He saw another man fall, his face a rictus of pain. The knot reforming, smaller now. Fragile. Hopeless. It wouldn't be much longer.

Ian was paralyzed with fear. He couldn't bring himself to move, couldn't bring himself to join the crew and fight. What good would it do anyway...

Where was the Captain? Ian looked around, frantic. All his hope now tied to the idea that the Captain was still alive and knew how to defend the ship. Maybe he could make this awful situation right again. Before he could find any sign of him, Ian felt a powerful hand grasp his hair and haul him bodily upwards.

He was halfway out of the hatch, his legs dangling, his scalp on fire, spinning in the grasp of a large native man. As if in a dream he saw the man's arm rise up, drenched in blood to the elbow, a wicked-looking axe in his hand, poised to come down on Ian's skull. Ian's thoughts were disjointed, incongruous. His mind stuck on the idea of a butcher. Memories of the meat market back home.

His eyes were locked on the native man. Brown skin, brown eyes, tattooed face, sweat glistening on his forehead, his shoulder muscles standing out in his exertion and frenzy. His executioner. The axe on its way down. The certainty of death entered his mind with stunning force. In the intensity of this experience he couldn't sort out what was real and what was vision. It all felt real. It had all been for nothing. He'd never learned what he was supposed to do. He would never see Amy again. He was going to die. Right here. Right now. It was upon him. He had no more moments left.

And then he felt himself falling, the native man's grip slipping from his hair as his ribbon came unbound. The axe swung down, the arc of it inexorable. And then a sickening impact. Axe on skull. The feeling of his skin peeling free, his skull caving, a splash of wet heat on his face, a flash of the brightest white, and then he was tumbling through the hatch into darkness. The darkness overtaking him.

He hit the floor with a reverberating thud, his body crumpled and lifeless – a marionette whose strings had been cut.

CHAPTER 35

Where were all the trees?

If this was Hurst Island, what had happened to all the trees? She turned to Steve and fixed him with a glare, "Where are we?"

He withered under her look, his hand dropping slowly to his side, "On the South Coast darling. You know that." He attempted a dazzling smile, but it died on his face.

"South Coast of what? Are we on an island?"

He was starting to look concerned. "Yes, of course, we are on an island. We've never left. Oh... I see... you were confused by our little flight, weren't you my peach. You are just so adorable."

Her glare intensified as she advanced on him, causing him to take an involuntary step back. "What. Island. Are. We. On." She was staring him down, he was shrinking under the force of her questioning.

"Hurst Island. We are on Hurst Island. What's the matter with you?" He appeared to be on the verge of tears.

So she had been right. Hurst Island. Buildings everywhere, people crowding the streets, the night lit up, overpowering the stars and the moon. What had happened to the beautiful, desolate, wild island that she remembered? She turned to Steve again, "What happened to all the trees?"

"Um... what?"

"This island used to be entirely covered with trees. What happened to them?"

"They were cut down?"

"When? Why? I don't understand... what happened?" She trailed off feeling lost. Not sure how to ask what she needed to know.

Seeing her uncertainty, Steve gained some of his confidence back. "You will feel so much better with food and a drink. Especially a drink. Probably several drinks." He watched for a reaction and then added, "Come on, let's go." He hooked his arm in hers, pulling her down the strand toward their restaurant.

It was the largest, flashiest establishment on the beach. There was a line of people waiting to get in and a bigger crowd standing nearby, just to watch the action. Steve waltzed up to a roped-off gate, said a few words to the man standing there and just like that, they were in.

The inside of the restaurant was styled like a tropical jungle. They walked through a space filled with giant tree trunks, soft carpet underfoot, colorful animals scampering in the branches above them. It was impossible for these trees to fit inside a building, she couldn't tell what was real and what was fake.

The smells of jungle were all around her, fragrant flowers and ripe greenery overlaid with the rich, sweet scent of tropical fruit. The air was filled with bird calls, monkeys crying out, and the soft sounds of leaves moving in the breeze. Occasionally they'd walk through a spritz of water, the air warm and humid on her skin.

Steve led her through one more set of trees and then they were in a large atrium, the sky visible above through a domed, glass ceiling. A maitre d' was standing at a podium with a long line of people waiting to be seated. Behind him, on the wall, was a large screen showing scenes from the restaurant. People dining, a dance floor, the crowd outside, rotating images of glamorous people having the time of their lives.

Soon after they entered, the screen showed Steve, huge, larger than life. As if on cue he raised his arms and waved, smiling broadly, some of the people near them turning to stare and a few of them even starting to clap. He pulled Amy in toward him, clasping her to his side as he continued to wave. Amy could see herself on the screen, looking horrified. She tried to relax, tried to look normal, she wasn't cut out for this sort of thing. A set of fireworks went off in her right eye, distracting her, the number 4.5k flashing rapidly.

The maitre d' snapped his fingers and a host appeared to guide them to a table, deftly maneuvering them past the crowd and through a doorway to a smaller, private room with plush booths and wall-length windows overlooking the ocean. Steve kept smiling and waving until he'd reached the doorway, then he turned to Amy, "That should get you a few thousand followers. Don't you just love it? You can thank me later!"

The room they were in was decorated like an old-fashioned ship, the theme distinctly nautical. There was a small ship's wheel, the booths were built from distressed, darkened wood and shaped as if they came from the interior of an old boat. The walls were covered with digitized pictures and paintings from the past, islands covered in trees, whales breaching, sea lions on a rock, a winter storm pounding a rugged shoreline with waves and spray.

There were pictures of people too. A man standing at the wheel of an old ship, sails straining, rain lashing his face as he peered into the gloom, trying to steer his ship to safety. Another showed a group of old-fashioned sailors in small boats, approaching a native village, the villagers crowded on the beach to welcome their arrival.

One of the paintings caught her eye. It was a blonde man wearing a woolen coat, his collar pulled up against the cold. He was turned away so that his face was in profile, watching a Captain take a gun from the hands of a native chief. The painting was wonderfully done, the details stood out so that she could clearly see the emotions on each of their faces. The Captain and the Chief looked angry, others in the party seemed upset as well, the intensity of expression varying from person to person.

But the blonde man, he looked different. He wasn't angry. He was scared. But that wasn't what caught her eye. What had caught her eye was that the man looked so much like Ian. The way he was wearing his hair was different than she remembered and the clothing was unlike anything she'd seen him wear. But the face was was startlingly familiar. The set of his mouth, the color of his eyes, even the shape of his cheekbones and forehead – if she hadn't known better, she'd have said that this was a painting of Ian standing on the deck of a sailing ship, hundreds of years in the past.

She looked at the placard below the painting, wanting to know more. All it said was, "Before the massacre, Captain Salter argues with Maquinna, Nootka Sound, 1805." Steve was sitting down when she called across the room to him. "Do you know anything about this painting? About these men?"

He stood up and walked over, steepling his hands under his chin in an attempt to look studious. "Let's see, that looks like a captain. They are on a boat. Hmm, that tribe member looks angry. I wonder why they gave him a gun?" He stared at the picture a little longer, "Yes. Yes, I see. This was probably before the tribes were scattered and homeless. Serves them right, doesn't it?" Then he turned back to the table and sat down to peruse a tablet with a menu on it.

Amy gave the picture one last look, trying to commit the image to memory, and then she joined Steve at the table. Maybe a drink wasn't such a bad idea after all.

CHAPTER 36

When Ian regained consciousness, he didn't know where he was. His first thoughts were for Amy. He hoped she was safe. His next thoughts were reserved entirely for the magnitude of pain in his head. It felt like someone had knocked his skull to pieces, glued it back together, and then knocked it apart a few more times for good measure. The pain was beyond anything he had ever experienced. He lay groaning for many long minutes, lost in the agony of it, eventually passing back into unconsciousness, thereby gaining a welcome respite in oblivion.

He heard Amy's voice, as if from a distance, "Do you know anything about this painting? About these men?" Her voice was distorted and fuzzy, fading into the darkness with him. Amy... where are you?

When he came to again, he had regained more of his faculties. He could hear the sound of the battle raging above him, shouts and thumps, and the occasional pistol shot. He realized he was still alive and decided he wanted to keep it that way. His face felt wrong. It wasn't just the pain – he felt hugely swollen, puffy, and broken. He could only see out of one eye, the right side of his face too damaged to allow the other eye to open. He reached a hand up and winced as his fingers touched skin. It didn't feel like a part of him, the sensations confused and awry.

When he pulled his fingers away, they were wet and sticky, his face covered in a steady stream of blood flowing from somewhere higher on his scalp. He tried to roll over, moving his head in the process, and promptly passed out again.

Opening his eyes for the third time, he realized that his situation was truly dire. The noises above were decreasing with no indication of who was winning. The screams were less frequent, there were fewer footsteps, and no more gunfire. Whatever was happening in the battle, it seemed like it would be over soon. He was in no shape to defend himself and even uninjured, he couldn't have managed much against the attackers. He felt helpless and exposed, laying prone at the base of the main-deck ladder.

Squinting his one good eye, he noticed that the hatch above him was closed and barred. That was something. He would have some warning if someone were to come down – the hatch would make some noise. But since it was barred from the outside, it also meant he couldn't escape. He levered himself into a seated position, leaning against the ladder for support. The pounding in his head increased, a pitch of pain he hadn't known was possible. He felt dizzy and nauseous, his stomach rebelling against him, his head wobbling randomly on the stick of his neck.

He clutched the ladder as hard as he could, willing his body to normalcy, willing the pain to recede. His good eye was having trouble blinking, the lashes sticking together with congealed blood and grime. He closed his eye and wiped a sleeve across the left side of his face, careful not to push too hard on damaged flesh, gritting his teeth and moaning against the intensity of it.

His sleeve came away soaked with blood, but his eye was working better, he could see a bit more clearly. He felt less trapped inside his head. More in control. His neck was feeling stronger, his head more solid on his body. The pain was easing up, not a lot, but enough to allow lucid thought.

How had he survived? He remembered being struck in the head with an axe and he knew he'd fallen a good ten feet through the hatch into the hold below. He recalled that his assailant had lost his grip at the last minute. He must have been struck a glancing blow and he was alive because of it.

It was time to take stock of his injuries. He wiggled fingers and toes, tried to move both his arms and his legs. Fingers were working ok. Left arm didn't want to move – his shoulder was very sore. Left leg was injured too, but seemed to be working. All in all, not too bad. His head was the epicenter of his pain, the rest of his body was hurting, but would recover. His head... he wasn't so sure about that.

Blood was still dripping down his face. He could feel it warm on his forehead, trickling down his nose and cheek before falling off his chin and dripping into his lap. He used a hand to probe gently along his scalp, afraid of what he might find. Needing to know. The top of his head, above his right ear, was where most of the pain was. He avoided the worst of it, letting his fingers examine other parts of his head.

He found the source of the bleeding first. Just above his right eye he found a flap of skin hanging down over his forehead. It felt like wet, sticky paper, curling down and over itself, ragged at the edges, oddly numb. Above the flap his fingers touched something slick, hard and cool to the touch. He prayed he wasn't touching the exposed bone of his skull, knew without a doubt that that's what it was. Above that it was too painful to consider touching. He left it alone.

He needed to stop the bleeding. Do something to reduce the chance of infection. His thoughts were muddled, it felt like he was pushing his brain through thick porridge. He remembered that he had clean, cotton handkerchiefs in his bag near the hammock. Unwilling to attempt standing, he shuffled himself backwards. Still seated, he slid himself painfully along the boards to the darkened corner where he kept his things.

By the time he got there, his vision was swimming. Stars were exploding in his peripheral vision, hands shaking, the pain an earthquake in his head, a volcano erupting. He sat still, waiting for it to pass, waiting for it to get better, urging his body to come back under his control. When the pounding in his head lessened and his hands became useful again, he bent to his task. After several tries, he had his bag un-knotted and opened. Digging around, his hand stubbed into something dense and hard. Pulling it out, he found his pocket knife - a wicked little blade folded into a wooden handle. Deciding that it could be useful, he put it carefully into his pocket before retrieving the handkerchief.

It took several attempts, but he managed to hold the flap of skin up against his skull long enough to wrap the handkerchief around his head. There. That should hold it in place. Carefully, oh so carefully, he tightened it and then tied a knot to hold it. The handkerchief covered his forehead and obscured his right eye. That eye wouldn't open anyway. It didn't matter.

The pressure was uncomfortable, but it helped to ease some of the deep pain in his head. The bleeding was slowing, the handkerchief was soaking through, but blood was no longer flowing down his face. He was making progress. It was time to try standing up.

Gritting his teeth, one hand on the hammock, the other on the hull he slowly pulled himself onto his feet. His legs were shaking and wobbly, but he was able to stay up, braced as he was between the hull and hammock. He realized he'd been so focused on getting himself bandaged that he hadn't been paying attention to what was happening elsewhere on the ship. It was strangely quiet now, the sounds of battle gone.

He cocked his ears, trying to hear something. Anything. Silence... and then he heard three loud shouts. Native shouts. All of them yelling together. Victory.

A feeling of utter hopelessness swept over him. Dread nearly knocking him off his feet, a claw-like grip on the hammock all that saved him from falling. What would happen now? What would become of him? He pressed himself up against the hull, into the darkest corner, and tried to make himself as small as possible.

CHAPTER 37

The rest of the dinner passed uneventfully. Amy was distracted by the painting, trying to understand the implications, thinking it through. She realized that there was no-one she could talk to about it. For the first time since she'd arrived in this place she felt truly lonely. Novelty had carried her this far, had kept her from thinking about how long she'd be here or how she'd get back, but now she needed a friend. Steve was useless. She needed someone to help her figure this out.

Was that Ian in the painting? Could it really be him? She knew that he'd gone on a vision quest too, knew that he must be having a strange experience like her. But she'd imagined him in a city somewhere, making similar discoveries as she was. But this... was he really in the past? Surrounded by sailors and angry natives? Was he safe?

Was it possible that their vision quests were overlapping somehow? If Ian was in her past, could she reach him somehow? Could he reach her? If this was anything like lucid dreaming then she knew she could exert some control over her surroundings, bend reality around her. But how? It all felt so real, not like a dream at all.

Steve prattled and Amy responded without thinking. It didn't matter what she said – he was carrying on a conversation with himself more than with her anyway. That realization only intensified her loneliness and isolation. The food came in waves. All delicious. Interesting flavors mixed in subtle ways. But it might as well have been dust to her. The flavors passed without making an impression.

She ordered a drink and gulped it down. Ordered another and drank it, her eyes unfocused, staring toward the sea. Ordered a third, Steve's eyebrows rose at that, but he didn't interfere. She nursed that one, starting to feel numb, her troubles receding, pushed away by the alcohol toward the distant horizon.

After the fourth drink, Steve pulled her away, said it was time to go. On the way out she leaned on him for support, looking for all the world like a real couple. Lovers who couldn't keep their hands off each other. She knew she was drunk, but she didn't care. As they made their exit he leaned over and whispered in her ear, his breath heavy and warm, "Nice work Allison, this will make a good narrative. You were interesting. We both were. Follower engagement should spike after tonight. You'll see." Amy could see something floating in the corner of her eye, but it was too blurry to make out the details. Indistinct and wavering. She closed her eyes and leaned her head on Steve's shoulder. Let him guide her back to his apartment.

Amy opened her eyes, sunshine drenching the room with a white, morning light. She looked around, keeping her head still, not yet wanting to move her body. She was on her side, laying in a strange bed. The covers were draped over her and... under the covers? A nightgown, soft and comfortable, warm where it touched her body.

She was facing the windows, sun rising over the mountains, conveniently darkened so that it didn't hurt her eyes. There was a nightstand next to the bed, a clock and a lamp. A paperback book. The clock said 8:15 am. Time to get up.

She rolled over and let out a yelp of surprise. There was somebody on the other side of the bed. Somebody's back facing her, covered in striped pajamas. In response to her yelp, it groaned, shifted slightly and then went still. Who the hell was in bed with her?

She gingerly lifted the covers and stepped out as quietly as she could, her feet sinking into a thick, plush carpet. She padded around the foot of the bed, far enough so she could see his face. Steve. Of course. But why was she in his bed? She turned her back on him, furious, and stared out the window. It took her a moment, but after she'd calmed down, she noticed that the clouds were gone and she was looking at a panoramic view of the island.

It was like the view that she and Ian and had gotten from the top of the hill but she was much higher now, the vista that much more expansive. The shape of the shoreline was familiar, tracing the same coves and bays that she remembered. But every portion of the island was covered in streets and buildings, vehicles moving everywhere, both on the ground and in the air. It was a hive of human activity.

She could see the little cove that had housed God's Pocket Resort, where they'd taken their shelter. It appeared to be a ferry landing now, a large passenger boat arriving as she watched, another working its way across Goletas Channel toward Vancouver Island, moving fast, appearing to fly over the water. There was a scattering of other islands lined up to the north, all of them fully developed cities. There wasn't a tree in sight, tall buildings covered every part of every island she could see.

Vancouver Island was hazy to the west, but she could see the outlines of cities over there too. She turned to the east, toward the mountains and the sea, and saw that the ocean was busy with boats. There were large boats, maybe freighters, working their way ponderously north and south. Mixed among the larger ships were mid-sized boats, skimming the top of the ocean, moving fast. The mainland was too far away to make out detail, but the characteristic green of the coastal mountains was gone, replaced with browns and greys. It was impossible to tell at this distance if she was seeing buildings or merely denuded mountainsides.

Her mouth was hanging open, eyes wide, gaping at what had been revealed to her. It was like seeing Los Angeles laid down over mid-coast British Columbia, draped over the islands and covering them with the detritus of human civilization. Her hands were fluttering, one on her chest just below her neck, as if she was trying to hold her heart from rising up and choking her.

A swell of panic overtook her as the strangeness of this place finally hit home. She felt a deep sorrow at what had been lost, wondering what, if anything could be done about it.

Her eyes dropped, nearly to the base of the building. Way down there, midway between this building and the sea, was a small oasis of green. A park. Some trees. She remembered it from yesterday. It was where she had met Norman. Perhaps he knew what had happened to this place and could help her understand. Without bothering to say goodbye, she threw on some clothes, strode out of the apartment and into the elevator. She was on her way to find some answers.

CHAPTER 38

Ian was pressed into the corner, trying to make himself as small and silent as possible, when the hatch opened.

"John, are you down there? I know you are hurt. Come to me. I will help you."

It was Maquinna. Ian recognized his voice and crouched down further, as still as could be, curled up around his pain. He was breathing in shallow gasps, his head throbbing, leg aching.

He heard someone step onto the ladder, the light changing as the sunlight through the hatch was obstructed. Footsteps in the hold. He whimpered involuntarily. Someone was trying to find him.

Maquinna's voice again, "John, I won't hurt you. Let me see you." The footsteps came closer, "Ah, there you are. Come with me."

Ian flinched as he felt Maquinna's hand on his arm, tremors of pain working their way through his head and over his body. He wanted to jump up, to scream, to fight, to claw and punch and destroy. Instead, he whimpered again, his body closing in on itself, unable to take any action at all. He was helpless in his fear and his agony.

Maquinna pulled him gently to a standing position, placed his shoulder under his arm and guided him slowly to the light where he could get a look at him. "Eh. You don't look good. You are hurt badly." Maquinna frowned, looked up, and called to someone in his native language.

A moment later strong hands reached down and he felt himself pulled from above, pushed from below, and then he was standing on the main deck, swaying and squinting, unable to make out details, the light so much brighter than what his eyes had grown accustomed to.

He heard Maquinna emerge behind him and say something to his people. Ian felt hands on him, then a wet cloth being used to wipe at the blood on his face and head, other hands pulled his jacket and pants from his body, cleaning him and binding his wounds.

After his face had been cleaned and his eye had adjusted to the light, he could see again. His right eye was still useless and his sight was flat and dim through his left eye as he peered at the natives around him. They were a fearsome group, blood-soaked, amped up from the battle, stamping their feet, and letting out yips and snarls as they paced the deck looking for weapons and other trophies of their victory. The ship was lost. Ian couldn't see another living member of the crew.

Several of the natives formed around him, daggers in hand, teeth bared. They were covered in blood from wrist to shoulder, evidence of the many throats they had cut. The King stood between him and this group, speaking to them, arms outstretched, palms down, trying to calm them. At the moment it seemed like a stalemate. The natives weren't killing him yet, but they weren't backing down either.

"John, these ones feel that you must die like the others."

Ian was unsure what to do, how to plead for his life without making things worse. He stood silent, his heart pounding in his chest.

"I have told them you are useful to us. You know how to make daggers and axes. You can repair guns. You know much that is useful. I have told them this."

Ian took a step back as the group moved toward him threateningly. Maquinna said a few more words in his native tongue, trying to calm them. The largest took another step forward, his dagger held high, eyes flashing, words spilling from him, angry and guttural.

Maquinna kept his eyes on the man while speaking to Ian. "John, I cannot hold this one back much longer. You must kiss my feet." He said a few more words to the other man.

"John. You must do this now."

Ian's eyes locked on the man with the dagger. He knew he was close to death. His will had left him, weakness taking its place. He was frozen, a deer in the headlights.

"John! Now!" Maquinna roared.

Without conscious thought, Ian knelt before Maquinna. He bent his lips to the top of Maquinna's feet.

"You must promise to be my slave. Promise to fight my battles for me. Promise to repair our daggers and our guns. Promise to submit your will to mine."

Ian promised.

"Now you must kiss my feet once more."

Ian kissed his feet.

"Now you must stand and kiss my hands."

Ian stood and kissed Maquinna's hands.

The group of natives looked angry, but they backed off, shaking their heads, spitting out a few more words.

"For this John, I have saved your life. From this day forward, your life is mine."

Ian was shaking like a leaf. Shock and cold overpowering him, swaying, barely able to keep his footing. He was having a hard time believing that he was still alive. A hard time grasping that he was now a slave.

Maquinna walked into the Captain's quarters, returning moments later with the Captain's greatcoat and a bottle of rum. He wrapped the coat around Ian's shoulders, propping him up as he did so, and forced the bottle of rum into his hands. "You are cold, so I clothe you. You are weak, so I sustain you. Drink this and become strong."

Ian's shaking subsided to small tremors under the coat. He pulled the cork from the bottle and took a drink, feeling the warmth of it rush down his throat, coating his stomach, spreading fingers of warmth into him. He took another drink, his tremors subsiding, his body relaxing.

"Yes. That is good. Now come with me."

Maquinna led Ian up the stairs to the quarterdeck, positioning him in front of a line of heads on the deck. "You will tell me who is each." He pointed to the first head. "Who?"

Ian had no idea. John would have known, but Ian hadn't been on the ship long enough. He shrugged and shook his head.

Maquinna asked more insistently, picking up the head by its hair and holding it in front of Ian's face. "Who?"

Ian felt sick. His gut was heaving and twisting on the rum as he stared into the head's sightless eyes.

Maquinna shook the head at him, drops of blood spattering the front of Ian's coat and pants. "Who?"

Ian closed his eyes and swallowed painfully, deciding to make up a name, hoping desperately that Maquinna would believe him. "Mark. It is Mark."

"Ok. Who?" and he pointed to another head. The next in the line. This head was so disfigured that nobody could have known who it was, the features were unrecognizable, face caved in by a heavy blow.

"Abe. That one is Abe."

"Ok. Who?"

Maquinna continued his inquiry through the entire line. Twenty-five heads. Twenty-five crew murdered, beheaded and lined up on the quarterdeck for this grisly census. Their blood had pooled beneath the stubs of their necks, a small stream trickling into a scupper where it drained to the ocean. The Captain's head was there, and so was the Mate's. Ian felt his last shred of hope die when he saw those two heads. Saw that they too had fallen to the axes and daggers of the native attackers. The natives must have killed the Captain as he defended the ship and then gone to shore to kill the fishing party, catching the Mate and his small group of men unawares.

When the task was done, Ian slumped against the rail. Drained. Sick. Unable and unwilling to do any more. Momentarily wishing that he had been killed and that this misery would end. What would happen to him if he died in this vision? The experience felt so real, his sense of self-preservation so strong. He couldn't take the risk.

He began to doubt his sanity. Was he really in a vision? Maybe he *was* John Jewitt. Everyone else thought he was. Maybe he'd had a mental break and his other memories were a psychosis. Could he trust his memories? Could he even trust his senses? How could he know what was real?

He dismissed those thoughts. That path led to madness. He needed to find his way back home. He knew there must be a way back. He wouldn't allow himself to be stuck here forever. He just needed to find the way. He thought about his earlier excitement at arriving in this time. The age of sail! What had he been thinking? He grimaced in morbid humor, his face protesting the sudden movement, the swelling of his flesh pushing back against his lips and mouth.

Meanwhile, the natives had cut the anchor cables, setting the ship adrift in the cove. Men were climbing the rigging, raising sails, and pulling lines to get the boat moving. Ian stared in wonder. The natives knew how to sail the ship?

Evidently, they did. Maquinna was at the wheel, grinning from ear to ear, capering, yelling at his men, compelling them to action. Ian watched as the mainsails pulled tight and a few of the foresails were raised, flogging and backing in the wind. Slowly the *Boston* began to make way, easing out of the cove and into the open sound.

The ship felt alive and a small part of Ian came back to life as well. He felt the sea breeze on his face. Felt the deck working beneath his feet. The natives were clambering excitedly over the ship, pulling on lines and rigging, helping the *Boston* along, catching the wind more efficiently as they figured out what each control was meant to do.

After a few slow downwind jibes, they were well away from the cove, sailing west toward the lowering sun and the open expanse of the Pacific Ocean. Ian turned to look behind them, the wind blowing directly into his face. He could see the sound narrowing to the east where it cut into the bulk of Vancouver Island. On the eastern horizon, past the head of the sound, Ian could see a jumble of mountains, the tallest with a touch of snow on the top. Other mountains surrounded this tallest peak, a wall of steep tree-covered slopes. So like the mountains he and Amy had seen as they had sailed north together. So similar, but so far away.

He felt the boat shift beneath him and turned to face forward again, pulling his greatcoat closer around himself. Maquinna had turned them into the last bay before the mouth of the sound. Close enough to the ocean that swells were rolling beneath the boat, forcing him to adjust his balance as the boat steadily climbed and fell. The bay was a tight semicircle, densely wooded on the right, rocky pinnacles on the left, open in the middle where a dozen longhouses pressed close against the shore.

The light was fading, but Ian could see people moving on the beach and standing on the longhouse roofs. When the villagers saw the *Boston* round into the bay, they sent up a ululating cry that echoed amongst the rocks and skipped across the water, reaching Ian's ears as a tremulous high pitched keen, raising and lowering in pitch and volume. He could see men holding torches, more torches fastened to the sides and roofs of the longhouses, sending smoky pillars of flame up toward heaven.

Maquinna steered the ship into the bay, toward the center of the beach. Dozens of villagers were pounding on the walls of the longhouses with sticks, creating a syncopated rhythm that reverberated through Ian's chest. He could see men and women running across the beach in excitement, close enough now that he could see their faces flickering orange in the torchlight, the sun completely down.

Behind them, a trail of phosphorescent wake. Before them, the firelit village, filled with shouts of excitement, war cries and the pounding of sticks. The beach was very close and Ian realized that the ship wasn't going to stop. He grabbed the rail hard, just as the *Boston* ran aground with a tremendous grinding, her bow rising up over rocks, driftwood and sand, the ships immense momentum driving them further up the beach than Ian would have thought possible, the wind in her sails pressing her ever further aground.

With a crackling of timbers, the *Boston* slowed to a stop. Like the final breath of a fallen giant, Ian felt the great rending of her hull as she tipped steeply to starboard. Her side pressed hard against the beach, hull caving, supports buckling, the sails flapping loudly overhead as she settled into her final resting place at the front of Maquinna's village. Ian clung to the rail, his feet scrabbling against the angle of the deck. Below, a multitude of firelit faces: looking up, dancing, arms raised in celebration of their great victory.

CHAPTER 39

Amy ran all the way to the park from Steve's apartment. She was standing on the sidewalk where she had last seen Norman, breathing hard, but he was nowhere in sight. She kicked herself. Why should she expect to find him in the exact same place as before? She wasn't even sure why she wanted to find him so badly. Would he really have answers to her questions? She sighed and walked further in, toward the center of the park. He probably couldn't help her, maybe he wouldn't have any answers, but she had to try.

In amongst the cedar trees, it was almost peaceful. The sounds of the city were muted and she was by herself for the first time since she'd arrived. She could take some time to think. She was on Hurst Island, that was clear, but it wasn't at all like she'd left it. The whole island was paved over, the beautiful forest gone. The majesty of the island diminished to this one remaining park.

The fear she'd felt while walking across the island with Ian was gone now. She had been scared before because she'd felt trapped inside something so much bigger and more powerful than herself. The wilderness was scary because of its unpredictability, scary because it was unknown and unknowable. That fear had been replaced by a fear of progress. What would happen if every last bit of the earth was developed, civilized and converted strictly to human use. What if there was nothing left unknown? Nothing left to explore? What if the only thing left were buildings and vehicles and people, all scrambling on top of each other – scrambling to be the best, fighting for power and influence and... what then? She felt claustrophobic. The Earth was too small. There was nowhere left to hide.

She was lost in these thoughts when Norman stepped into her field of vision. "Hello Amy, how are you doing?"

"Oh hi. I'm ok. I... wait... what did you call me?"

"I called you Amy. That's your name isn't it?"

"Yes, but how do you know that? I told you I was Allison. Steve called me Allison."

"Steve. Yes. He would call you Allison wouldn't he? Interesting man, Steve."

Amy raised an eyebrow at him. Interesting? That was one way of putting it.

Norman cleared his throat. "Ahem. Well... Amy, would you follow me?"

Amy had sought out Norman so they could talk, but this was a bit too much. Why should she go where he told her at the drop of a hat? What did she know about this guy anyway? And how could he possibly know her real name?

He turned and walked away toward a line of bushes on the far side of the park.

Amy hesitated. Shit. Shit! She let out an exasperated huff and hurried to catch up with him.

"Norman? Is that even your real name? Why in the world should I come with you?"

"You tell me. You *are* following me, aren't you?" He looked over his shoulder and grinned, "and I assure you that Norman is *not* my real name."

Amy took a moment to think that through. Why was she following him? She wanted answers, that's why. Wait, not his real name? What?

"I want answers! What am I doing here? Who *are* you? What happened to this island?"

Norman kept walking, long strides until they were right up against the bushes. There were small red berries peeking through the branches, hiding behind the leafy greens. He turned to her and smiled, a little too smugly in Amy's opinion, and then said, "What are you doing here, hmm? The age-old question. Every human has asked themselves that doozy. Why am I here? What's my purpose? Why am I alive? Indeed!" He finished this little speech with a hand on his chest, head thrown back dramatically.

Amy waited for more but Norman just stood there, a silly smile plastered on his face. He was actually kind of cute when he looked at her like that, but she wasn't going to give him any ground. "You seem different than last time. Not as nice," she said.

Norman responded, "Yes. That's true. I am different. Every moment of our lives, every experience, it changes us. You seem different too. Not as naive."

He was infuriating. She thought about turning and leaving, then thought better of it. She almost stamped her foot, then she realized it would look childlike. Instead she gave him her iciest glare.

He didn't wilt. Not even a little bit. He was impervious to it, his smile unchanging.

She sighed, "Ok. I'll bite. Yes, I'm different. I've learned a few things since I saw you yesterday. What I've seen is... well, it's sad."

And that was true. The strongest feeling she'd had during this experience was sorrow. She missed the forest. She missed the wild seas filled with life. She missed the knowledge that a voyage north would be an adventure to test her soul and test her skill while traversing a wild and unpopulated landscape. In this place, traveling north would mean more cities, more restaurants, more buildings, and more people like Steve, wrapped up in themselves with no thought for anything other than what they could do to get more people to pay attention to them.

She spoke again, her voice breaking with the intensity of her feeling, "Norman, what happened to this island? What happened to the native people? How could they have let this happen?"

Norman's smile faded, replaced by a new warmth in his eyes. "Those are the right questions. Now, come with me." He checked to see if anyone was looking, then ducked through a break in the bushes.

Shaking her head she followed him and found herself in a tunnel carved into the thicket. She followed as it wound deeper into the brush, occasionally catching a glimpse of Norman's foot or the back of his head, just enough to keep her moving forward, all the while a strangely familiar musky scent grew in her nostrils.

Eventually, she found herself at a door set into a steep hillside, overgrown with wild rose and blackberry. The sound of bees surrounded her. They flew from blossom to blossom, little furry bodies busily ignoring her as she stood there uncertain. The door was both strange and incongruous. It looked like someone had transported the front door of a house into the middle of the bushes, had painted it bright blue and then set a small cedar-bark doormat on the doorstep.

"Um, hello?" Amy called out, looking around, hoping Norman was somewhere nearby. He couldn't have gone into the door already could he? She lifted her hand tentatively to knock, when she saw there was a small doorbell set into the doorframe. She let her hand drift down so that her finger hovered over the button. Should she push it?

She touched the button lightly, pressing it in until she heard a loud, jarring ring from behind the door, causing her to step back, startled. She heard movement inside and then the sound of the door unlatching and opening.

"Hi there! Fancy seeing you here! So glad you could make it!" It was Norman. He was dressed in a smoking jacket, a cigar in one hand and a snifter of whiskey in the other. "Come in, come in. Don't be shy!" He held the door open, waving her into the room.

Speechless, she followed him in. It was a warmly furnished room, fire roaring, two leather chairs pulled up, a small wooden table next to each. Norman sat down on one of the chairs and motioned her to the other. "Sit. Sit. Go on, make yourself comfortable."

She sat down. It *was* comfortable, she had to give him that.

"What is this place? Where are we?"

"Oh this? It's nothing. Just a place for us to chat. We won't be bothered here, hmm?"

"No, I suppose not... Can you answer my questions now?"

"Amy, you will be leaving soon and there are a few things I am compelled to tell you before you go. Listen carefully." He leaned back, sighed comfortably and took a sip of his whiskey. "Ahh. This never gets old does it? Simple pleasures."

Amy was on the edge of her chair, looking at him intently, silently urging him on.

"Ugh. Humans. Always so impatient. So tense. You never do learn to appreciate the moment do you?" He winked at her, "Have you enjoyed your time here?"

"Here? In these bushes? Um... I suppose?"

"No... bah!" He looked exasperated. "Not in the bushes! Here..." he waved his arms around his head, "in this vision, this island, this city, meeting Steve. All that."

"Enjoyed? No. Not exactly."

"Ok good. That's what I was hoping." He leaned back, satisfied.

"Norman?"

"Yes?"

"Weren't you going to answer my questions?"

"Who are you? Who am I? What's my purpose? Why? Why? Why? That kind of thing?"

"Yes."

"So impatient! Ok... ok. Yes, I'll tell you something."

Amy waited.

Norman looked over at her. "You mean now?"

Amy waited. She felt she was getting the hang of this.

Norman sighed. "Ok. There are some things I'm supposed to tell you." He looked straight forward and spoke in a forced monotone, "You were placed here to see what you need to see. You now have seen what can happen if no-one is able to stop it. Nature is dead. Sasahevas is dead. Humans are ascendant." He looked at her for a moment with a creepy smile, showing too many teeth, "but not for long."

Amy waited for more, but Norman stayed silent, creepy smile rigid on his face.

"Is that all?"

"Damn it, that was my best smile! No... Yes... there's more." He sighed dramatically and then returned to his monotone. "You must find a way to stop this from happening."

Amy waited.

Still nothing. Norman was staring into the fire. Amy waited.

"Ok that's it! You're done! Time's up!" Norman looked at her and gave a little wave as the room faded to black.

When she opened her eyes she was sitting cross-legged in the moss, Richard curled up snoring behind her, the morning sun peeking through the branches around her.

CHAPTER 40

Maquinna led Ian limping from the wreckage of the *Boston* past the villagers and through an open space populated with large, wooden statues. They were at least twice as tall as he was, looming over him in the dark, torchlight flickering over their features. The first was a woman, mouth agape in an unnaturally large 'O', nothing but blackness inside. She had a basket on her back, her arms stretched forward grasping for something, looking across the beach and out to sea.

Tsonoqua.

He felt a shock of recognition when he looked at the second statue. It was a massive hairy creature, arms slack at its sides, head protruding forward on a thick neck, face furrowed, huge feet, legs planted into the ground like tree trunks.

Sasahevas.

Ian felt a deep unease as he passed them, the torchlight imbuing them with the illusion of life, making it seem as if their eyes were following him. He limped on, following Maquinna, picking his way past a series of totems – massive logs carved into fantastic shapes, animal and human, twisted together to tell the story of his tribe and his rule. Maquinna led him up a steep hill, to the village where it was perched safely above the beach, through the thick posts of his longhouse, and into a warm and smoky gloom.

Once inside, Ian was surrounded by Maquinna's many wives. They gathered around him, touching his hair, pulling at his jacket, asking questions, using words that he didn't understand. When he didn't answer, they looked to Maquinna with curious eyes, but he responded brusquely, brushing them aside as he pulled Ian to the back wall. Up against the wall of the long-house, Maquinna pointed to a pile of bedding on the floor, "Sleep here. You need rest. I must go back to the ship."

Ian laid himself down, turned his head away from the light of the fire and closed his eyes, trying to shut out where he was, what had happened to him, what he had become. Despite the clamor of the villagers on the beach and the steady murmuring of the woman around him, he fell into a deep unconsciousness, sleeping the sleep of the dead.

The next morning, Ian awoke with a start. Maquinna was squatting over him, shaking him by the shoulder. "Come with me. We have found something."

Ian followed Maquinna back down to the beach where he saw that the natives had spent the night looting the ship. There was equipment spread across the beach, up the hill and in the grass. Cannons, muskets, and pistols piled near the ship. Clothing, sails, and bedding carelessly strewn through the sand. Bunches of hemp rope, anchor cables, and the anchors themselves laid about carelessly, intermingled with tables, chairs, broken boards, and other bits of wood unidentifiable from where Ian stood. The ship looked like a beached whale, body left to rot in the steady drizzle bleeding from a grey and overcast sky. Ian pulled his coat around him, trying to get the front to button up, shivering from the chill that was growing within him.

Maquinna looked to where Ian was surveying the scene and waved him onward, impatient. They were heading toward a cluster of natives, gathered around something right up against the keel of the boat where it pressed into the beach. When he got closer, Ian saw that the thing they had gathered around was a person curled up on the beach, the natives kicking him, shouting insults, beating at him with sticks, and spitting upon his head.

From where Ian stood, he couldn't tell who it was. It didn't look like a native and he wasn't moving, nor was he making any sound in response to the steady drumbeat of blows upon his body. Ian feared for the worst.

Maquinna shouted at them and they stopped their abuse, hauling the man up by his armpits and dragging him close enough that Ian could see his face. It was Thompson, the burly sailmaker, one of the few members of the crew who had deigned to speak with him while he'd been aboard. His eyes were closed, face swollen, body limp, head lolling, clearly unconscious.

While Ian was inspecting Thompson, Maquinna was speaking with the other men. After some back and forth, he turned to Ian, "We found him in the ship. He was hiding from the battle. No honor. We will kill him now while he sleeps." He turned to his men, said a few quick words and made a motion across his throat.

"No!" Ian said it without thinking. He couldn't bear to see anyone else killed. As far as he knew this was the last of the crew, the only person left that he had any affinity to. He couldn't bear it.

Maquinna looked at Ian startled, "What did you say?"

"Please, no. Let him live."

Maquinna grabbed the man's hair, pulling his head upright so they could see his face. "Why? Who is this?"

Ian thought fast. Thompson was one of the oldest members of the crew, over fifty, it could work. Maybe.

He drew himself upright and looked Maquinna in the eye. "Do you love your father?"

Surprised, Maquinna answered. "Yes. Of course. It is my duty."

"Would you allow him to be killed?"

Maquinna looked puzzled, Thompson's hair still in his grip. "No. Of course not. I would die first."

Ian drew on all the confidence he could muster, tried to let it shine through his eyes, his face, and his posture as he stood tall. "Maquinna, as you love your father and would die for him, do not kill my father for I would die first."

Maquinna looked at Ian, startled. Then at Thompson and back at Ian again. "Your Father?"

"Yes. My Father."

Maquinna released Thompson's head, letting it drop forward, his chin thumping into his chest. "It is your duty. You must die first."

Ian felt a panic rising in him. He wanted to save Thompson, but he didn't want to die. He'd faced death already, was twisted and beaten down by it, he wasn't ready to face it again.

Maquinna pondered. "You are my slave. I do not wish you to die. I will not destroy my property."

Ian relaxed a little.

Maquinna turned to his men and gave them a few commands so that they dragged Thompson up the beach, his heels digging furrows in the sand, two long trails pointing toward Maquinna's longhouse.

"Your father will live. He will be my slave. Come." Maquinna said, and walked up the beach following his men. Ian followed too.

As Ian walked back past the carved statues, he could have sworn that Tsonoqua's head looked different. It appeared tilted whereas it has been straight before. She was looking to the side, toward him, no longer looking out to sea. Her eyes were narrowed, eyebrows raised. He didn't remember seeing eyebrows before. It had been dark last night. There had been torches. He'd been tired. He must be mistaken.

Back in the longhouse, Maquinna was in the mood to talk. They were seated on the floor, comfortable atop cedar-bark mats, cross-legged, and facing each other. Thompson was in the corner, tended by the women. Ian could see by his movements that he was coming back into consciousness, but he seemed out of it, not fully aware of his situation yet.

Maquinna spoke first, "We will have to burn the ship and hide what we have taken."

Ian was surprised. "Burn it? Why?"

"There will be other ships. They cannot know what has

happened here. It would cause problems."

Ian wasn't sure if he should ask the question, but forged ahead anyway. "Why did you do it? Why did you attack us?"

Maquinna didn't seem to mind and responded in an even tone. "Captain Salter insulted me. He could not live."

"Because of the gun?" Ian asked.

"Yes. I was very angry. My heart would not stay in my chest. It rose into my throat, choking me." Maquinna looked upset as he remembered it. "Your ship was powerful. So I made a plan to split your men. Then we could win. We did win. It has brought me much honor with my people. With my ancestors. With my gods."

"Gods? There are many?"

Maquinna looked at him curiously. "Yes there are many. You don't know?"

"I ... I guess I do." Ian responded.

Maquinna nodded, satisfied. "We must trade with your people. We must stay strong against the other tribes. Your people must not know what happened. The ship will burn tonight. Then it will be gone. It is over."

"What will happen to me? To Thompson?" Ian asked.

It was Maquinna's turn to look surprised. "You are my slave. You will do as I say. You will live in my tribe. We will take care of you. Don't worry."

Maquinna looked away for a moment, troubled. "Come with me John. There is someone you must meet."

Maquinna led him out of the longhouse, but instead of going toward the beach they turned so that they were walking deeper into the village. Once they had passed the longhouses, they were standing on the edge of an open slope. Blackberry and wild rose grew rampant, the sound of bees thick in the air.

Maquinna paused, uncharacteristically uncertain. "You must go see him now." Maquinna pointed toward a trail that had been cut out of the bushes, the outlines of a small hut evident through a screen of leaves.

"Who? See who?" Ian asked.

"You will find him there." Maquinna pointed to the hut. "Be careful." Then he walked back to the village, leaving Ian alone.

Ian watched Maquinna disappear around the front of the longhouse and then he turned and limped down the trail. It was narrow so he had to be careful to avoid overhanging thorns as he pushed aside branches, stepping over lumps and roots. The sound of bees surrounded him, all-pervading, entering his ears forcefully and seeming to thrum in his chest. But he couldn't see any, there wasn't a single insect in sight.

As he walked, he passed wild rose blossoms heavy on their stalks, the scent sticky in his nose. A rich, familiar musk mingled with the roses, reminding him of something, but he couldn't place it.

When he was close to the hut, the sound of bees stopped. One moment, the buzzing was everywhere, the next there was nothing. Just a slight ringing in his ears. No other sound.

The hut was dilapidated. Walls of rough wood, grey with age, gaps showing, green lichen in bright, scaly spots. The roof was cedar shake, grey and split, moss growing thick and drooping over the eaves. The door was strange. It was bright blue, surrounded by a solid frame, a cedar mat on the doorstep, incongruous with the rest of the structure.

"Hello?" Ian called out. Not sure what else to do.

There was no response.

"Anyone um... home?" He felt self-conscious.

There was still no response.

He lifted his hand to knock. Pausing in mid-air, unsure. Maybe he should turn around and go back to Maquinna. There was no-one here.

He steeled himself and knocked. A solid, resonant thump. Not at all in keeping with the frailty of the hut. He heard some movement inside. Footsteps. And then the sound of the door unlatching and opening.

"Hello. Welcome. I've been expecting you."

It was an old man, slightly hunched, white hair long and

hanging over his cedar-bark shirt. He held the door open for Ian to step through.

Ian sat on the floor, next to a fire pit filled with ash, the old man next to him, looking at him intently.

"Maquinna told me that you wanted to talk to me. Why?" Ian asked.

The old man remained silent, moving his head as he examined Ian from various angles. Looking for something, or trying to judge something.

Apparently satisfied, he grunted and nodded firmly. "So, Ian, have you enjoyed your time here?"

"Enjoyed? No. It has not been enjoyable. Wait... what did you call me? How do you know my name?"

The old man nodded once more. "No, I'd think not." He contemplated Ian's face, "You've been injured, haven't you?"

"Who *are* you?"

The old man smiled. "I am sorry. Manners. I've been here so long. I've forgotten my manners." He extended his small wrinkled hand for Ian to shake. "My name is Norem. How do you do?"

"How do you know my name? Everyone here calls me John."

Norem looked solemn, "Yes, I know. Here you are John. I knew that." He trailed off, muttering to himself.

Ian didn't know what to think. Was the old man crazy? What was going on? Norem stood up, still muttering and started rummaging through a pile in the corner. As he flung small scraps of wood left and right, Ian decided to ask another question. "Are you a part of this tribe?"

"Yes, I guess so. They think of me as their medicine man. I help them and they leave me alone. I think they are scared of me." His voice was slightly muffled. "Aha! Here it is!" He hobbled back and sat down, cradling something in his arms.

"This is an artifact of power. It is important." Norem intoned.

Ian waited for Norem to say more. When the silence became intolerable, he spoke up, "Ok?"

Norem startled slightly and then held the object up. It was like one of the carved statues by the village but on a much smaller scale. It was made of dark wood, cut and polished until it glowed softly in the dim light of the hut. The figure was Sasahevas, perfect down to the last detail, solid and dense in Norem's outstretched arms.

"I took this artifact from their Whale Shrine. Their medicine man would use it to call the whales to the village. The whales would hear the call and one of their number would choose to come here to Yuquot." Norem said, the figure still held before him.

"Come here? Why?" Ian asked.

"For the good of the tribe. So that they would live through the winter. Without the whale, they would starve. They would freeze. The sacrifice was necessary or the tribe would be no more.

"The whale would present itself to the village. They would kill it in the cove, then pull the carcass up on the beach for the people to take what they needed. They would burn what was left, spend the night celebrating, thanking the whale for what it had done for them.

"Sometimes the village would be too weak and the whale would drive itself up onto the beach. Sometimes this was necessary. Without the strength of the whale, the people would not have survived. It was a necessary sacrifice."

Norem placed the artifact into Ian's hands, reverent. "Ian, you must remember this artifact. It is important."

Ian was surprised by the weight of it, marveled at how Norem had held it so effortlessly. It nestled warm and thick in his arms.

"Your time here is almost over. There is one more thing I must tell you." Norem tilted his head, observing Ian and the artifact in his arms. He nodded again, satisfied. "As Maquinna has had mercy on you. As you have had mercy on Thompson. As you have seen the sacrifice. As you now know the price. You must extend mercy to these people. They are important. Without them you will be lost. Remember. It is important."

With Norem's last words, Ian's vision faded to black. When he opened his eyes he was laying on hard granite, his head cradled in Tum's lap. Tum was looking down at him, lines of worry etched into his face. The sky was pink overhead, the sun rising over a wall of jagged, snow-capped mountains to the east.

PART 4: THE VILLAGE

CHAPTER 41

It was a beautiful morning. The sun was peeking through the branches overhead, painting the moss a dappled, emerald green. Wisps of night mist clung to the dark roots of giant cedars, slowly dissipating as the air grew warmer.

Amy stood and stretched her back, her knees creaking as she straightened her legs.

"Hey Richard, wake up."

Richard was snoring. He must have had a rough night. Amy wondered how long she'd been gone in the vision quest and what, if anything, he'd had to do to protect her. What an experience it had been! Her mind was full of questions. There was so much to discuss.

The radio in Richard's pack came to life. "Richard, are you there? This is Tum. I have a situation."

That woke him up. With a groan he uncurled and sat up, looking groggy. He blinked a few times, still bleary. "Amy? Are you awake?"

Amy nodded her head, amused at Richard's sleepiness.

"Amy! You're back!" Fully awake, he stood up and rushed toward her. He looked like he wanted to give her a hug but stopped short, putting his hands on her shoulders instead. "I'm so glad you're back. Are you ok?"

"Yes, I'm fine. It was... the most amazing experience of my life. I learned so much. There is so much I want to tell you."

Richard was at a loss for words, overcome by emotion.

"Richard, it's ok. Really." She remembered the radio, "Hey, shouldn't you answer Tum? He called for you."

"Right!" He dove into his pack, pulled the radio free and keyed the mic, "Tum, this is Richard. Go ahead."

"There's something wrong with Ian. You need to come fast."

All the joy drained out of Amy. In her delight to be back, she'd forgotten that Ian had had his own experience and they had no idea, yet, what it had been like for him. She remembered the painting she'd seen in the restaurant. The painting with Ian in it. One word stood out. Massacre. Amy and Richard shouldered their packs and started a fast hike back.

Dispensing with caution they found Sasahevas's trail, the trail they had avoided before, but that they knew would lead them west to Ian and Tum. They set out double time, packs bouncing, trees and bushes flashing past, worry driving them forward. With all that had happened, with the vision quests complete, with Ian in trouble, they needed to use the fastest path possible. Amy couldn't help but wonder – what were they going to find at the end of this trail? What was wrong with Ian?

The bushes were the first thing Amy noticed as she approached the top of the men's hill. Cresting the final rise and breaking out onto the rocky hilltop, she saw bushes uprooted and scattered everywhere on the ground. There were at least a dozen, pulled up whole and thrown violently, clumps of soil and bits of root trailing behind. The sight of that mayhem nearly stopped her in her tracks, but her concern for Ian propelled her forward, a slight stumble the only outward sign.

The next thing she noticed was Ian. He was laying on the ground, eyes closed, and he wasn't moving. Tum was standing over him, looking worried. "I don't know what's wrong with him. He opened his eyes and tried to talk a few times, but nothing coherent."

"Tum, what happened to the bushes?" Amy asked.

"Bushes..." he looked around as if just noticing, "Oh, yeah. Ian was restless all night. He wouldn't sit still, pacing around the hilltop, yelling at things that only he could see. Later, he spent at least an hour cowered up against that rock." He pointed at a granite block. "I was trying to keep him calm when I heard noises in the dark... terrible noises." Tum shuddered. "When the sun rose, I saw what had happened."

"Is Ian ok?" Richard asked.

"I don't know. When he calmed down, I was able to lay him down. This morning, around sunrise, he opened his eyes and... well, you know the rest."

Amy had heard enough, she put her pack down and walked to where Ian was laying. Kneeling carefully next to him, she put a hand on his forehead. He was clammy, cool to the touch, a sheen of sweat visible on his face.

He stirred and opened his eyes. "Ahmee?"

His voice was slurred, and only half of his face was moving. Amy recognized her name, but just barely, and she drew away from him in surprise, shocked to see him so incapacitated. It wasn't just his voice. One of his eyes wasn't opening all the way and he seemed like he was having trouble focusing. She couldn't tell if he was looking at her or through her.

He spoke again. "Ahmee?"

"Yes Ian, it's me. I'm here."

"Amy, what happened to me?" His breathing was labored, each word forced past an unwilling tongue and uncooperative lips.

"You were on a vision quest Ian. Just like me. But you're back now. How do you feel?"

"A vision quest?"

"Yes, don't you remember?"

"Amy?"

"Yes"

"What happened to me?"

Richard and Tum looked as alarmed as she felt.

"What do we do?" she asked. Hoping one of them would have an answer.

Richard spoke first. "We need to get him to the lodge and take care of him there. Between the three of us, we should be able to manage it. We'll carry him if we have to. Once we're back, we can put him in bed, regroup, and figure out what to do next."

Amy nodded and turned back to Ian. “Don’t worry. We’re going to help you now. Everything is going to be ok.” She put as much confidence as she could muster into her words and hoped he couldn’t tell what she was really feeling. Hoped that he couldn’t see the raw panic that she felt when she looked into his lost and bewildered eyes.

“Amy?” he asked again, “what happened to me?”

Tum took one arm, Richard the other and Amy cradled his head to protect his neck as they slowly lifted him into a standing position. Once up, he was able to stay standing – swaying, but not quite falling, while they supported him.

“Ian, can you try walking? We need to get back to the lodge. It’s safer for us there.” Richard nodded encouragingly, “That’s it. One foot in front of the other.”

Ian was able to walk, sort of, with their help. His head lolled from side to side, and his left leg didn’t work very well, but they were able to make their way down the hill, along the orange trail and finally to the lodge. Exhausted, on edge and uncertain, they laid him carefully into one of the beds and then sat around the table, the three of them trying to decide what to do.

CHAPTER 42

"I think we need to let Ian rest," Richard said, "he needs more time to recover from his experience. I've heard of this happening before. The body gets confused, doesn't know how to sort out what's real from what's not. Part of him might still be lost in the vision... we need to give him time."

Amy hoped Richard was right. If Ian was permanently disabled, she would never be able to forgive herself. She put her head in her hands. This was a nightmare.

"Amy, while we're waiting, why don't you tell us about your vision. Maybe by the time you're done talking, Ian will have recovered enough to tell us about what happened to him. Then we can make a plan to get off the island."

Amy took a deep breath and organized her thoughts. It seemed like so much to convey, how would she get it all across to them? The only thing she could do was start talking and do her best.

"I saw the future. I don't know for sure when it was, but it couldn't have been more than a couple of hundred years from now. It was awful. This island, all the islands around here, were covered in cities. Richard, your people, they were scattered and homeless. There were no animals, hardly any trees, they'd destroyed it all..."

Amy proceeded to tell them all that she had seen and heard and felt. All that she had learned, starting with Steve and ending with her encounter with Norman at the end.

"The strange thing about Norman was that he seemed familiar. He reminded me a lot of our Norm. Do you think that was a coincidence or do you think it means something?" Amy asked.

Before Richard could answer, they were distracted by Ian as he limped into the room to join them. "Amy, did you say that you met someone who reminded you of Norm?"

"Ian! It's nice to see you up again!" Amy jumped up and hugged him, but he didn't reciprocate. He stood rigid, his arms hanging by his sides. Amy backed up a few steps to get a better look. "How are you feeling?"

Ian ignored the question. "I met someone in my vision who reminded me of Norm too." He spoke to the room, without looking Amy in the eyes, and then he limped to a chair and sat down. He lifted a hand, fingers trembling, and gently touched the right side of his face.

Amy watched Ian, concerned, but she chose not to say anything, not wanting him to feel self-conscious. Instead she turned to Richard, "Speaking of Norm, where is he? I'm starting to worry about him... shouldn't he have shown up by now, or responded on the radio?"

Richard looked confused. "Norm? Norm who?"

"You know? Norm? The guy on the boat with you and Tum. He went to the southwest corner of the island while we went to the two hills. Remember?"

"Amy, I don't know what you're talking about. There isn't anyone named Norm with us, just the two of you, Tum, and I."

Amy threw a bewildered look at Tum, who nodded silently to confirm – no Norm.

"What the hell is going on? Ian, you remember Norm right?" Ian stayed silent, so she turned on Richard again. "He was part of your crew for God's sake! He might be in danger for all we know. We need to find him!"

Richard stood up and put a calming hand on Amy's shoulder. "I know you're upset. I think the vision quest confused you. There's never been anyone named Norm on my crew."

Amy brushed Richard's hand off her shoulder and stood up. "Ian, answer me. Do you remember Norm?"

Ian's hand was still probing his face, his eyes vacant, staring ahead. "Yeah. I remember. Norm."

"See Richard? Ian remembers him."

Richard looked from Ian to Amy, his eyes sad. "Yeah, I heard him." He sat down across from Ian, looking tired, his shoulders drooping. "Ok, Ian. Why don't you tell us about your vision quest. Let's hear what happened."

Ian didn't look up, but he told his story, starting with his arrival on the *Boston*. He told of meeting Maquinna, trying to fit into the ship's crew, the disagreement with the Captain and the broken gun, and then stopped abruptly. "I don't want to talk any more. I've said enough."

"Ian, what you experienced in the vision quest is important. You need to share it with us."

"No."

Richard looked to Amy, his eyes pleading for her to help.

She sighed, sat down next to Ian and took one of his hands. "Richard's right, we need to know more. My vision quest showed us a future we want to avoid. Yours showed you the past. There's something there that we need to know. We need you to keep going."

"No." Ian turned toward Amy. "I remember what happened to me now. I remember everything." His breathing was rapid and shaky, his face flushed. "I can still feel it all. My leg... it doesn't work right. Neither does my arm. My face... The right side of my face is numb... it tingles. My eye... it doesn't work. I can only see out of one eye, Amy." He looked like he was about to break down. "I can't relive it. I can't."

Amy was horrified. He'd clearly been through a traumatic experience, but all they'd been thinking about was how they could pump him for information. She cursed herself for her thoughtlessness.

"I'm sorry, Ian. If you aren't ready to talk about it yet, that's ok. We can talk later."

Ian nodded, slumped forward, placed his head on his arms, and closed his eyes.

Richard wasn't ready to give up so easily. "Ian we really need you to tell us what you know. All of our safety may depend on it."

"Leave me alone, I don't want to talk about it!"

"Well, that's that I guess," Richard said as he stood up. "Let's get off this island." He and Tum walked out the door leaving Amy alone with Ian, catatonic at the table.

In the silence that was left behind, punctuated by the steady hush of Ian's breathing, she felt very alone. Alone and confused. What had happened to Ian? What, if anything, could she do to bring him back to himself? What in the world had happened to Norm?

She thought back to that first night on the island. She'd been terrified, but the beauty of that night stuck with her. It haunted her. She and Ian had been a team then. They'd made it to the lodge together through a strange and hostile forest. They'd survived together and then they'd shared that incredible vision in the cove. Now... now what?

Everything was broken, and she didn't know how to fix it.

She had to make a choice. Sit down at the table, lay her head down, join Ian in his misery, and give up. Or... what? Fight to get Ian off the island, help him get better, make it up to him for what she'd done. If it hadn't been for her stupid mistakes, they wouldn't be stuck here. It was up to her to make things right.

"Come on Ian, get up. Let's get out of here." She grabbed him by the elbow and forced him to follow her out of the lodge and into the light.

Richard and Tum were on the dock, manhandling kayaks into the water. Amy shielded her eyes, "I wonder what they're doing?" When Ian didn't respond, she walked to the dock, pulling him behind her.

"Are we going kayaking?" Amy asked.

Richard grunted as he heaved a kayak into the water, then tied it's bowline to a cleat. "Yeah, this is our only option now. We don't have radio or cell reception and my boat doesn't have enough fuel to get back."

"If we couldn't get through the fog in your boat, how are

we going to make it in these little kayaks?"

Richard jerked his head toward the cove, pulling her eyes out to sea. Something had changed. There was a gap in the fog, an opening that they could paddle through.

"We are going to go through that?"

"Yup."

"Do you think it's safe? It looks unnatural."

"Yup."

"What do you mean? Yes it's safe, or yes it's unnatural?"

"Both I hope. But definitely unnatural. Now that the vision quests are complete, I think Sasahevas is giving us an invitation to leave. I suggest we take it."

"Yes." Ian said.

They both turned, surprised to hear him talking. He seemed better than before, he was standing straighter, and he didn't look so pale.

"What?" Amy asked.

"Yes. We should leave. We can't stay here any longer. We need to leave."

Amy shared a look with Richard, eyebrows raised in puzzlement, and then she bent to help him with the next kayak. It was time to go.

CHAPTER 43

Once the kayaks were ready, they gathered food and water from the lodge, loaded the supplies, and secured the hatches. Richard showed Amy how to get into the boats without tipping them, gave her a paddle and a lifejacket, and then showed her how to attach the spray skirt so that she wouldn't get swamped and sunk by waves.

Sitting in the boat, Amy felt small and vulnerable. With each shift of weight she felt like the kayak would tip over and spill her into the water. She put her hand on the dock to steady herself, happy for the relative stability of the wood beneath her hand. She watched as Ian, reluctantly using Richard's arm to support him, got into his kayak. After Richard stepped away, when he must have thought nobody was watching, Ian's hand furtively drifted up to the right side of his face, probing, exploring his cheek and forehead with gentle fingers.

"Ok everyone, this is it," Richard said. "These kayaks are beginner-friendly. As long as you don't lean too far, you won't tip over. If you feel like you're losing your balance, use your paddle on that side to push yourself back up." He paused a moment to see if everyone understood. "If you do tip into the water, don't panic. You'll feel trapped under your boat, but if you detach your spray skirt, you'll float right back to the surface. Be sure to stay with your boat and I'll help you get back in."

Amy knew that Richard was trying to help, but it was making her nervous. She did not want to tip over... the chances of her not panicking if that happened were just about zero. She could pretty much count on panicking. She decided to think about cute baby seals so she didn't start to panic right then and there.

Leaving was strangely anticlimactic. So much had happened to her on this island and now they were leaving. Just like that. She wasn't the same person she'd been when they'd arrived. Wow, she had stories to tell. Stories that no-one would believe. The shipwreck, Sassahevas and Tsonoqua, the vision quests, and Norm... What had happened to Norm? Why wouldn't Richard acknowledge his existence?

"Alright, let's get going," Richard said. He untied them from the dock and gave each of them a push so that they were bobbing calmly in the protected cove, well away from the dock. Richard clambered into his kayak, snapped his spray skirt on and pushed off to join them. After making sure they were all ready, he started paddling, steady strokes, headed straight for the gap in the fog.

Ian turned to Amy, frowning, "Who died and made him the leader? That's what I want to know." Then he paddled away before she could form an answer.

The closer they got to the gap in the fog, the more unnatural it seemed. The bank of fog swirled and moved in front of her, looking the same as she remembered, but now it had a tunnel cut into it, edges straight and sharp. Amy stopped paddling and let herself drift as she peered nervously into it – the interior grey and uninviting.

Looking into the gloom, she had a strange desire to stay, to live on this island and forget everything else. She could stay here cut off from the rest of the world, cut off from the future. She could learn to forget everything she'd seen. Maybe she could be happy here.

The rest of the group was getting ahead of her and were already in the tunnel, strangely indistinct in the dim light, fading as they got further away. She gripped her paddle, steeled herself, and pulled hard – propelling herself forward to stay with her friends, paddling toward an uncertain fate, the kayak wobbling underneath her.

Inside the tunnel was a different world. A world without color or warmth. Water condensed on her face and arms, her paddle dripping on her as as she propelled her kayak forward. Sometimes she could hear the water splashing around her as if the fog walls were made of solid rock. Other times she couldn't hear the water at all, instead she would hear Richard breathing or Ian muttering as if they were right next to her, the sounds projecting unnaturally into her ears.

The walls were close on either side – close enough that she had to concentrate to keep herself in the middle, unwilling to touch the unnatural fog with her paddle or her kayak. She didn't like looking at the fog either. It was hypnotizing. The swirls and eddies forming and reforming, patterns and almost-patterns, shapes and almost-shapes, tricking her eyes and stealing her concentration, willing her to the right or to the left, her bow drifting steadily off course.

Once she came dangerously close to the fog only to correct course at the last moment. She pinched herself, trying to force her eyes to focus, indistinct thoughts floating through her mind, neck, and shoulders aching under the strain.

The water was smooth and dark, inky black, swallowing her paddle on each stroke. The water stirred beneath her, unnaturally viscous, flat and dead. She sensed no sign of life, her friends out of sight. She was alone with her kayak – paddle dipping in the water – her breathing and heartbeat echoing in her ears. She felt out of control, she could only follow the tunnel, hoping it would take her somewhere safe. Still deeper she went, paddling further into the belly of the infernal fog.

She found herself praying for the first time in years. "Heavenly Father, I am lost, but I trust you to be my guide. Heavenly Father, I am lost, but I place my life in your hands. Heavenly Father, I am lost, but I have faith that you will lead me from this darkness and bring me into the light."

She glanced back and saw the tunnel closing up behind her – a solid, swirling wall of dark grey fog, ten feet away. Panic rose in her. It broke her paddling rhythm, water splashing as her kayak twisted left and right, out of control, flailing.

She pulled the paddle out of the water and rested it on the

deck of her kayak as she took a couple of deep breaths to compose herself. When she felt she was ready, she planted her paddle in the water and moved forward once more. She didn't look back again.

After an interminable time. Hours? Days? Weeks? She heard Richard talking, but he was too far away for her to make out words, everything was garbled. A few minutes later, the group came into view. They had stopped paddling and she drifted up to join them.

"What is it?" She asked.

Richard looked weary and drawn. "Look up there. I think that's the exit."

Amy saw that the tunnel curved one last time and just beyond, there was a hint of light, the fog's grey giving way to a lighter white.

"Where do you think it will take us?" she asked.

"I have no idea. Let's find out."

A few more minutes of paddling and they could see the exit out of the fog, framing ocean, rocks, and a shoreline beyond. When they emerged, blinking and relieved, they found themselves half a mile from land, a deserted village rising from the shore, structures abandoned and overgrown. The fog swirled behind them, a solid wall, the tunnel had closed.

"Where are we?" Ian asked.

"Mamalilikulla," Richard replied. His eyes were flat, mouth set. "We are miles from any other village, anything else will be farther than we can travel in the remaining light." He looked resigned. "I guess we'll have to stay here for the night." He paddled ahead, assuming they would follow.

Ian spoke loudly towards Richard's retreating back, "Why the hell did you bring us here Richard? We want to go home, not to some godforsaken, abandoned village."

Amy didn't like the look of the place either. "Tum, what is Mamalilikulla?"

"It's one of our villages. The people were relocated fifty years ago and its abandoned now. Place gives me the creeps."

Great. Just great. Amy gritted her teeth and followed Richard toward the shore.

CHAPTER 44

They pulled their boats up onto a shore that was slimy with seaweed and algae. The tide was low and the ocean had uncovered a vast collection of garbage. Rusted pieces of iron, twisted and deformed by years of exposure to salt water and salty air, lay half-buried in the sucking sand. They looked like tortured fingers reaching toward the sky, blood-red flakes falling when disturbed, sharp to the touch, dangerous, and unwelcoming.

They floundered knee-deep through sand and mud, clams squirting water into the air in waves around them, signaling their presence with bivalve panic. Eventually, they emerged on higher ground. Above the tideline the sand was slimy, punctuated by slippery rocks, and covered with debris. Amy bent down to get a closer look, dropping the kayak's nose, a dark furrow tracing behind her from where she had dragged the boat, already closing up as the saturated sand collapsed into itself.

She ran her fingers through the sand, straining out shards of pottery and glass. The pieces were no bigger than her fingernail and they appeared very old. The chunks of glass were rounded and polished by the sea, glowing faintly in the flat light. The shards of pottery were white with patterns of blue and red. One had a perfect flower painted on it, whole and unblemished, the rest of the shard pitted and scarred, the flower an improbable survivor. She gently placed it in her pocket. A reminder. A charm perhaps.

Lifting her eyes, she took in the rest of the beach. More debris. A shoe, partly chewed through. Another shoe, just the sole, pitted leather and rubber. A small toy soldier, forlorn and lost, dwarfed by the seascape around it, buried to the waist, sand-spattered and tarnished.

The beach extended for at least half a mile in each direction, all of it covered in remnants of a civilization abandoned. In the near distance, the skeletal remains of a pier, only the posts remaining, half rotten, shattered, birds perched on top, water lapping at their feet.

The sky was grey. The sea was grey. The sand too. The entire world was monochrome, leeched of color, drizzle falling into the sea, the line between earth and sky blurred and indistinct. The seabirds were the only sign of life besides the four of them, the ocean still and desolate, nothing moving as far as the eye could see, smudges that must be islands on the edge of the world.

A log poked out of the bank above the beach. It was laying horizontally, suspended ten feet above the sand, its far end grounded in the top of the bank, covered in a thick tangle of blackberry bushes. The end of the log was carved into the head of a wolf, snarling and defiant, pointed toward the sea. Their welcoming totem. Beneath the head of the wolf was a narrow, sandy path leading straight up the bank and into the bushes.

Richard must have seen the path as well, because he was pulling his kayak toward it, Tum following close behind. Amy looked for Ian, and found him well behind her, sitting on the bow of his kayak, deep in the muck, head in his hands, resting. She left her boat where it was and headed back to see if he needed help.

When she arrived, he raised his head and gave her a wan smile. “Sorry Amy, I guess I’m still pretty tired.”

“What? Are you kidding? You’re doing great! I can’t believe you paddled so far. You deserve the rest.” She sat down next to him and put a hand on his arm.

“Thanks. I just don’t want to hold you back. And this place. It reminds me too much of where I was. I want to tell you about it… I really do. I’m just not ready yet.”

“It’s ok. I understand. The vision quest was intense. Really intense. And I think you went through a lot more than I did.

Don't worry about it. I'll be here to listen when you're ready, ok?"

Ian smiled again. "Ok. Thanks." He stood up and began to pull his kayak forward. Slow steps, sinking to the knee each time, struggling to lift his feet and move through it.

Amy moved to the back of his kayak and pushed, lifting a little to help ease his way. It was easier when they worked together. As a team they got his kayak up to where Richard was waiting, returned to her kayak and brought it up as well.

Richard looked at her, quirked an eyebrow up, then climbed up the path, disappearing into the bushes. Amy let Ian go first and then she followed him in. The bushes blocked the outside world completely. Within a few feet she was surrounded by leaves and thorns. She couldn't see more than a couple of feet in any direction. Wild rose intertwined with the blackberries, little pink flowers poking through and scenting the air around her.

She was wary of cutting herself or tearing her jacket, so she walked through the overhanging branches carefully, moving slowly, letting the others get well ahead. Her feet trod on small plants, the smell of mint rising from the ground as she crushed the leaves. She found herself alone, but she felt safe. Ensconced. It was familiar somehow. She let her fingers trail along the leaves, touched the velvety softness of flower petals, marveling at how they contrasted with the sharp thorns. There was a sudden movement by her feet, a small snake crossing the path. She could hear it slither into the thick bushes, a smaller predator avoiding a much larger one.

When she found the others, they were standing at a trail junction, the bushes giving way to provide enough space for them all to stand and talk. There was a steady humming buzz, the bushes here covered with bees, feeding upon rose and blackberry blossoms, their legs and bellies heavy with pollen. The sound was all around, as if it were coming from inside her, permeating her, a part of her.

"Amy? Did you hear me?" It was Richard. He'd been talking

to her about something.

"What? Sorry, I got distracted."

"I was just saying that we need to decide where we are going to sleep tonight. I've only been here once. It was years ago, but I can't imagine it's changed much. If we turn right, we'll enter the old village." He gestured down the path where Amy could see dilapidated, peaked roofs emerging from the bushes. "The other direction is the old school."

Amy looked but she couldn't see the school, just more bushes. "I suppose the school is the better choice, I imagine there would be plenty of room, right?"

"Yes, but... ok, I feel stupid saying this, but the school is kind of creepy. It wasn't only used as a school. During the epidemic, it was used as a TB hospital. It has a really bad feeling. I think there was a lot of suffering in there. A lot of death and sadness."

Amy could understand his reluctance. "Ok then. Let's stay in one of the houses."

They turned right and pushed through the brush, increasingly thick, the path narrowing until they were hacking away at it to cut away the branches and make it wide enough for them to pass. The first house they found had collapsed in on itself, the windows empty, the roof concave, timbers falling in toward the floor.

"How old did you say this village was?" Amy asked.

"It was abandoned in the 1950s. The people here were relocated to other towns where the provincial government thought they would be better off. More services. Easier access." He looked at the house and shrugged. "I don't think this one is going to work."

They walked further and found a strange wooden structure. Two large log posts, topped by another log to create a square entrance that went nowhere. It stood alone, framing nothing but bushes behind it.

"What is that?" Amy asked.

"That's the entrance to one of the old longhouses. This

was a village site for a very long time. The modern structures were built in the 1920s. Before that, the people lived in traditional longhouses."

"Where did they find logs that big? They must be fifteen feet across!"

Richard looked at her oddly. "All the trees around here used to be that big Amy."

"Why aren't they now? Aren't all of these forests old growth?"

"No. Not even close. Some of it is second growth, but most of it is third. This whole area has been logged and logged and logged again. Started with hand loggers, then logging crews, and now it's totally mechanized. They come in with diggers and chainsaws, backhoes and helicopters, and they can wipe miles of forest clean in a matter of months."

"I had no idea. Even Hurst Island?"

"Hurst is different. Old growth is unmistakable. The trees are massive and they are spread far from each other so it's very open. There is little undergrowth, the ground is dry and clear because the trees take all the light and water. It's like being in a cathedral, sacred and quiet. Hurst is special, most of this area has already been exploited by mankind. Very little is truly wild or pristine. Not anymore."

They walked on, leaving the remains of the old longhouse behind.

The trail dead-ended at a craftsman style house that looked promising. It was set atop a small rise, the front porch level with the tops of the bushes. The windows were gone, but the structure seemed intact, the roof rising clean and strong. The steps to the front porch were missing, as was the front door, but there were a couple of old planks laid between the porch and the ground, providing a slippery, rotten bridge up. Richard tested it with his weight first. The planks bent and complained, but they held, so he carefully walked up, picking each step carefully, arms out, balancing on the greasy wood. Tum followed, then Ian, and finally Amy.

Amy found the porch unpleasant. Floorboards were missing in places, dark gaps through which she could see the brushy ground below. Old, faded, aluminum beer cans littered the ground, a messy pile of them stacked in the corner. Through the door she saw more floorboards missing, a bed with springs showing naked and rusty, an old stove, and cupboards with doors hanging open and broken. Just inside the room was a single shoe. Patent leather. Tiny. A child's shoe. In strangely perfect shape, white leather gleaming and polished.

Amy shuddered. "I don't like it here."

Richard's face was grim. "I don't either. But I think the school is going to be worse. Come on, let's see what's inside." He took two steps and his foot broke through the floor, plunging him down to his knee, his lower leg disappearing into the hole. Richard screamed, his face a rictus of pain as he fell over sideways, clutching at his upper leg where it emerged from the porch floor.

Tum rushed forward, grabbing him and trying to pull him up but failing. "Amy, Ian. Help!"

Amy rushed over to Richard, trying to free his leg where it was pinned, feeling him writhe and groan beneath her. "Ian, come help. We need you."

Ian was looking at Richard strangely. He had a smile on his face, canines exposed, eyes feverish. He was standing on the edge of the porch, one hand on the railing, one foot already on the ramp, looking like he was ready to leave Richard where he lay.

"Ian! Come here now!" Amy yelled through gritted teeth, pulling as hard as she could.

The urgency in her voice seemed to get through to him. He rushed over, and with his help they got Richard out of the hole. Richard was on his back, laying on a solid section of the porch, panting and grimacing.

"Richard? Are you ok?" Amy asked.

"Give me a minute. I think so." His pants were torn, and his lower leg looked like it had a pretty deep cut, the blood welling up thick and red.

After a couple of minutes, Richard stood up, gingerly putting weight on his leg, testing it. "I think I can walk. Slowly though." He looked back through the door into the house and shook his head. "It's not safe here. We need to go to the school."

From her vantage point on the porch, Amy could see a flat grey building in the distance. It was up amongst the trees, bulky and dark, empty windows staring back at her.

Chilling her to the bone.

CHAPTER 45

They returned to the kayaks to tie them up and gather their food and water. The boats were well above the high tide line, but Richard felt it would be best to tie them to the roots sticking out of the bank, just to be safe. Losing the kayaks would be a disaster not worth contemplating.

The path to the school was overgrown, like the path to the village, until they broke into the trees. The ground opened up and the trail, covered with grass and pine needles, softened underfoot. Amy felt like she could breathe again. After several minutes of walking, the grey concrete school building loomed into view. The roof was collapsed in parts, the walls pitted, and the foundation partly eroded, exposing concrete and rebar. Trees were growing in the basement, and had pushed their branches out broken windows, a few reaching as far as the roof where they'd dropped seeds, allowing saplings to take root on top of the building. A door was hanging ajar, crooked on its hinges, pushed in at an odd angle. Beneath the dirt and grime, Amy could see that the door had once been bright blue.

Richard was standing in front of the door with his back to them, and as Amy got close she could hear him speaking softly. "Great Spirit, please bless us in this endeavor. Great Spirit, please keep us safe and see us through danger into safety. Great Spirit, please give me wisdom that I might choose the right path in this time of hardship."

Amy stayed where she was, not wanting to disturb him. When he was done, he set his shoulders. "Let's go in and find a place to set up camp," and then he walked through the door.

Amy followed him in, brushing away spider webs, feeling them in her hair, a crawling sensation on her head. The hallway was dark and ruined, the walls no longer straight, the floor lumped up in dirt and roots, the ceiling stained and bulging, vines and branches, leaves and thorns everywhere.

They pushed through into an open atrium-like space, the roof partially collapsed, letting in air and light, the remaining roof giving shelter to half the room, where they could stay out of the rain. They didn't feel like going any further, no need to explore deeper into the building – this would do for their needs.

They dumped their food and water in one of the corners, and Richard set up a camp-stove in the other. They didn't have any bedding, so Amy and Tum returned to the forest to gather soft materials they could use as makeshift mats for sleeping.

Amy left the building with a palpable feeling of relief, happy to put her back to the door and walk in the open forest once more. She stepped carefully off the trail, sticks crackling, her feet sinking deep into the soft soil and decomposing leaves. She bent down to pick up soft duff, putting it into a bag she'd brought for the purpose. She carefully separated dry needles and leaves from moist soil, collecting what she needed from around the base of the trees where the rain had been kept at bay. Large grey mushrooms grew out of the tree trunks, little white mushrooms poking up through the soil. She gently touched the tiny mushroom caps, feeling a velvet smoothness under her fingertips, briefly wondering if they were edible before setting the idea aside as too risky.

Absorbed in what she was doing, she lost track of where Tum was, lost track of where she was too. The soft patter of the rain lulled her, as did the distant hum of the bees hard at work collecting for their hive – just like her. It was peaceful. She was at peace.

A new sound broke into her consciousness. She realized she had been hearing it for some time, but it was getting louder, loud enough to disturb her.

"Uh, huu. Uh, huu?" It sounded like someone trying to get her attention.

She stood up, looking around. "Tum? Is that you?"

"Uh, huu. Uh, huu?" Increasingly loud.

"Ian? Richard?" Spinning around. "Who is that?"

"Uh, huu. Uh, huu?" She couldn't tell where the voice was coming from. She cocked her head, trying to get a fix on it.

"Uh, huu. Uh, huu!" Very loud. Above her? The air was electric, sharp and acrid.

She looked up and saw dark eyes and a large mouth, round and red, a woman with wild hair and a basket on her back. She was perched in the tree, feet planted on a branch, heels on one side, toes on the other, squatting, knees at her ears, indistinct shapes floating around her shoulders, soft and translucent.

Amy recognized her from Richard's stories. This was Tsonoqua, solid and real before her. Amy stood up slowly, her hands up, palms facing out. "It's ok. I'll leave now. I'm sorry I disturbed you."

"Uh, huu. Uh, huu?" Tsonoqua's eyes were mournful, her voice expressive, her words nonsense.

"Ok. Ok. I'll just pick up my bag and go. I'll leave you alone, huh?"

Amy backed away slowly, Tsonoqua's dark eyes following her, voice quieter as the distance grew. Once she felt she was far enough, Amy turned and walked quickly back toward the school. At the door, she glanced behind her – the forest was empty, Tsonoqua was gone.

On the way down the hallway, she heard loud voices.

"You don't get to tell me what to do, you backward, uneducated savage. I don't have to listen to you! You can go to hell for all I care!" Ian yelled.

She could hear Richard next. He was speaking in quiet, calming tones, but she couldn't make out the words. When she entered the room, she saw Ian. His face was red, head thrust forward, enraged. Richard was next to him, hands up, trying to placate. When Ian noticed her in the room, he let out a huff, turned his back and stalked away.

"Richard, what happened?"

"I asked him to help me with dinner and he got upset.

I tried to calm him down, but nothing I said seemed to help. Maybe you could talk to him?"

Amy set her bag down and walked to the other side of the room where Ian was crouched, rocking back and forth, talking to himself. "Hey Ian, are you ok?"

"Yeah. I'm fine." He growled, then seeming to realize his tone, he stopped himself and gave Amy a thin smile. "I'm sorry. I'm just frazzled I guess. I feel like I'm walking on eggshells around here. No matter what I do, Richard is judging me. I can see how he looks at me. He thinks I'm weak. Thinks I'm no good. He doesn't know. He doesn't know what I've been through."

"Ian, none of that is true. Nobody is judging you. We all want you to feel better, that's all."

"Has he told you that? He's lying! He's a lying, no good, son of a whore!" Ian was worked up again, his face red, spittle flying from his mouth.

Amy was taken aback. She'd never seen Ian act like this, never heard him talk like this.

"Ok, Ian. Calm down. It's going to be ok." She put her hand on his shoulder to calm him. She could feel his breathing slow, some of the tension easing out of him. "Why don't you rest for a little while, huh? I'll help Richard with dinner and we'll let you know when it's ready. How's that?"

Ian nodded once and didn't say anything more, so Amy stood up and rejoined Richard.

"Is Tum back yet?" She asked.

"Not yet, he must still be gathering bedding. I've got dinner under control, do you want to go look for him."

"Yes. But... um... I saw something strange out there."

Richard paused from opening a can and gave her his full attention. "Strange how?"

"Strange as in a supernatural visitation by a spirit-creature. That kind of strange." She didn't know why, but she was feeling very comfortable with what had happened. In fact, she felt safer in the forest, even with Tsonoqua, than she did in this creepy school building.

"Are you pulling my leg?"

"No, I'm serious. I think I saw Tsonoqua. She was perched in a tree above me. I heard her first. Then I saw her."

"Tsonoqua. You think you saw Tsonoqua. In a tree..."

Richard didn't seem to believe her. Maybe she shouldn't have been flippant about it. "Never mind. I'll go look for Tum, ok?"

Richard went back to work on his can, shaking his head.

CHAPTER 46

Amy walked out of the school and back into the forest. She thought about yelling for Tum but decided not to break the silence. She stood on the trail for a long moment, trying to decide where she should go. To the right the trail disappeared over a small crest, deeper into the trees. To the left was the path into the bushes, toward the village.

She chose to walk straight ahead, off the trail, into the underbrush, amongst the giant trees. Within a few paces she picked up a game trail and followed it as it wound its way along the path of least resistance, the ground soft and spongy beneath her feet. The rain was coming down harder now, drumming on the leaves around her and hissing in the treetops. She pulled her hood up over her head and snugged it tight, isolating herself, the folds of synthetic cloth crinkling and echoing in her ears, the rain tapping on the top of her head and rolling down her nose.

There was still no sign of Tum when she broke out of the forest and onto the beach. But there was someone else on the beach, someone new. It was a woman, short and hunched over, wearing traditional clothing, a cedar cloak over her shoulders, wispy white hair sticking out of a round, conical hat. She was walking near the tideline, occasionally bending over and collecting tidbits off the beach.

Amy stepped down into the sand and walked toward the woman. She stopped several paces away, politely waiting for the woman to notice her, not wanting to startle her. The woman was focused on what she was doing, her back to Amy, and gave no indication that she'd sensed her presence.

"Hello, how are you?" Amy asked.

The woman straightened up and turned around, placing a

small stone in her pocket as she did so. "Why, hello dear. I'm very well thank you."

Amy was immediately entranced. The woman had a warm and open face, high cheekbones, almond colored eyes, honey colored skin, with beautiful wrinkles. She was a tiny little thing, less than five feet tall, stooped over, radiating happiness and good health.

"Do you, um, live around here?" Amy asked.

"Yes, I do. Right up there in the village." She gestured up the bank and past the bushes. "Not many of us left here anymore. Almost everyone is gone now, you know."

"I thought the village was abandoned. My friend told me everyone had left years ago."

"Oh, he was right. Mostly. Almost everyone left. But a few of us old timers still stick around. I don't know why. But here we are."

"Well, it's nice to meet you. My name is Amy"

"Hi Amy, my name is Eustochee. I know, it's hard to say. You can call me Molly."

"What are you looking for out here Molly."

"Oh, I don't know. Bits and pieces. This and that. I think I found what I was looking for though." She looked closely at Amy, nodded her head and smiled. "Yes, I think I did."

"What did you find?"

"It may not seem like much, but it's a treasure to me. Oh you never mind an old woman's wanderings. Tell me how you got here. Not many people come to this beach."

"That's a long story and I don't know how to tell it. We are trying to get home now and are spending the night here tonight."

"Home. That's important, isn't it?"

"Yes, I think so. Have you lived here a long time?"

"Oh yes. A very long time."

"Can you tell me what happened to this village? Why was it abandoned?"

"That's a sad story. But I'll tell it. I guess someone needs to hear it, don't they?"

Amy stayed silent, waiting for the old woman to continue.

"Well, let's sit down and get comfortable." The woman led her to a log on the edge of the beach, up against the forest, and they sat down, facing the sea, knees touching, angled toward each other, sitting close.

The old woman searched for words. "Where should I start? Well I guess the first thing should come first." She smiled. "That makes sense, doesn't it?"

Amy nodded.

"This is not where my ancestors lived, not originally. We were way over in Nootka Sound, far across the island from here. This was the village for another tribe, a tribe that weakened and died when the European diseases came. Many tribes weakened and died in those days. Some tribes combined with others for strength, some withered and died, disappearing completely, some were killed by other tribes who had stayed stronger. Everything changed. Everything was out of balance.

"We were one of the stronger tribes and we held out against the provincial government as long as we could. But they came down on us harder every year. First it was our whale shrine, then it was our potlatches, then it was our clothing and finally it was our children. Yes, that's right. I can see the surprise in your eyes. They came for our children. That's how they finally broke us.

"I need to start at the beginning. When we lost our whale shrine, we couldn't hunt the whales any more. We lost a sustenance that had supported us for so many generations. Without the whales we had to rely on the government for food and tools. Maybe that's why they stole the shrine... I don't know. Maybe they wanted us dependant. Last I heard, it was in the basement of the Smithsonian in New York City. Can you imagine that?"

Amy shook her head, no. She was captivated.

"That's right. They came in the dead of the night and stole it right from under us. Unimaginable. Next they told us that potlatches were illegal and we couldn't gather for them any longer. They used that as an excuse to keep us from gathering at all. Any group larger than fifteen was suspect. We got away with a few more potlatches, a couple more years, hiding and skulking. After some of us were arrested and sent to jail... well, we just stopped gathering I guess. We gave up." The old woman looked down for a moment, wiped away a tear and then looked at Amy with bright eyes. "Forgive me. I'm an old woman, my emotions get the better of me. I've grown weak in my old age."

"No, not at all! You aren't weak. I think you're wonderful." Amy put her hand on the woman's knee and smiled encouragingly.

"Thank you dear. You are sweet, aren't you? Let's see... where was I? Oh, yes. Next they made us wear their clothing. You should have seen us, all out in front of the longhouses, our salmon smoking on the rack, log canoes up on the sand, and they expected us to wear petticoats and suits! Preposterous! As soon as they'd leave we'd put our old clothes back on, but they'd catch us and punish us for breaking their rules. Eventually, we got used to it and then we were wearing their clothing more often than not. The children grew up not knowing any different. They'd already started to lose their heritage. That unbroken string of knowledge that had preserved us for centuries was fraying and soon would break.

"They moved us here, to this village, to keep an eye on us. They built us these houses and that school, all in European style. They said it was a great gift. A sign of their tolerance. They wanted us to live our lives inside, teach our children inside. We became strangers to the wild and lost our connection to nature. Can you imagine that? Spending all your time inside, never going outside, forgetting all of the natural rhythms? It was like a small death for us.... Then they came for our children.

"We didn't know how to teach them in a school. How could we? So they started something called a 'residential school' where our children would live away from the tribe, learning only what the government taught them. They called it 'assimilation' but it was conquest is what it was. They killed our culture. They cut our children away from us. You couldn't see the wound, but we bled. Yes we did." The old woman was crying again. After a minute she pulled herself together, wiping her nose on the hem of her cloak.

"It was a sad time Amy. A very dark time. We stayed in this village for years, the old longhouses rotting around us, while we lived in European houses and our children learned in a European school. Then the tuberculosis came. We thought we were done with the European diseases, but we were wrong. The school was filled with the sick, the air malignant, the sound of coughing, blood and sputum on the floor. Our children finally came home, but it was too late. The chain had been broken and they didn't look to us for knowledge and wisdom any more. We had nothing left to offer.

"Our tribe was broken. All the way broken. They moved us to Alert Bay after that. Close to their towns and hospitals. They said it was safer for us. Safer to finish our assimilation is what they meant. A few of us stayed here, in this old village. We try to remember the old times and retain the old wisdom. But there aren't many of us left, and we are all very old."

"I'm sorry Molly. That's a terrible story." Amy felt devastated, hearing all of this loss, the many layers of sadness that had been laid down here. The air felt heavy. She could feel the weight of history pressing on her.

"Yes, it is terrible isn't it? I've seen a lot of things change around here Amy. When I was young there were seals everywhere, sea otters too, and so many salmon it felt like you could walk on them. The humpback whales would come up against the rocks to scratch their backs and we would reach right down and give them a little scratch ourselves. There were herring balls so big it looked like the ocean was erupting. And eulachon... oh the eulachon, their oil so rich and delicious it would keep us fat all winter long. There were even basking sharks if you can believe that!"

"What happened? Why are the animals gone?"

"They were killed, that's what happened. The province put a bounty on seals, twenty five cents for each one you killed. The Coast Guard would shoot them with machine guns, there were so many. Then they put blades on the bows of their ships and ran the basking sharks down, killed them where they lay in the water, eating nothing but plankton, they weren't harming anything. The fish, they were killed by overfishing and logging mostly. Each time they'd log a river drainage, that river would coincidentally lose all of its salmon. Spawning streams that used to have millions of fish are now empty and dead, a cycle that ran for millenia broken beyond repair."

"That's horrible!" Amy exclaimed, horrified.

"Yes, it is. I've seen it all in my long life, seen all the depredations and exploitations. Of my people and of my world. It never ends. It won't be long before they destroy this village too, destroy my home. They'll tear down the houses and cut down the trees to make room for something new. Progress they'll call it. When will it stop? I'll tell you when. It will never stop. Not if no-one stands up against it."

"Is there anything you can do?"

"No honey, not me. I'm old and my time has passed. The young people need to take up the mantle now. They need to stand up for what's right. Stand up against the destruction. If my people can't stand up and speak against what's happening, who will?"

"Are your people doing that? Standing up and speaking out?"

"I'm afraid not, though some of them try. They are too broken, too spread out. They lack a focus. They don't have the old traditions. They've lost the ancient wisdom. No, they haven't been able to slow it down much. But I have hope, I think maybe that will change." She smiled warmly at Amy.

"What will change? How will it change? Is there anything I can do?"

The old women stood up, brushed herself off and settled her cloak around her shoulders. "Come with me, sweet one. I have something to show you."

Amy followed the old women into the forest, deep into an ancient grove of trees where she stopped in a little nook next to a giant, moss-encrusted log. Amy looked up and saw that the tree branches, far above her head, had wooden boxes hanging from them, five feet long and three feet wide. They looked very old and were suspended by crude rope, like ripe fruit, ready to fall and spill their contents upon the ground. In some of the branches, the ropes were hanging alone, frayed and broken, their burden long ago dropped to the forest floor.

The old woman had a hand on the log and was pointing into a crevice where the side of the log met the ground. "Amy look in there. Find what I want you to find."

Amy bent down, but she couldn't see anything, the crevice was too dark and too deep.

"Go ahead, it's ok to dig." The woman said.

Amy dug and the soft dirt moved aside easily until she had exposed a small hollow where something gleamed dull and white within the earth. Rain water was dripping from Amy's chin and her pants were soaked through.

An electric shock ran through her, from her feet to the top of her head, and she sat up rigid, in shock. She had just realized something. The rain had been steady, the water falling from her hood and her jacket the entire time she'd been talking to the old woman. But the woman, somehow, had never gotten wet. The rain had never touched her.

Amy turned slowly, still crouching, chills running up and down her spine. The forest was empty, the old woman was gone, not a trace of her remained.

She looked into the crevice and it took a long moment for her to take in what she was seeing. Deep within the earth, resting comfortably in the dark soil, was a skeleton. Small and fragile, wisps of white hair clinging to her skull, she was curled protectively around a wooden figure, the skeletal arms cradling it like a child.

The figure was of Sasahevas, perfect down to the last detail, solid and dense, polished and glowing.

CHAPTER 47

Amy walked, as if in a trance, back to the school, her arms wrapped protectively around the figure, cradling it gently. When she entered the room, Richard looked up from what he was doing and was about to greet her, but stopped when he saw the look on her face, and what she was holding. He stood slowly, approached her and placed his fingers delicately upon the figure, tracing it with his fingers, in wonder.

It was about three feet tall, carved from cedar and burnished with age. It looked like Sasahevas as she remembered him from the cove. A fur-covered body, long powerful arms, an ape-like face with thick brows, wide cheekbones and a strong mouth. The top half of his face was smooth, with shaggy fur above and below, like hair and a beard. He looked placid and wise, staring forward, arms at his side, shoulders relaxed.

"How? Where?" Richard asked, not taking his eyes from the figure as he continued to touch it.

"There was an old woman. She led me to it. She told me it was ok to dig."

He looked up at that. "An old woman? You had to dig?"

"She looked like an old woman, but I don't think she was alive. I found her skeleton."

"A spirit guide then. You were taken to that place and given this gift. I wonder what its purpose is?"

"I don't know. She didn't tell me. Just that she wanted me to find it. So... I brought it here." She swallowed visibly. "Did I do the right thing?"

"I... think so. I don't know. It's an important artifact, of that I'm sure. What should be done with it?" Richard looked uncertain. "I think we need to trust the spirit guide."

Tum had returned from gathering and was standing behind Richard, looking at the figure in awe. "This is important Amy. I don't know why, but I know that it is important. Thank you for finding it."

Ian was walking toward them, tentatively, from the other side of the room, curious to see what was happening. When he got close enough to see past Richard, his face turned white and he gasped in shock. "I've seen that before! It was in my vision quest!"

They all looked at Ian in surprise. Amy was the first to speak. "You've seen this before? This exact figure?"

"Yes. I didn't get far enough into my story to tell you. There were some horrible things that happened to me. I haven't been ready to talk about it."

"Will you tell us what happened now? Can you tell us what you know about this artifact?"

Ian nodded. "This might take a little while. Let's sit down." Then he told them about the rest of his vision quest, starting with the battle and his injury, then his slavery, how he had saved Thompson, and finally his experience with Norem, and how he had been given this artifact – the same figure that Amy was now holding.

Amy wiped away tears. She understood now. Ian had seen death, had felt near death himself, had been subjugated and powerless. But he had come out of it with two significant pieces of information. When it had mattered, he had stood up for Thompson and saved his life. That was an impressive act of bravery. And he had been told the origin of this figure. They knew what it was now.

"If it came from the whale shrine," Richard said, "then this artifact is imbued with enormous spiritual power. It was used to call forth the whales, to gather the tribes, and to strengthen our people. It has migrated across time and space, to be revealed to us now. But for what purpose?"

"Ian's vision was about the past, we know that. But I think it was also about conflict and division. It marked the first contact between the white people and the tribes and showed what life was like before our civilization encroached upon yours." Amy said.

Richard nodded in agreement.

Amy kept talking. "My vision showed the ultimate result of that conflict, the end of the wild, and the destruction of this land under the weight of our people and technology. This artifact is the thread that ties us to these visions. It's something solid and real that the visions have shown us."

"I think Sasahevas is expecting us to use this artifact to stop the destruction somehow," Richard said.

"That's what I think too. The old woman told me the story of her tribe. She was from Nootka, where Ian had his vision, and they were relocated here as their culture was being destroyed. Maybe she is one of your ancestors?"

"Yes, it's possible."

"She talked a lot about the destruction of the wilderness and animals. She said that someone needs to stand up and put a stop to it, but the tribes aren't strong enough to do it alone. She implied that they needed help. In my vision the tribes were even weaker, they were dispossessed. There had been a diaspora."

"I think I know what needs to be done," Richard said. "There is a village nearby that is being formed by a visionary chief in my tribe. The village is Tzatsisnukomi. The chief is trying to call the tribes together to live there. He's had some success, but not enough. He could use help. With this artifact to rally around, I think he might be able to achieve his goal. And if he does, our tribe would find a new center, a new foundation on which to rebuild our culture. From that foundation, with the knowledge we've gained from these visions, we could stand up against the destruction that is occurring and the destruction that is coming. We could make our voices heard."

"No." Ian said angrily.

They had forgotten about him, they'd been so excited about their realizations.

"No, what?" Amy asked.

"No, I'm not going to another village. I want to go home. No more side-trips. No more pit-stops. I want to go home and forget any of this happened. I want to live a normal life again."

"But Ian, we have to help. We can't just leave now."

"Why not? This isn't my problem. Even if your vision is true, it won't happen until after I'm dead. I don't care anymore. I just want to leave."

Amy felt frustrated, and if she was honest with herself, angry with Ian. She felt compelled to follow through on what the vision quest had shown them, but she wasn't willing to leave Ian behind. They had to do this together.

That night Amy dreamt vividly. She was back on Hurst Island, standing in the cove where the lodge stood. The hillsides around the lodge were denuded, bare of trees, stumps showing over slash-piles of shredded wood, gathered to be burned down to ash. The birds were gone, as were all the other animals, large and small. The island was covered in a blanket of silence so thick that she could hear only her own heart pounding in her chest and the breath rushing in and out of her lungs.

The ocean was at her feet, but it was oily, glistening and viscous, impenetrable, devoid of life. The phosphorescent plankton were gone, as were the underwater plants, the barnacles, clams, and fish. Further out she could see the stark, white curve of a giant rib-cage. The whales were dead and had washed up onto the shore.

Around her lay a profound stillness. The end of life. The end of nature. The wild was gone from this island and would not return. It was ready for the arrival of the cities. There was nothing left to save.

CHAPTER 48

They woke the next morning, nothing resolved. Amy was sore and exhausted from sleeping on the hard ground. The air was cold as she rolled out from under the jacket she'd used as a blanket and stood up, her body protesting, joints stiff, breath puffing in the moist air. Richard was already awake, working on breakfast at the camp stove, Tum sitting beside him with a steaming mug of coffee in his hands.

"Good morning, Amy. I'd ask how you slept, but if your night was anything like mine, it's best not to talk about it." He gave her a wink.

Amy stretched, arms over her head, trying to work out the kinks in her shoulders and back. "Yeah. Best not to talk about it."

Amy noticed that Ian was laying with his back to them, so she left him alone. When she joined Richard he gave her a cup of coffee and pointed his chin toward the milk and sugar in case she needed any. Grateful for the warmth, and the caffeine, Amy doctored her coffee and took a sip, closing her eyes as she savored the flavor.

"What are we going to do about him?" Amy asked, pitching her voice low so she couldn't be overheard, nodding toward Ian.

"I was thinking about that. Maybe overthinking... I didn't sleep much last night." Richard said.

"Yeah? Did you come to any conclusions?"

"I need to talk to him. We need to come to an understanding."

"What do you mean? What kind of an understanding?"

"Since he returned from the vision quest he's had a problem with me. I think it's because of who I am and what I remind him of."

"Because you're a tribe member?"

"Yes. His injury and his enslavement were traumatic. I think he blames me for it. I was instrumental in sending him on the vision quest and every time he looks at me, I remind him of what has happened to him."

"That's not fair. You didn't do anything wrong. You saved us and you got us off the island."

"It may not be a conscious decision on his part. Perhaps he's just reacting, like a wounded animal. Either way, I think it's time for us to have a reckoning."

Amy felt worried, but she couldn't think of a better idea, so she kept quiet. Richard stood up slowly, set his shoulders, took a deep breath, and walked across the room to where Ian was laying.

"Ian. We need to talk." Richard said.

"I don't have anything to say to you."

"Look Ian, I'm sorry for how my ancestors treated you in the vision quest. But I didn't have any control over what happened. It wasn't me who hurt you."

Ian was silent.

"You can ignore me if you want, but you are being selfish, and I think you know it. There are people who need you. We need you. You were chosen for the vision quest, and I believe you need to see this through to the end."

Ian stood up, erupting from where he had been laying. "How dare you call me selfish? You sent me on that vision quest for your own purposes. You knew what would happen to me and you sent me anyway. You sent me to die!"

Richard spoke softly. "Ian, that's not true. I did what I had to do to get us off the island. We were forced together by Sasahevas, and we had to work together to get away. We still need to work together. He's not done with us yet." Richard jerked his head toward the wooden figure where it stood by the wall.

"You and Sasahevas can both go to hell." Ian's words were laced with venom, spitting out of him.

"You don't mean that. Not really. You're a good kid, I know you are. I've seen it. You're overwhelmed right now, I understand that."

Ian was rigid with anger, his fists clenching and unclenching, his jaw working, the muscles in his neck stood out like cords.

"I've worked with lots of angry young men, I know..."

As Richard was talking, Ian tensed his shoulders and raised a fist. Amy saw it as if it were in slow motion, her body too slow to react. She was too far away, all the way across the room, unable to stop what she knew was about to happen.

With an animal roar of rage, Ian swung his fist at Richard's face, connecting with the point of his jaw, feet planted, all the weight of his arm and shoulder behind the punch. Whether Richard saw it coming or not, Amy would never know, but he didn't raise a hand to defend himself or duck his head to avoid the blow. He dropped hard to the ground, the back of his head bouncing off the concrete with a sickening thud.

Ian looked at his fist in wonder, eyes wide, in disbelief at what he had done. Amy rushed to Richard's side. Tum ran at Ian and tackled him, driving him to the ground, pinning his arms, immobilizing him. "What the hell did you do?!" He growled at Ian. "If you've killed Richard, I will kill you. Right here. Right now. With my own hands." He shook Ian, bouncing his head a few times off the floor. "Do you understand?"

Amy cradled Richard's head in her lap, blood soaking her hands from where the back of his head had split open. She desperately felt for a pulse and checked his breathing. "Richard, can you hear me? Are you ok?"

His pulse was light and thready, his breathing rapid and shallow. His eyes moved under his eyelids and he groaned heavily, his head twisting back and forth, as if he was trying to escape from something.

"Please be ok. Please be ok. Please be ok." She was repeating it like a mantra, repeating it and hoping it would be true. Tum was turned toward her, sitting on Ian, trying to see what was going on.

"How is he?" Tum asked.

"I don't know!" She was distraught. How could this have happened? How could Ian have done this?

Richard opened his eyes and groaned again. "Amy? What happened?"

"Oh thank God you're awake. Ian fucking punched you. I thought you were going to die."

"I feel like I was hit by a ton of bricks." He sat up working his jaw back and forth, rubbing it with his hand. "He hit me?"

Amy nodded, staring at the back of his head. It was dark and slick with his blood, the hair matted down.

Ian was quiet, no fight left in him, so Tum rushed over to Richard and knelt down. "How do you feel?"

"I have a headache. I'm going to sit here for a moment. I'm a little dizzy."

Amy approached Ian. "What were you thinking? You could have killed him!" She noticed he was crying, curled around himself, shaking and sobbing incoherently. "Bah!" She cried out in frustration. "To hell with you Ian."

When Amy turned away, Richard was right there, looking at Ian, concerned.

"Ian, it's ok," he said softly. "I forgive you."

"How can you forgive me? How can I forgive you? Too much has happened, it's gone too far." Ian was still curled up, speaking into the floor, shaking.

"It's never too late for forgiveness. I choose to forgive you, because I can't imagine living any other way." Richard kneeled down and put a gentle hand on Ian's shoulder.

Ian sat up and faced Richard, his face red, eyes watering. "Richard… I'm sorry."

"I know you are, son. It's ok. You shouldn't have hit me. But I understand. I guess I had it coming. I pushed you into this, and I didn't prepare you as well as I should have. I'm sorry too."

Amy watched in wonder as Ian sank into Richard's arms, hugging him tightly, releasing his misery in loud, heart-wrenching sobs.

CHAPTER 49

While Amy was tending to the wound on Richard's head and re-checking his injured leg, Tum and Ian packed the supplies into the kayaks and got them ready to travel again. Once she was done, Amy walked with Richard down to the beach and helped him pull his kayak into the water. It was a beautiful day, bright and warm, with a thin layer of clouds high in the sky, and no sign of the wretched fog.

Bobbing in the steady swell, Amy marveled at where she was and what she was doing. The world was lovely around her. The islands were emerald green, grey rocky shorelines, surrounded by a dark blue-black ocean. A seal head broke the surface of the sea in front of her, black watery eyes peering at her. Then it tipped its head back and disappeared into the water, sinking slowly down, nostrils the last to go. Further out in the strait, she heard the muffled blast and whump of a whale as it rose to breathe, slapping its flipper on the surface.

Richard had given Ian the artifact so that he could be the one to carry it to Tzatsisnukomi. It was a great honor. An honor that Richard said Ian deserved because he had been the one to see it in his vision quest. Amy was happy for him. She hoped that Ian could be happy too. She hoped that he could conquer his demons.

"Even with the tide in our favor, we have half a day of paddling before we make it to the village, so we'd better get going," Richard said.

Ian and Richard paddled together. They had bonded in an inscrutably male way that Amy didn't understand. Tum was behind them, keeping a watchful eye on Ian, still not willing to trust him completely. Amy took up the rear, paddling and admiring the beauty that surrounded her, grateful.

The islands slipped smoothly past her, paddle strokes blending together into a continuous, steady effort. The tide was in their favor, making progress easy. They passed through a narrow section of rocks and the water boiled under them, turbulent as it was forced through the constriction. Amy let her kayak drift, enjoying the acceleration, the bumps and lumps, not caring if she was facing forward or back, the kayak spinning of its own accord. She was happy that they knew where they were going, happy that they finally were going in the right direction, trusting in the current to bring her ever closer to their destination.

When the village came into view, Amy's arms and shoulders were tired, burning from the extended exercise. She paddled hard for a few more minutes and then lifted the paddle up and out of the water as the kayak glided the final distance, the shoreline visibly rising beneath her, seaweed and fish flashing past, and then the nose of the kayak drove itself up and onto the beach.

The other three were already on shore, their boats pulled up and tied to driftwood logs. Ian ran down when he saw her, grabbed her bowline, and pulled her higher up the beach so she wouldn't have to get her feet wet.

"Thanks."

He smiled, eyes down. "No problem."

Together they dragged the boat the rest of the way up and tied it alongside the others.

"We made it! What's next?" she asked.

Before Richard could answer, three large dogs emerged from a set of trees between the beach and the village. They gathered around, jumping up on Richard, wagging their tails, slobbering, and shoving themselves under his hand to be petted.

"Ok, ok, what a welcoming committee. Hello, old friends, I hope you've been well." Richard was laughing and trying to pet them all at once.

Amy watched, bemused. She was glad the dogs were friendly and that they recognized Richard. Two of them were the size of regular dogs, but very wolfish in aspect. The third was massive, his head well above Richard's waist, towering over the others.

After the dogs had settled down, and moved away to explore other things, Richard was able to answer Amy's question. "Tum and I will go into the village and let them know we are here. You two need to wait. You can't enter without permission. After I find the Elder and tell him about you, I'll come back and get you, ok?"

"Ok. We'll sit tight I guess. See you soon." Amy said, feeling perturbed to be left behind. Unsure if she wanted to be alone with Ian.

Richard reverently took the artifact from Ian's kayak, and then he and Tum walked into the trees toward the village.

Amy waited, feeling awkward, until Ian broke the silence. "Amy, I'm sorry for how I've been acting."

Amy nodded and folded her arms. "Ok. Thanks." She wasn't ready to trust him completely. Not yet.

They continued to wait, facing the sea, the sound of the dogs crashing and playing in the forest behind them. As she stood there, quietly absorbing the seascape with Ian, something small and insistent got her attention. A feeling at the base of her spine that they were no longer alone. She turned slowly, afraid of what she might see, and found herself face to face with Norm.

"Norm! What are you doing here?" Amy exclaimed.

"Oh, I wouldn't miss this for the world. You've come a long way and accomplished so much!"

Ian was looking at Norm, a funny expression on his face, his head tilted. "You look so much like him."

"Yes, I know."

"Just like Norem. But younger."

"Yes, that's right."

Amy looked at him more closely. "And you look so much like Norman."

"Yes." Norm was nodding. "That's right."

"Were you actually in our visions?" Ian asked.

"Yes, I was." He cocked an eyebrow. "You two are a little slow on the uptake aren't you?"

Amy was shaking her head. "Who are you?"

"I'm Norm. Remember?"

"No, I mean who are you really?"

"That's harder to answer. Who are any of us, really?" Norm threw his head back, mock dramatic.

There was something wrong with Norm, his eyes were too bright, his mouth too big, and when he smiled it was too elastic, too expressive. Amy found him exceptionally creepy. How had she not noticed how inhuman he seemed before now?

"What are you?"

"You've met me before, and you'll meet me again. I'm many things to many people. I've been helping you, you know?"

"Helping us? How?"

"First of all, I showed myself to Richard, pretended to be his grandfather, and told him to find you on the island. How's that? Happy?"

"You told Richard to go to Hurst Island and find us?"

"Yes!"

"You pretended to be his grandfather?"

"You really can't trust any of your senses when I'm around. You should know that by now." He blew a small wisp of fog out of his mouth. "I also hitched a ride on Richard's boat to make sure he found you. I didn't let him see me of course."

"How did you know we were on Hurst Island?" Ian interjected, looking suspicious.

"Umm.... Hmm. I'm not sure I want to tell you that. Are you sure you want to know?"

"Yes!" They both said at once.

"You may not like it."

"Tell us," Ian said.

"I... kind of... forced you onto the island." Norm responded.

"You what? Are you mad?" Ian advanced on Norm, looking angry, losing all sense of his earlier nervousness.

"Now, now, hold on. It was necessary."

"Why. Was. It. Necessary." Ian had stopped a few feet from Norm, fists clenching and unclenching.

"Because I needed you on the island, that's why. I'd been waiting for someone like you. When I saw you passing by, I couldn't let you go to waste, could I? Two young humans. One girl, one boy. Healthy and fit. You seemed likely to survive." He looked at them more closely. "And you did survive didn't you? Well done!"

"Why did you need us on the island?" Amy asked.

"For Sasahevas, that's why." Norm looked like he thought that made sense.

"For Sasahevas?" Amy asked, incredulous.

"Yes!"

"I don't understand," Amy said.

"Do I have to explain everything? Sasahevas can provide visions. That's what he does. He has one big, stinky foot in the physical plane and the other foot in the spiritual plane... so to speak. He doesn't talk much though. Have you noticed that?"

Amy gave Norm a blank stare. What in the hell was going on? This couldn't be real.

"Ok, well... My job is to draw you into the visions. He can't do that by himself. Not without my help anyway. I'm rather proud of that. Some of my finest work, making that happen. Gives me something to do. I'm stuck here in the physical plane. Most of me anyway. Parts of me are in each of his visions, that's what you met, one of my shards. I kind of... shattered, when I forced myself into this role."

"Why did you need to draw us into the vision?" Amy asked, choosing to ignore the rest of it.

Norm grew serious, took a step closer, and talked in a low voice. "This world is going to end. Just like your little boat. You've wrecked it."

"What?!"

"The natural world anyway. It's not going to last much longer. Maybe a few more of your generations. And when nature dies, she will take all of us with her. That's all."

"But why?" Amy asked.

"Sasahevas tried to show you. He showed you, didn't he? The world can't survive that kind of destruction. Not for long. Once enough of the plants and animals are extinguished, the entire web will collapse."

"Why did you pull us into this? What good is it telling us all this?"

"Oh you're just one small part. But an important part! Don't get me wrong, I'm not trying to belittle you."

"Ok?"

"Look. I don't care what you humans do. You could all die, for all I care. But if you destroy the world, you are going to take me with you. I can't have that. I've been around too long to die now."

"I still don't understand."

"Look, you saw what is going to happen here. Your friend over there," he gestured to Ian, "he saw what started it."

"Yes?"

"I'm trying to slow it down. I don't think I can stop it, but maybe I can give myself a little more time before I'm swept away. You're helping me with that. As a side effect, you humans may last a little longer too."

"We are helping?"

"Yes. That artifact is important, that's why I showed it to Ian. That's why I brought you to Mamalilikulla to find it. It will strengthen the tribes. The people will gather. They will try to push back the tide. They may not be able to stop it, but they can slow it down. That's as much as I can ask for."

"What should we do next?"

"I don't know. Do whatever you like. Live your little human lives. It doesn't make a difference to me." Norm turned to go, then paused. "You have my thanks for your help, unwitting though it was. I've left a present for you in the village. I hope you like it."

Amy and Ian, stupefied, watched Norm walk away. At the edge of the forest the lines that defined him began to waver. The thing that was Norm expanded, filling more space, growing taller and broader, wild hair rising out of his scalp, a basket appearing on his back.

What was once Norm, turned its head and looked at them, eyes deep black, mouth huge and red, shapes flitting about its shoulders, transparent and indistinct – the spirits of those who had been lost at sea. "Uh, huu, huu!" it said, the noise blasting over them, forcing them to cover their ears, cowering.

Tsonoqua strode into the forest and disappeared.

CHAPTER 50

When Richard returned to the beach to retrieve them, Amy and Ian were still in shock. They remained utterly silent as he led them through the forest and toward the village. If he noticed anything odd about their lack of conversation he didn't mention it.

They emerged from the trees at the back of a large, newly constructed longhouse flanked on both sides by the many houses of the village, all built from local materials, wood and stone. Richard led them to the front where there was a group of people waiting on a wide lawn, fronting the sea. The wind was whipping around them, clothes flapping and snapping.

"Amy, Ian, let me introduce you to the people of Tzatsisn-ukomi."

An old man, grey-haired, vigorous and healthy looking, broke from the group and nodded solemnly at them. "Welcome. I am Russ, Elder of this village."

Amy nodded back, Ian doing likewise.

"Richard has told me of what you have done. What you have seen. He has shared with me the visions that you have acquired."

Russ looked intently at them, before going on. "I want to thank you for finding and returning this important artifact to us." He gestured toward his wife, who was holding the figure. "It will bring us great strength."

"You're welcome," Amy said. Ian stood silently beside her.

"We have decided that it is time to resume the vision quests of our tribe. We have decided to revive this ancient tradition."

"I am glad to hear that," Amy said.

"You may stay with us tonight, if you'd like. You may visit us whenever you want. You will be honored guests of this village."

"Thank you."

"There is something else I want to show you. Come with me."

The old man walked across the lawn, down the hill, and toward the village dock. Amy and Ian followed, walking past the group of men, women, and children who watched them, some of them reaching out to pat them on the back or on the shoulder as they passed. The group was silent and solemn, even the children, who seemed to have picked up the mood from the adults.

The old man led them along a gravel path that wound amongst the village buildings to the dock, crowded with fishing boats and aluminum runabouts. At the end of the dock, past a large ocean-going trawler, Amy could see a single mast sticking up. There was a sailboat docked here.

The old man clumped slowly down the dock, not looking back, merely expecting them to follow. When they got to the end, past the trawler, Ian's sailboat came into view. Clean and ship-shape, tied up neatly, prim and proper, bobbing on the small waves, straining on her lines against the receding tide.

Ian stopped in his tracks, his mouth opening and closing in surprise. "How? What? How is this possible?"

"Richard told me this might be your boat. Coast Guard brought it to us this morning. Said they'd found it drifting south of Hurst Island no crew on board. Asked us if we'd hold onto it for a few days while they continued their missing persons search."

"But, we saw it sink!" Ian said.

"Are you sure? It seems to me like it's floating." The old man shrugged his shoulders.

He was right. It was quite evidently floating in front of them. Amy remembered what Tsonoqua had said. When she was around, you couldn't trust your senses. Perhaps the shipwreck hadn't been what it had seemed. This must be her gift. Ian's boat was back. Amy hadn't sunk it. She could let go of her guilt.

As Ian got over his shock, she could see the realization hit him. The boat he loved was back. They could continue their journey north. They were alive, and they were free, and they had everything they needed.

EPILOGUE

Amy stood in the cockpit, her hair streaming in the wind and spray, blissfully happy. Ian was at the wheel, joyful, the boat heeled hard over, driving forward, a bit in her teeth. They crested a massive wave and Amy laughed out loud, the sound bubbling up from deep within her. Ian flashed a huge smile, his eyes crinkling adorably. She grabbed his hand and he let go of the wheel, letting the ship tend to itself for a brief moment, as they balanced together, feeling the ocean under their feet, feeling it through the living hull of this sailboat that they both loved.

They were on their way to Alaska, sailing in a vast wilderness of waves and water, edged up against a seemingly endless expanse of mountains and glaciers, temperate rainforest, huge trees, bears and whales, animals of every type. On their starboard side, the coast range, roadless and untamed. On their port side, Haida Gwaii, ancestral home of the Haida people.

They had seen the violence and depredations of the past. They were aware of the destruction that was coming. But for now they were in the present, their bow pointed north, taking them further into the wild. Further into what they loved, further into what made their lives worth living. Further into their dreams.

For now, that was enough. For now, they were happy.

HISTORICAL ACCURACY

The historical events in this book are based upon true events and many of the historical figures are based upon real people. In pivotal scenes, I have tried to stay true not only to the general events that took place but also to specific words spoken and actions taken. As described in the book, John Jewitt was enslaved by Maquinna after the *Boston* was taken by the natives and the motivation for the attack was as I described in the story: Maquinna had broken a fowling piece that Captain Salter had given him, the Captain was angry, and there was an argument. Deeply insulted, Maquinna felt that the only way he could restore his pride was to attack the ship and kill the crew. The scene in which Maquinna tries to press his heart back down from his throat into his chest is a wonderful historical tidbit based upon how Maquinna later described his feelings during the argument.

I suppose it is true that fact can be stranger than fiction. Many of the events in John's account are hard to believe: his narrow escape from death, how he was saved and then enslaved by Maquinna, as well as the natives actions in sailing the ship, running it aground and then burning it. I found myself in the peculiar situation of trying to decide if I should write the story as it had happened or fictionalize it and make it more 'believable'. I decided to stay true to history. Thompson's story is incredible too. He did in fact survive the attack by hiding in the hold and he was later saved when John claimed him as his father. If you want to learn more, I highly recommend John Jewitt's book: *The*

Adventures and Sufferings of John R. Jewitt: Captive of Maquinna.

My time in the Salish Sea has been enriched by reading Captain Vancouver's journals. During my own journeys, I've followed his progress as he mapped the coastline through the summer of 1792. After entering Puget Sound, Vancouver described an empty landscape populated by deformed people and beaches littered with human bones. He marveled at the park-like meadows just above the shoreline, never realizing that these lush parks were the remnants of a bustling civilization that had been decimated by smallpox and other diseases brought by the first European explorers twenty years prior. The land was empty when Vancouver explored it, because it had been depopulated. Even today, sailing through many parts of British Columbia, I will get the feeling that I am tiptoeing through a graveyard. The remnants of a lost civilization are buried beneath long years and dense vegetation, but if you know where to look you can still find the signs: totems, clam gardens, longhouse posts, and canoe haulouts.

After his surveying was complete, Vancouver sailed to Friendly Cove, Nootka Sound in an attempt to resolve an ongoing territorial dispute that had erupted between the English and the Spanish. Amazingly, this was not Vancouver's first time in Nootka Sound. As a young midshipman, he had traveled with Captain Cook on the *HMS Resolution* and had been among the first Europeans to set foot on Vancouver Island, initiating first contact in 1778. Continuously inhabited by the Mowachaht tribe for over a four thousand years, Friendly Cove is a hugely important historical site both for the tribes that live there and because of the incredible stories from European explorers such as Cook, Vancouver, and John Jewitt.

The migration of the tribes, as described in Part 2, including the fact that the forests didn't yet exist when humans first arrived, the movement of sea levels over time and the discovery of villages which are now deep underwater is based upon current archaeological research. The Pacific Northwest is a region that holds many secrets and has an incredible history to tell.

The integration of the tribes into Canadian culture happened very much as I described it, including the outlawing of the Potlatch ceremonies and the creation of a residential school system where children were torn from their families and forced to integrate into the mainstream western culture.

The legendary creatures in *End of the Wild* are for the most part described as depicted by the native legends, including their physical characteristics and their roles in Salish mythology. I did invent a few things in order to further the narrative, including Sasahevas's role in the vision quests and Tsonoqua's active role in helping Amy and Ian. None of these types of interactions are described in legend, although many other strange and fantastic stories have been told about these interesting characters. If you would like to learn more about the native legends, I recommend *Indian Myths & Legends from the North Pacific Coast of America: A Translation of Franz Boas' 1895 Edition of Indianische Sagen von der Nord-Pacifischen Küste Amerikas*.

It is fascinating to me that these early anthropologists were faced with a storytelling culture so foreign to their European sensitivities that the translators struggled to put it into words. Many of the legends they encountered were so graphic, so visceral, and so obscene that the anthropologists would write them in Latin so that a casual reader could not be accidentally exposed. Even today, these legends can shock – they are so relaxed in their descriptions of violence and physical degradation that it can be hard to imagine the culture from which they sprung. The legends do not follow any type of story arc or narrative structure that I can recognize, often reading like a series of random events strung together with one event following the next, for no apparent reason. The villain wins, the maiden becomes depraved, the monster kills with impunity and is rewarded for it. It is very different from the European storytelling culture that I am familiar with and it strikes me that the Salish culture was perhaps one of the most alien cultures we have ever encountered and it is now all but destroyed.

The behavior of Sasahevas, the banging of sticks to communicate and the creation of a nest by breaking off the tops of trees, are based upon stories that were told to me by locals. Based on this folklore, the creature's behavior is realistic in terms of what people have reportedly experienced. Many locations in the Salish Sea feel wonderfully haunted and oppressive. I've heard people say that they can recognize old village sites by the feel of the atmosphere alone. I've felt it myself.

While *End of the Wild* is a work of fiction, I have tried to keep it as true to life as I can in terms of what it feels like to spend time there. The most important books I've read that have helped me to understand the psychology of this area are *The Curve of Time* and *Klee Wyck.*

WHY I WROTE THE BOOK

When I started writing this book, I didn't know what I was getting myself into. All my life I'd wanted to write a novel, but I'd never found the time or the courage to give it a real go. I wrote short stories and tried to hone my writing style, but I had never worked myself up to attempting anything longer. Time went by. I read avidly, consuming anything I could get my hands on, learning from each author, what I liked and what I didn't.

The years went by and still no novel.

My Grandpa loved writing. He'd always wanted to write and publish a book. We'd have long conversations about writing, how I could finish his current manuscript for him and publish it. I'd nod my head and we'd talk and talk, but still no novel.

The years went by and my Grandpa died. My Grandma too. My chance to write a novel that he could read and be proud of was gone. The years continued to slide by.

Then I bought an anthology of John Steinbeck and spent a few weeks in the fall reading his stories. *The Pearl. The Moon is Down. Cannery Row. East of Eden.* I was entranced and inspired. This was art, I thought. This was genius. I wanted to try my hand at it. I knew I couldn't be a Steinbeck, but I could let him inspire me.

So I started thinking about a novel more seriously and I started to wonder what I could write about. And then tragedy struck. In my small hometown, an avalanche took the lives of a young couple, striking them down in their prime. I could see myself in them. We all could. My tribe was in deep, deep mourning over this loss, grappling to understand. These feelings were thrust into the mix.

Why are some of us so drawn to the wild? Even at our own peril, we are drawn to it like moths to the flame, like an addict to the fix.

Why are so many people so disillusioned with modern life? Why do we feel so disconnected, as if we are separated from some great truth that is receding further and further from view?

What does it mean to be human at this point in history? We are so powerful that we have changed the world with our technology, but we are not yet powerful enough to protect ourselves from the catastrophe that may result.

We cannot go backward – back into the wild, even if we wanted to. That path is closed to us forever. Yet, we cannot continue to live as we do; it is unsustainable, dehumanizing, and too alien to what our bodies and minds have been designed for.

We can only move forward. But forward to what? Where are we going and what will we find when we get there?

The islands of Queen Charlotte Strait are wild and mysterious. Dense and impenetrable. Rich in First Nation's history and mythology. And yet, they are not a wilderness – not in the ways that I had expected. I witnessed clearcuts scarring the mountains, fish farms in remote coves and small marinas scattered throughout. In the summer there are super-yachts and cruise ships. In the winter there is rain and storms and everything is covered with a foggy mist that blurs and smears. I have come to the realization that this is a frontier, not a wilderness. A working frontier for loggers, and fisherman, and for tourism as well.

I listened to stories from the old timers who told me about what used to be: pristine old growth forests, salmon running in the million, countless eulachon, massive herring balls, basking sharks, seals, and sea otters. Much of this is now gone, lost to progress and to the hunger of the cities.

Billy Proctor was hugely influential. He is over 80 now and has lived in the Broughton Islands all of his life. He told my family and I about his time as a hand logger, as a fisherman, as a seal hunter, and now as a conservationist. He has seen the salmon disappear, the river valleys destroyed, the basking sharks massacred, the seals hunted for 25c per 'head'. He's seen what people, himself included, have done to this area and he has realized it cannot continue. He's decided to take a stand.

I asked myself then – what happens to a frontier? The answer is obvious. A frontier doesn't revert back to wilderness, and the animals don't magically come back. A frontier becomes further developed. A frontier becomes civilized until all that is left are the old stories, the faded pictures, and the animals mounted on the wall. I live in Montana and I've seen what a frontier becomes. Progress brings many benefits, but it comes with a cost.

In *End of the Wild* I've tried to convey the complex impressions and feelings I've had while exploring the fascinating, beautiful British Columbia coast – from the Gulf Islands in the south, up north as far as Cape Scott, and around the wild, exposed western reaches of Vancouver Island. I hope that you've enjoyed the journey and I hope that it inspires you to learn more and perhaps even spend some time in this unique and very special place.

CONNECT

To see a photo album containing pictures of locations from *End of the Wild,* visit my wife's photo site: https://kirstentaylorphotography.smugmug.com

To see videos filmed in the area and more, subscribe to my YouTube channel: https://www.youtube.com/user/tlaloc75

If you'd like to contact me, please send email to endofthewild@gmail.com

If you enjoyed this story, please write a review on Amazon.com or Goodreads. I would love to hear what you thought of *End of the Wild.*

If you liked *End of the Wild,* check out my next book *Ganymede.* You can find it on Amazon in both eBook and paperback: https://www.amazon.com/dp/B07N8KNDRQ

ABOUT THE AUTHOR

Jason Taylor spends his life in the mountains and at sea. A native of Montana, coastal BC is his second home. No stranger to the pull of wilderness on the human psyche, his writing explores the themes of what makes us human and our place on this planet.